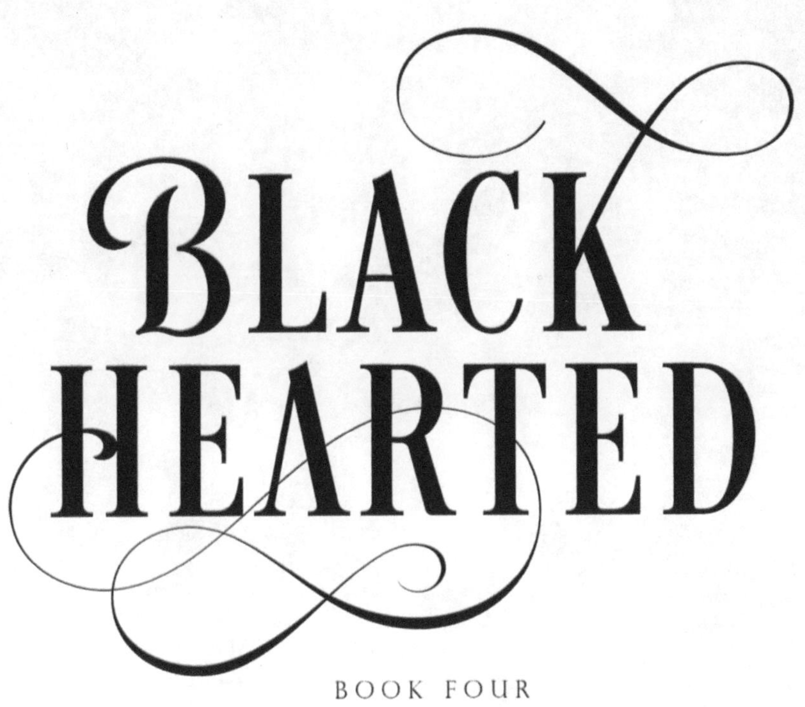

BOOK FOUR

CURSED FAE SERIES

CURSED FAE BOOK FOUR

BLACK HEARTED

USA TODAY BESTSELLING AUTHORS

LEIA STONE & JULIE HALL

Black Hearted (Cursed Fae Book 4)

Cover by Fay Lane

Map by Brina Boyle

ISBN (paperback): 978-1-951578-52-7

ISBN (hardcover): 978-1-951578-53-4

To our readers.

Books by Leia Stone

LEIASTONE.COM/BOOKS

FANTASY

Vampire Hunter Society

Shifter Island Series

Wolf Girl Series

Daughter of Light Series

The Titan's Saga

Supernatural Bounty Hunter Series

Dream Wars Series

Fallen Academy Series

Dragons & Druids Series

Matefinder Series

Matefinder: Next Generation

Hive Trilogy

NYC Mecca Series

Night War Saga

Water Realm Series

The Kings of Avalier Series

Gilded City Series

ALL TITLES

LeiaStone.com/books

Books by Julie Hall

JULIEHALLAUTHOR.COM/BOOKS

CREATURES OF CHAOS SERIES

Creatures of Chaos

Kingdom of Chaos

FALLEN LEGACIES SERIES

Stealing Embers

Forging Darkness

Unleashing Fire

Supernova

LIFE AFTER SERIES

Huntress

Warfare

Dominion

Logan

SHADOW ANGEL SERIES

Shadow Angel Book One

Shadow Angel Book Two

Shadow Angel Book Three

Julie's books have won or were finalists in over 20 awards.

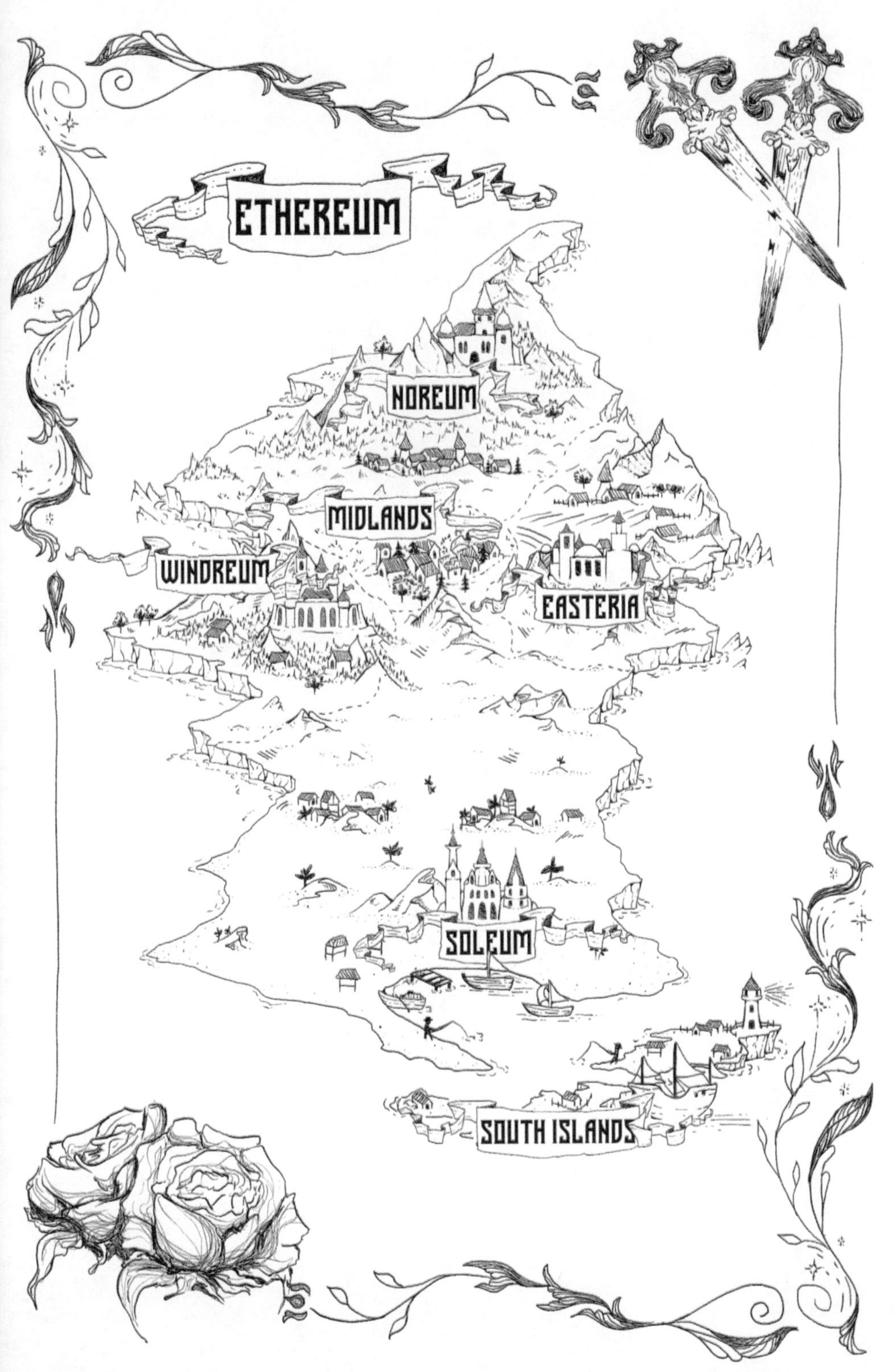
ETHEREUM
NOREUM
MIDLANDS
WINDREUM
EASTERIA
SOLEUM
SOUTH ISLANDS

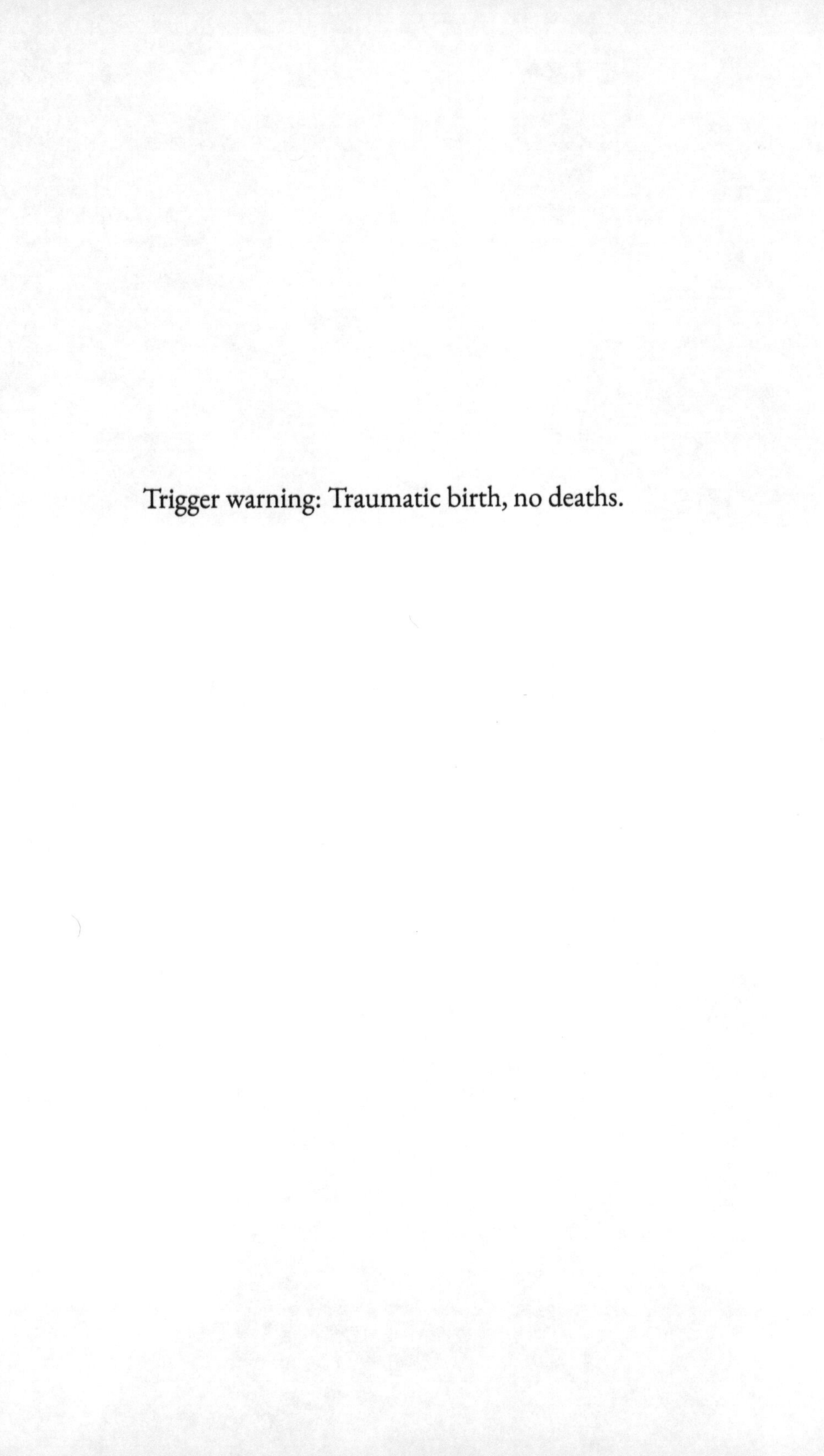

Trigger warning: Traumatic birth, no deaths.

Prologue

A reminder . . .

Isolde

What happened next was one of the most beautiful things I'd ever seen.

It started with Zander. A golden glow rose up from where he crouched and moved to Stryker, washing over him like a wave and then going to Adrien. It covered my husband and then disappeared into the earth before popping up around Zane and cocooning him.

"Wow," Dawn breathed beside me.

I inched forward, still clinging to Aribella and Dawn. The

golden magic seemed to solidify over Zane as he grunted, no doubt trying to make his portal.

"The image of Faerie in my mind's eye isn't enough," Zane growled.

I had an idea then of what might help. Letting go of Dawn's and Aribella's hands, I rushed into the center of the circle, feeling a buzz come over my skin as I crossed the threshold.

Zane peered up at me pleadingly as I reached into the satchel around his hip. I grasped the two stones from Dawn's and Aribella's daggers and then my own and pulled them out, placing them under his palms between his skin and the earth. The second I did this, I was nearly blown off my feet with a force of power.

"What was that?" Zander shouted.

I stumbled out of the circle and looked back to see a small window had opened in front of Zane. A window to our world. But it wasn't large enough for Zane to go through, and it was flickering.

"Those are the Harvest Mountains," Aribella exclaimed.

They were indeed the Harvest Mountains of Fall Court, and they were as black as night, covered in what looked like oil. The image flickered in and out.

"I can't hold on much longer," Adrien cried.

Zane grunted in defiance. "I just need it to get a little bigger so I can jump through."

Should he be going through on the other side of the Harvest Mountains? It wasn't Spring Court, it wasn't healthy. But it was his only shot, so I knew he would, no matter what.

"Maybe we can help them," Dawn said, rushing forward to kneel beside Zander.

"No, stay back," Zander grunted, sweat beading down his face.

She dug her hands into the earth next to him, and I could see sunlight beams pouring out of her fingertips and into the soil.

The portal suddenly stopped flickering and blew open wider.

It worked!

Aribella and I rushed to kneel next to our husbands without another word and added our magic as well. I fed my icy tendrils into the earth and then felt as it took what I offered. It was like a drain had been pulled from a tub, and magic started sucking out of me.

I peered up to see the portal open to the size of a door, and black, sludgy water poured inside our world as Zane met my gaze.

"No, it's too dangerous. We'll try again another day," I yelled at him. This wasn't the Spring Court.

"I'll stop the curse or die trying, and I won't let a hair on Lorelei's head be harmed." He declared like an oath and then leaped into the portal, ripping his hands from the earth and barreling through just as it snapped shut behind him.

The rest of us fell backward, panting as exhaustion pulled at our limbs. Laying on the forest floor, I peered over at Adrien, and my heart broke for Zane. We all had each other, and he'd just gone on a one-man mission to save both of our worlds.

May the stars be with you.

Lorelei

One second, Isolde and the handsome Lord Zane were standing in front of me in the garden, and the next, Queen Liliana showed up, and they disappeared.

"I knew I couldn't trust you," the Summer queen seethed, her face contorting into a reflection of rage as she stalked toward me.

I backed up a few paces, holding my hands up in surrender. "I didn't know they would be here."

She shook her head. "You can't save us." Her words hit me in the chest like arrows, piercing me deep.

"I want to," I said more timidly than I'd intended.

I wasn't a warrior: it literally went against my magic. I gave life, I didn't take it. But even so, I hadn't lied. I did want to save our world.

As the queen advanced, I backpedaled until my shoulders hit the tree behind me. I held my breath as Queen Liliana walked right up to me. "You fancied him, didn't you? That lord who said he was coming for you?"

She'd heard?

My heart pounded in my chest. The letter Isolde sent to me had sounded unbelievable, but now I wondered if it was true.

"Are they our mates?" I dared to ask, my voice no louder than a whisper. "Is it true?"

We didn't have mates in Faerie, but I still understood the concept. I'd only ever heard the term in fairy tales: myths and fables our parents read to us as children. It was said there was no connection stronger than mates. It wasn't just love that bonded the pair, but magic as well.

The queen's upper lip curled, sneering at me. "Yes. A small price to pay to bring peace for a hundred years."

I whimpered at the confession, despair filling my heart. All these years, the Summer princess champions had been sent to Ethereum to kill their mates. And Queen Liliana expected the same of me now.

I shook my head, a tear falling down my face. "I can't. I won't hurt him."

If the handsome man who'd come in the vision with Isolde was my mate, I wouldn't harm him.

Queen Liliana nodded, a slow smile streaking her lips and causing a foreboding shiver to slither down my spine. "I know you won't, delicate Lorelei. That's why I'm going to use you as bait to bring him to me so *I* can carve his heart from his chest myself and end this once and for all."

"What?"

No! I can't let her use me like that.

I burst forward, intending to run, when she reached out with something shiny and cracked the side of my head.

I had about two seconds to process the fact that the Summer queen had just struck me, and then everything went black.

Chapter One

ZANE

The moment my feet landed on the oily incline, I slipped, landing hard on my back, and began to slide. I'd leaped through the portal without a second thought, and now I was gliding feet-first down a mountain.

I kicked my heels, trying to dig into the earth for purchase and slow my descent, but to no avail. The ground beneath me was slick, like the mountain itself was made of black cooking oil and there was nothing that I could grab onto either.

Desperately, I reached for my power, hoping to use my lightning magic to lasso a nearby tree, but I was horrified to feel a drain on my power. It was nothing like as strong as it normally was in Ethereum, so here I was struggling. I still managed to summon some lightning, but it was difficult.

My brothers and I all shared some ability to control shadows, but each of us had a unique variation of magic. Mine was the ability to create and manipulate black lightning, which alone would do nothing to slow my descent unless I coated it in shadows so it didn't burn through the trees I was hoping to lasso.

As quickly as possible, I created a bolt of lightning and wrapped shadows around it. Lightning could be dangerous when I intended it to be, but when coated this way in shadows, it could be used as a rope. Flicking my wrist, I curled the shadow whip around the base of a thick tree. The second it pulled taut, I was yanked to a stop. I breathed out heavily with relief.

I was now halfway down the mountain, and the only thing keeping me from sliding the rest of the way was my grip on the lightning rope. My butt was likely bruised, and I might have a few cuts on my back, but the black oil pouring around and below me was so thick it had actually cushioned some of the impact. It was also terrible to look at. There was so much black, oily liquid rushing down the whole of this mountain like a mighty stream.

I glanced outward, and my breath caught as I gazed upon miles and miles of gloom in what must have once been a beautiful land. Withered trees stood stark against the bleak backdrop. Farms were submerged in what looked to be the same black substance I'd slipped on, with only the top halves of houses peeking out.

Everything, as far as the eye could see, was shrouded in shadows and blackened fields of dying vegetation. The sky was overcast, the sun completely hidden from sight, leaving me no clue as to what time of day it was.

Now I understood Dawn, Aribella, and Isolde's anxiety about stopping the curse. It was much worse here than in our world. Well, that might not be a fair statement since it was also affecting our people in Ethereum, but this . . . this land was ruined. Is this what lay in store for Ethereum, too?

Panic shot through me, and I quickly checked to make sure

the satchel was still slung over my shoulder. I let out a relieved sigh when I patted it with my free hand, feeling it still bulging with its contents. Everything I needed to end the curse was inside: a map of Faerie, the daggers and their stones, the Shadow Heart, the accompanying vial, and the note with Lorelei's name on it. I was determined to find her and give it to her. The Spring Court princess who could end the curse.

My mate.

I'd waited my whole life for a love like the one my brothers had with their wives. I was incredibly happy for them, but I was also lonely. For a moment, I had thought Isolde was meant for me, but it was clear with just one kiss how wrong I'd been. There weren't any lingering doubts in my mind that Isolde was meant for Adrien, but even if there had been, they would have been shattered to pieces the second I laid eyes on Lorelei.

She'd been wearing a pretty yellow dress and singing softly to herself as she carried a basket of vegetables through the palace gardens in the Spring Court. The attraction and protective feelings that rose up in me the moment I saw her for the first time were undeniable. The brown-haired woman with a soft-spoken voice and a penchant for flowers was the one for me. I knew it in my soul.

Now I just had to get down this mountain and find her.

Using my free hand, I created another shadow-coated lightning whip and lassoed a nearby tree farther down the steep mountain. Releasing my hold on the higher tree, I slid downward quickly but was pulled taut once my lightning shadow rope reached the end of its length.

I repeated this process several times, slowly sliding downward and using my lightning magic to lasso nearby trees and control my descent. Finally, I neared a cliff where the black oil poured over the side like a waterfall. At the cliff's edge sat a small, half-submerged cottage.

Lassoing a tree that butted up against the cottage, I pulled myself closer, shortening the length of the shadow-coated lightning rope until I grasped the railing of the porch and hefted myself onto the oil-slicked deck.

Glancing over the side, I began to plan my way down the cliff. Attaching my lightning rope to the railing, I could rappel down the side—

A clank from inside the house made the hairs on my arms stand on end. Was that a door closing? And footsteps?

Spinning, I peered up at the top floor of the cottage and bellowed, "Hello!"

Another clank, followed by footsteps. This time, they sounded like someone running. From inside the house, a small hand fiddled with the window latch, and then it flew open, revealing the face of a wild-eyed young girl.

"Oh, thank the stars," she said. "I thought I was going to die here." Her voice was so eager.

She had pointed ears, pink cheeks, and red hair wrapped into a bun at the top of her head. Across her nose was a smattering of freckles. If I had to guess, I'd say she was eleven or twelve.

"Hi," was all I could manage. I hadn't expected a kid to be all the way out here. "Are you alone?"

She nodded. "The oil took my nana over the cliff when she was trying to braid us a rope down. I've been alone for weeks."

Weeks? How had she survived?

Her gaze fell to my shadow-coated lightning rope, and her eyes widened to the size of coins, and terror flashed across her face. She backed away from the window and disappeared out of sight.

Oh no. I'd forgotten that the fae in this world all thought my magic was evil.

"I won't hurt you," I called out.

Quiet footsteps moved inside the house, but she said nothing.

I didn't need this right now. An untrusting kid slowing me down wasn't part of the plan, but I couldn't leave her here. This was the Fall Court. The curse had descended on this land months ago. It was a wonder she'd survived this long, but if she stayed here, she'd surely die.

Sludging through at least a foot of the oil on the porch, I went to the front door, and, with great effort, I pried it open and waded inside. The living room and kitchen were completely dark. No candles, which made sense because this oily substance might be flammable.

"I have shadow magic, but I'm not a bad person," I yelled into the house.

"That's exactly what a bad person would say," she called back from somewhere upstairs, and I hated the terror I heard in her voice.

I blew out a frustrated breath. She was right.

"I'm friends with Princess Aribella of the Fall Court. I'm here on a mission to help the Spring Court princess."

"Liar! Go away. I'd rather die here alone than trust someone from Ethereum."

I began to walk up the steps. "How do you know where I'm from?"

"My nana told me things. Shadow magic means you're a bad guy from Ethereum," she called from a room off to the left.

I sighed. I couldn't deny that I was from Ethereum. She'd seen my magic for herself, but maybe I could convince her I wasn't bad. "I'm going to the Spring Court. Would you like a ride there? I can use my magic to get us out of this oil."

I stood in the open doorway of the room I'd heard her voice come from and stared at the closed closet door. Black footprints covered the upper floor, along with plates, dried food, and clothes smeared with oil in the corner. No one should have to live like this, let alone a child without an adult to depend on.

"I have powerful magic," she called back, her voice muffled from the closet. "And if you don't leave right now, I'll jump out and blast you with it."

The little fae might have great power, but she sounded terrified. I didn't want to scare her any more by taking her by force.

"Please don't hurt me. And I promise I won't hurt you," I said. "I don't know anything about this land, and I really need to get to the Spring Court to see Princess Lorelei."

Silence.

"So you can kill her?" she asked.

I huffed a humorless half-laugh. So I can marry her was more like it. "No, so I can bring her a letter and help her destroy the curse."

The door handle turned, creaking open. The little girl poked her sweaty red face out of the closet. "Destroy the curse?"

I nodded, holding my hands up in a gesture of peace. "I'm here on strict orders from Princesses Dawn, Aribella, and Isolde to help destroy the curse."

She frowned. "But all those princesses are dead. That's what Nana told me. Otherwise, the curse would have stopped by now."

I shook my head. "They aren't. They're alive and doing everything they can to end the curse forever, not just for another hundred years."

She looked me up and down, as if sizing me up. "What's in the bag, huh?" she asked skeptically.

I opened my satchel and let her see the meager belongings inside. "The things I need to get to Princess Lorelei. Will you help me?"

She chewed her lip. "I have an aunt in the Spring Court. If you get me there safely, I won't kill you."

I had to control the smile that threatened to spread across my face. "Absolutely. I'd love to return you to your aunt."

She lifted her hand, palm out, and aimed it at my chest. "I mean it. I'm really powerful. If I think my life is in danger from you at any time, I'll kill you."

I held my hands up again. "I will not harm a hair on your head. But I'd like to get down this mountain before night falls. I imagine it gets very dark here."

She shivered. "Unnaturally dark."

Squaring her shoulders she peered up at me with a steely look of determination. "Okay, fine. Let's go. But remember—"

"You have super scary powers, and you'll kill me if I try to hurt you," I finished for her, and she nodded.

"Yep."

"I'm Zane," I said, holding out my hand and dropping the lord from my title so as not to scare her even more.

"Nellie." She shook my hand quickly.

"Shall we go?" I offered her my hand again, but this time to help her step up out of the closet. But she shook her head and climbed down herself.

She walked over to a cupboard, grabbed something that I

couldn't see, and then tucked it inside her clothes. It must have been small.

"You okay?" I asked.

She swallowed and looked around the room and although we really had to move on, she paused and said, "It's just my nana's favorite necklace. I want to keep it with me."

I realized how hard this must be for her, leaving her home in fear of what might happen to her if she stayed.

"Okay, take a few more minutes if you need it."

But then she shook her head.

"Okay, I'm ready," she said. And with that, we left the house.

When we reached the porch, we both stood there, black liquid almost up to Nellie's knees and my shins. Going to the railing, I glanced out over the edge of the cliff, where the oil poured over like a dark waterfall.

Nellie hooked her hands into the straps of her backpack. "How are we getting down?"

"You ever ridden piggyback?" I asked.

She made a sour face. "Not since I was five. And that was a *long* time ago."

I shrugged. "Well, how about just this once because I can't think of another way?"

She didn't look at all impressed with me but nodded, and I crouched down to make it easier for her. When she climbed onto my back, she pinched my ribs with her knees and hooked her arms around my neck.

"Hold on tight and close your eyes," I told her. She did exactly that. Actually, she held on so tight that she squeezed my throat and restricted my breathing.

"Could you just release your grip a little bit?" I asked in a bit of a muffled voice.

"You just told me to hold on tight!" she huffed.

Phew, this was going to be hard work in more ways than one.

"Fine," she said, but there was a wobble in her voice that betrayed her fear.

I hated that I didn't know what was on the other side of this cliff. How far down did it go? How flooded was it at the bottom? I had no idea, but we couldn't stay here, so what other choice did we have than to descend?

When I went to pull for my magic, it didn't come at first. Fear knotted my chest, but before I could panic, a bolt of lightning grew from my palm, and the knot of dread loosened. I threaded the black lightning's edges with shadows even as I grew it and then lassoed the large willow tree next to the cottage.

I took my time braiding the thick rope of magic so that it would hold our combined weight. I was more proficient with my lightning magic than I was with the shadows, so it had taken me a long time to figure out how to do this, but I was glad I'd had the patience to learn. This shadow-coated lightning rope was going to save both of our lives.

"Okay, don't be afraid. I'm not going to let anything happen to you," I said as I began to wade further into the deep, oily water.

"My nana said that right before she died," Nellie sniffled in my ear.

"Did your nana have shadow powers?" I asked her as the current of the thick substance rushed past my knees and up to my thighs as I walked down the porch steps.

"No," she answered, and I could hear a touch of disgust in her voice. "Nobody here has powers like that."

I was about to respond when I lost my footing, and we went down. Nellie screamed. Keeping my grip on the lightning rope, I twisted onto my stomach so that Nellie was above the liquid as it pushed us toward the edge.

"We're okay. We're going to go over the edge, but my lightning rope will keep us from falling. Don't be afraid."

"We're gonna dieeeeee!" Nellie screamed in my ear so loudly as we went over the edge and began to free fall so quickly that I winced.

But then, just when I was hoping that the lightning rope would pull taut, it suddenly did, stopping our descent with a sharp jerk that made my shoulder ache.

We hung in midair, black oil raining down on us. Concentrating, I slowly extended the rope, trying to look down to gauge how far it was to the bottom, but every time I did, black oil dripped into my eyes.

Nellie sputtered behind me.

"Don't swallow it," I warned her.

"I'm trying," she snapped, and then I felt one of her hands fall away from around my neck. She cried out.

"Keep both hands on me." Fear gripped me as her legs slipped down my waist.

"I'm slipping! Zane!" she cried, and then she was gone, no longer hanging onto me.

A surge of desperation slammed into me, and I felt sick. It was as if time stopped, and my brain processed a million thoughts in a single second. The way she had said my name clawed at my heart. I had promised nothing would happen to her, and now . . .

I did the only thing I could think of.

Keeping the lightning rope connected to the tree above, I

released the tension, allowing myself to plummet downward as I frantically searched the falling water below until I caught sight of Nellie, about to smack face-first into a lake of thick oil.

I pulled harder than ever before for my power. As I felt my gift respond, I flicked my free hand quickly toward her, wrapped another rope around her waist, and yanked her back up to me. The second I had her in my arms, I pulled the upper shadow rope taut, slowing our descent before jerking to a stop.

But something was wrong. I felt it briefly, and then, perhaps because my conjuring the two ropes had been too much, the one connected to the tree above snapped. We both began to fall again. Nellie's scream didn't last as long this time.

Luckily, we were only ten feet from the lake of oil, and we went in with a splash.

I bobbed up immediately, searching for Nellie.

"Zane, I can't swim," she called out, flailing in the thick oil a little ways from me.

I still had one rope attached to her, so I pulled on it, and she came closer as I treaded to keep us from sinking.

She reached me and frantically climbed onto my back, clinging to my neck. "I thought I was a goner," she sobbed.

"You're okay," I said. I tried to console her, but I was shaken myself. Why had my power failed? Two ropes should not have been too much. But I hardly had time to think about it as I searched for the shore.

The lake that we'd fallen into funneled us into a river of oil. Since I could keep our heads above the thick substance, I decided to let it carry us farther down, away from the mountain. As we traveled, Nellie held on tightly, and I tried to imagine how scary this was for her. She was a young girl stuck with a strange person from another place, and she was unable to swim in a thick river of black oil. I spoke calmly to her, and eventually, she seemed to become less tense.

It wasn't long before I saw a town with a desolate landscape. It wasn't as bad as what we'd just come from. There were withered crops, but oil didn't cover the ground as it had the mountain.

Pulling us from the river, I rolled onto the shore, panting as Nellie lay beside me, both of us covered head to toe in the foul stuff.

Her chest heaved as she stared at me wide-eyed. "We're alive."

I chuckled at her assessment. "We are."

She peered at the town and shook her head. "Sad that Orange Hills looks like this now."

I perked up, remembering Orange Hills on the map.

"How far is the capital of the Spring Court from here?" I asked her.

"Three or four days' walk. Less by horse."

We needed a horse. Lorelei was so close.

I helped her up. "Come on, let's see if we can find some people that can help us get a horse."

Chapter Two

LORELEI

The creaking of metal had my eyes snapping open. I pushed myself to a seated position just as Queen Liliana strolled into the small stone cell and peered down at me.

"Oh, what a mess you've forced me to make," she clicked her tongue.

I don't think I'd ever hated anyone in my life until this moment. Dawn's mother was positively evil. She'd kidnapped me and forced me into a cell.

"When my mother—"

Queen Liliana laughed, the sound grating on my nerves. "Your mother and father are about as useless as you are, dear. Your magic makes the world pretty, but it won't stop this curse."

I reached for my magic, testing the earth beneath me, searching for a seed, a root, anything I could make grow and wrap around Queen Liliana's throat. But there was nothing. Almost like she'd taken me to a barren wasteland on purpose.

"You're sick," I spat. "How fierce and loyal Dawn could be your daughter, I'll never know."

The hurt that crossed her face had me regretting my words instantly. Losing Dawn must have been hard on her, and my words were cruel.

"I'm sorry," I mumbled.

But just as fast as the hurt had been on Queen Liliana's face, it was replaced with stone-cold anger. "Lorelei, I never want to hear 'I'm sorry' from your mouth again. It's weak. Like Dawn, like Aribella, like Isolde. You're all weak," she snapped so loud I jumped.

Reaching down, she grabbed my arm and hauled me into a standing position. The second her skin made contact with mine, I became aware of her headache. When touching people, I could detect their maladies and then heal them, but even though it went against my nature, I didn't allow myself to heal her headache; she could live with it for how she was treating me.

As she marched me out of the cell, I glanced down at the heart locket at her throat. The glass casing held the smallest shriveled black heart I'd ever seen. A tiny purple glow emanated from it, and I felt sick now that I knew what it was. The heart of a mate of Dawn's great-great-grandmother Mae.

If what Isolde told me was true, the princesses of Faerie had been going to Ethereum for centuries and killing their beloveds. It was enough to bring tears to my eyes.

Queen Liliana gave me a side glance, looking disgusted with me. "You're crying."

I felt bad for Dawn, for what it must have been like growing up under this woman's rule. Yet somehow, the Summer princess still managed to retain her decency.

"Where are you taking me?" I asked as we moved down a dark hallway. I had no idea where we were, only that there were no flowers or trees for miles around us. If there were, I would have been able to feel them, but instead, the energy of this place was dark, desolate, unforgiving.

When we finally stepped into the underground stone room, Queen Liliana released me, and I skidded to a stop.

We were in some sort of study. There was a desk and shelves packed with books. Texts and papers were strewn about, and in the center of the open space was the mirror portal, the same one that normally sat polished in the Spring Court's throne room. My pink moonstone dagger lay on the floor beneath the mirror.

"Did you hurt my parents? My sisters?"

My knees felt weak. I couldn't remember much about my abduction. She'd knocked me out before I even knew what she was up to, but she would have had to fight half the castle staff to get the mirror portal out.

She rolled her eyes. "I didn't need to. They were dumb enough to give me the mirror for *training purposes*."

Training purposes . . .

My stomach dropped. Did my parents know she'd taken me? Had she convinced them that I was off training?

The one hope I'd been clinging to was that my mother and her guards would burst in here any moment and rescue me, but now that hope was dashed. I did not know how I would escape. But I did know what I was capable of.

Lifting my chin, I crossed my arms over my chest and leveled the queen with a hard stare. "I won't kill any of the Ethereum lords. So asking me to go through that will be pointless."

The look that washed over her face was nothing short of evil and caused a full-body chill to creep over my skin.

"Oh, I know that, dear." She reached out and grasped my shoulder hard, pushing me down and forcing me to kneel before her.

"That's why *I'm* going to do it. If your Ethereum lord doesn't come for you like I hope, I'll go into his realm and carve his black heart from his chest myself."

Zane. The handsome man I'd met only briefly already had my heart beating frantically just thinking of him.

"Or any of the others. It's nice that I have so many to choose from." She grinned as she dug her nails deeper into my shoulder, and I whimpered at the pain.

"You can't. Only a Spring Court royal can go through our portal when it opens," I told her.

"Yes, that's what you're here for, dear." Bending down, she picked up my faestone dagger and fisted it in her palm, and my heart rate spiked.

"You know, there is a lot about these daggers that is unknown. How they are capable of harnessing the power of Ethereum to open the portal home, among many other things. But I read a curious thing recently . . ."

I felt a tug at my navel and then a sharp stabbing pain in my stomach that caused me to keel forward, splaying out my hands to catch myself. The dagger in Queen Liliana's fist glowed a light pink, the same color as the moonstone embedded in the hilt, and I gasped as I felt my magic being sucked from my body.

"They can also transfer power from one fae to another." She grinned, her eyes going from blue to . . . purple. Like mine.

No.

I writhed out of her hold, trying to kick out, but it felt like someone had sliced my stomach open, and I was bleeding out all over the floor. Except it wasn't blood, it was my magic.

I wasn't prepared for the sudden weakness that washed over me, making my eyelids droop. My breathing slowed, and I struggled to stay conscious.

Fear flashed in Queen Liliana's eyes when she saw how weak I was getting, and she released my shoulder just as the darkness took me.

Chapter Three

ZANE

It was unnaturally quiet as Nellie and I left the oil river behind us and headed toward the town of Orange Hills. There were no birds flying through the air, no leaves rustling in the trees, no insects chirping or detectable life of any kind as we walked over the blackened, dead grass. Even the wind itself seemed to be holding its breath.

As fae, we shared a close relationship with nature. We respected and nurtured it. Some even had their magic rooted in the life-giving properties of nature itself, which I was told was the case with Lorelei and the fae in Faerie, who had seasonal-based magic. But as I looked around, it was obvious there was no life here anymore, and it made the hair on the back of my neck stand up.

Everything about this place was unnatural. Wrong.

This land was nothing but death.

Nellie and I remained silent as we reached the first house on the outskirts of town. It was a small cottage painted blue with red shutters and a thatched roof. Even the colors of the home, which were probably bright and vibrant at one time, were faded and muted, covered in a layer of what looked like gray soot.

As we passed, I noted that the front door was open and hanging awkwardly from only one of the three hinges. Whoever lived there was long gone.

We walked deeper into town, passing boarded-up storefronts and homes with shattered windows. There wasn't a single sign of life. Not so much as a lit candle flickering in a window. I supposed that made sense. The residents must have fled to another court for shelter because who could survive in this land of death?

Everything in the town appeared to be covered in what looked like a fine layer of dark dust or soot, dulling any colors that would have given this village a livelier look. The sun was still nowhere to be seen in the sky above, but the daylight had darkened, telling me that night was going to fall soon.

I wanted to press on. The need to reach Lorelei was like a living beast, constantly rattling in my chest, but when I glanced over at Nellie, her eyes were drooping, and her steps were unsteady. It was clear she was exhausted, and unless I wanted to carry her through the dark in an unfamiliar and most likely hostile land, we had no choice but to stop here for the night. With any luck, maybe one of these homes still had running water. I would give half my fortune right now to get cleaned up or at least find a fresh set of clothes that weren't covered in the oily substance we had basically just bathed in.

"We should stay here for the night and get some rest," I said to Nellie, and she nodded woodenly. "We can set off first thing in the morning when it's light."

Nellie glanced up, and the look she gave me was nothing short of eerie. "The sun's never up anymore," she said, her voice hollow.

I swallowed, thinking of how much trauma she'd been through recently, how much she'd lost already, and at such a young age. I vowed to myself then and there that I'd make sure I got her to her aunt in the Spring Court, no matter what it took.

"When it's lighter, then," I told her, and she made a noise that I think meant she agreed.

We'd walked about two-thirds of the way through the town already, and rather than backtracking, I steered her toward the first home that looked mostly intact. It was a squat, A-framed wooden house set back from the street. There was a small decorative fence in the front yard that only reached my hips. It was once white but now held the same grayish hue that everything else did in the village.

The gate was open and, much like the door of the first cottage we passed, hanging from only a single hinge. The front door of the house was still attached, though, and the windows weren't shattered or broken, which I took as a good sign.

We walked up to the door, and just as I was reaching for the knob, I paused, my ears picking up noise coming from something other than Nellie or me for the first time since entering the town.

"What?" Nellie asked, looking up at me with wide, scared eyes.

I held a hand out toward her. "Stay here," I ordered and then started around the side of the house in the direction of what sounded like a faint grunting noise.

When I reached the back of the house, I froze, taking in what I assumed was once open space for the town's members to enjoy but was now a makeshift graveyard.

Dozens, maybe even up to a hundred piles of turned dirt, were laid out in front of me, each one with its own rough stone marker. The marker was similar to what we did back in Ethereum to honor our dead.

Off to the side, I spotted an older man digging another hole in the ground, grunting with each stab of his shovel into the dirt.

"What's going . . . ?" Nellie started as she came up next to me, having completely ignored my command to stay put. I rolled my eyes. She crossed her arms.

The man's head whipped up, and his gaze landed on Nellie and me immediately. I didn't fear him. Even with my powers somewhat unreliable at the moment, a single fae wasn't any match for me, but I still nudged Nellie behind me.

"Who goes there?" the fae called, a touch of mistrust in his voice, and I didn't blame him. Even if it wasn't obvious that we weren't from his town, Nellie and I were covered in oil from head to toe. We had to be a sight to behold.

Lifting a hand in what I hoped was received as a friendly gesture, I started to slowly walk toward him. "Just a pair passing through on our way to the Spring Court. We were hoping to take shelter here in town tonight before moving on."

I stopped before drawing too close, not wanting to spook him more than I already had. Nellie stayed a step behind me, and for that, I was grateful.

With my hand, I gestured up and down my body. "As you can see, we ran into a bit of trouble."

The fae's grip on his shovel loosened a little as I spoke. He opened his mouth to reply, but a hacking cough racked his body, and I could hear an underlying wetness to it. When it cleared, he said, "Decided to take a swim in the river of darkness, did you?"

That was an apt name for what we'd just floated in.

Reaching back, I rubbed the back of my neck and chuckled. "Something like that. I'm Zane, by the way."

He nodded at me. "Evander." He wheezed, coughing again.

By the lines on his face, I'd guess that Evander was older than me by at least three decades, but he had a strong build and was clearly fit despite the slightly gaunt look of his face. His shoulders were almost as broad as my own, and he was also a tall fae. Again, not quite as tall as me—very few fae were—but almost. His beard was speckled with brown and white, and his gaze was both wary and tired at the same time.

Nellie poked out from behind me, and Evander's eyes shifted to her and warmed before returning to me.

"And this is Nellie," I added.

"Did you say you were passing through?" he asked, and I nodded. "Where from?"

He didn't seem suspicious of us, more curious, but even so, I had no intention of telling him the truth. "The other side of the Harvest Mountains," I told him, then gave him the name of a town I remembered from the map.

Out of the corner of my eye, I caught Nellie shooting me a look that I ignored. I might not have been able to hide that I was from Ethereum from her because she'd seen my powers, but it wasn't something I wanted to broadcast. From what Isolde and the other princesses had told me, these seelie had deep-rooted prejudice against our realm, and if this fae had any help to offer us, I planned to take it.

"What happened here?" I asked, waving a hand toward the graves and then the fresh hole he was digging.

I hadn't missed that just behind him was something wrapped in a dirty sheet that was approximately the size and shape of a body. I didn't think this man was a murderer. What killer dug graves for their victims? But just in case, I reached for my magic so that I was ready to lash out if he tried anything.

Evander grunted a half-laugh that was completely devoid of humor. "What do you think? The curse, of course. Many of us stayed, thinking we could hold out and withstand it, but . . ." He let his words trail off, and sorrow filled his gaze. He shook his head, glancing over his shoulder at the wrapped figure. "This was our neighbor. He passed just this morning. It's just me and my wife now. Everyone else either left or—" He gestured to the graves around us before hacking into his fist, this time releasing a gray puff of dust from his mouth.

It was clear the cough was because of the dust.

"Cover your mouth with your shirt," I whispered to Nellie.

Evander waved me off. "She won't get the powder lung from one night."

Powder lung. "Is that how they . . . ?" I nodded toward the grave closest to us.

He just nodded.

I cast my gaze around the area, once again taking note of the gray and blackened earth that stretched as far as the eye could see. I didn't know Aribella very well. Out of all the princesses, I'd spent the most time with Isolde, but even so, I knew with certainty that her heart would be broken if she could see her beloved court reduced to this uninhabitable wasteland.

"Why didn't you leave when the curse started poisoning your lands?"

Evander shook his head, and a stubborn glint entered his eyes. "My family has lived and farmed these lands for dozens of generations, just as most of the families in Orange Hills. This is our home."

He glanced at the half-dug grave at his feet, and then the hardness in his gaze melted away, revealing a deep well of sadness and vulnerability. "We just kept hoping, kept believing, that one of the princesses would return with an Ethereum lord's black heart. If just one of the princesses had succeeded in killing one of those evil bastards, none of this would have happened. But now—" He coughed and had to clear his throat before going on. "Now I think Elida and I have no choice. It's abandon our home, or end up like so many of our friends and fellow townspeople."

I didn't take offense to his words. Just like Dawn and the other princesses, the fae in this realm only knew what lies they'd been fed about Ethereum and my brothers and me. This man's grief was raw and real and founded on so much loss.

For the first time ever, I stopped to wonder if perhaps we'd been wrong all along. What was one life compared to all this death? Was my life, or any one of my brothers', really worth more than any other fae's?

I never considered myself better just because of the power flowing through my veins. The only thing that made me different from the man standing before me was that I'd been born with a black heart and the destiny to become an Ethereum lord. But in the face of all this death, was it selfish to not offer myself as a sacrifice to stop this curse?

I took a shaky breath and tried to center myself, hardening my resolve. What the princesses and all my brothers have worked so hard for, and the reason I'd traveled to this barren and hostile realm, was true and right.

Even if I wanted to forfeit my life to restore these lands, it wouldn't be possible without one of the princesses' faestone daggers to carve my heart from my chest. And we didn't even know if that would stop the curse in Ethereum as well. Maybe the magic from my heart would only stop the curse here in Faerie, leaving my realm and everyone in it doomed. And even if the best happened, and it did stop the curse in both realms, in a hundred years, this cycle of death and destruction would just start over again until another Faerie princess murdered her Ethereum lord mate.

No, I was doing the right thing. What this curse was doing to all our lands and subjects was wrong. Evil. It had to be destroyed once and for all, not just postponed.

"I'm sorry for your losses," I said to Evander, knowing my words wouldn't even begin to soothe his apparent pain, but they were all I had to offer.

"We've all experienced loss these days. But thank you, just the same." He cleared his throat again, reining in his emotions. "You two look like you could use a bath and a good night's rest. There's another shovel over there," he said, nodding toward a shed a little ways away. "If you help me dig the rest of this grave, my wife and I can offer you both of those things."

"We'd appreciate that," I answered him and went to grab the extra shovel.

We made quick work of digging the rest of the hole he'd already started. He stopped many times to cough up gray soot and phlegm, and I had to agree with his earlier statement that he'd end up like the fae wrapped in the sheet at our feet if he didn't leave this town soon.

When the hole was deep enough, I helped him carefully lower the body of his neighbor into the grave and covered him with dirt again. By the time we finished, Nellie was curled up against the side of the shed, fast asleep, so I scooped her up into my arms and followed Evander to his home, only a short walk away.

When we reached the house, I was introduced to his kind wife, Elida, who was short in stature as Evander was tall, with a round face, a kind smile, and the brightest green eyes I'd ever seen. Once I got a sleeping Nellie settled, she showed me to the washroom, and after using half a bar of soap and two buckets of boiled water, which Evander explained was still fresh as they had a deep well, I was clean.

It wasn't until I was standing with a towel wrapped around my waist and looking down at my soiled clothes, that I remembered to check my satchel. It was covered in the black sludge from the mountain and the river we'd basically swam in, but it was an oilskin bag and could be cleaned.

The items inside didn't fare quite as well. The map of Faerie was completely ruined. My heart sank, but then I thought that I knew fae here now, so I could ask them the way. Isolde's faestone dagger, the other princesses' faestones, as well as the pieces of the Shadow Heart, were covered in the black oily substance. It wasn't great, but they could all be cleaned.

It took me a little bit to find the vial and, specifically, the rolled-up note for Lorelei in the bag, but when I did, I sighed in relief. They'd been at the very bottom of the bag, protected by the oilskin and covered with the other items, so they were miraculously relatively unharmed.

The clothes I'd arrived in were ruined from my slide down the mountain and dip in the river of darkness. Since Evander was almost as tall and broad as me, he graciously gave me some of his clothes to wear, telling me he'd had a pair of pants that were too long for him anyway. Elida had gone to the house of one of the neighbors who used to have a girl around Nellie's age and found some clean clothes for her to put on when she woke.

After gulping down a small bowl of stew Elida had made with roots and lettuce she'd grown indoors, I stared at Nellie's sleeping form, wondering if I should let her sleep and if the oil sitting on her skin might be harmful. I decided in the end to wake her, and Elida helped her clean up and dress in the fresh clothes she found for her and eat a bowl of stew.

When we finally settled into bedrolls in front of the fireplace, my mind was wrought with worry.

How were things back home in Ethereum? Were Dawn and the babies okay? Was Lorelei waiting for me in the Spring Court? And what if Dawn's mother hurt her?

I felt absolutely feral just thinking about Lorelei being subjected to Queen Liliana's brutality. It was a long time before I drifted off, but when I did, it was with Lorelei on my mind.

Chapter Four

LORELEI

My magic was unique in many ways. I might not be an incredible warrior like Dawn or able to freeze someone where they stood like Isolde, but I could do other things. One of those things was a gift I kept secret from anyone outside my family. It frightened other fae, and I rarely used it unless it was an emergency. Like now.

My connection to all living things allowed me to remain cognizant during sleep or unconsciousness and move through dreams to visit the people I wanted, as long as they were asleep, too. The moment I collapsed on the floor in front of Queen Liliana, my subconscious mind became aware, and I dream-walked to my mother, only to find her awake and unreachable. It was like a closed door, even screaming and banging on it would get me nowhere.

I tried my father next. Door closed. Then my eldest sister. Still no luck.

Finally, I reached my three-year-old sister, Daisey, and relief washed over me when I saw the door to her mind wide open. She must be napping.

I rushed through the door, peering around at her dream landscape. We were in an open field of wildflowers, and Daisey was running through the colorful blooms, laughing and holding a cupcake in each hand. I'd never dream-walked with her before. I had always felt she was too young, but I had no choice now.

"Daisey, dear," I called, using her family nickname. She spun to look at me with a goofy grin, holding up the cupcakes in her hands as if to show her excitement.

"Lorly!" She couldn't say my name when she was a baby, and *Lorly* just stuck.

My heart pinched as she ran to me and fell into my arms.

"Want a cupcake?" She handed me one, and I took it but didn't eat it.

"Daisey," I began gently, "I know this is going to sound silly, but I need you to give a message to Mother for me when you wake."

"Wake?" She cocked her head to the side.

I had trained my other sisters and parents to sense when they were dreaming, but not Daisey, not yet, because of her age.

I nodded. "You're dreaming right now. But I can visit you in your sleep with magic."

"Fun." She bounced up and down, shoving the cupcake into her mouth and smearing frosting all over her face and nose.

"Daisey," I said, crouching to her eye level, "when you wake up, tell Mother that Queen Liliana took me. Tell her I'm being held somewhere with no trees or flowers for miles and miles."

Daisey's bottom lip quivered. "Took you? No fwowers?"

I didn't want to turn this into a nightmare for her.

I nodded, keeping my voice calm. "I'm going to be just fine, but I need you to tell Mother the second you wake up, okay?"

She frowned but nodded. Then, the sound of her heartbeat grew louder around us as the edges of the dream landscape began to dissolve. She was waking, probably because I had scared her.

I needed to leave. One thing I knew about this type of magic was never to get stuck in someone's mind when they woke. It could be dangerous for the fae and for me.

I rushed backward out of the door before the dream collapsed and found myself back in the blackness of my empty mind.

My dreamscape was void on purpose. I kept it that way so no one could enter uninvited. Something I had learned from my grandmother, who had the same gift. In her days of ruling, another fae who was a dream walker had implanted thoughts into her mind, trying to manipulate the outcome of certain events.

Because of her experience, I guarded myself. I sat alone in the blackness for hours, waiting to wake naturally, until a thought came to me.

What if Zane was here in Faerie?

I didn't think I could dream-walk into another realm, but he'd said he was coming for me. If he had found a portal into Faerie, that meant I could reach him, assuming he was asleep.

I'd never tried to dream-walk into the mind of someone I hadn't met in real life before, but in theory, I should still be able to reach Zane. Even though we hadn't technically met face-to-face, we had crossed paths briefly. That short interaction had left more of an impression on me than any other moment in my life.

His ghost-like image was seared into my brain. Dark auburn hair, shorn close to his scalp on the sides but longer on top. A sharp jawline, chiseled cheekbones, and a defined brow that might have made him look intimidating if it weren't for his kind, dark blue eyes. My favorite part was the splash of brown in one of them.

And he was tall, perhaps taller than any fae I'd ever met before. He had broad shoulders that tapered down to a narrow waist, long legs, and thick, muscular thighs.

Even in my dream state, I felt heat rise to my cheeks just thinking about the handsome lord. My reaction to the mere thought of Lord Zane was alarming. There were plenty of handsome men in the Spring Court, some arguably more so than the mysterious Ethereum lord, so having such a strong physical attraction to a fae I barely knew was unnerving.

I didn't know Zane's character or anything about him yet, so I was undecided whether I should be running toward these feelings or guarding myself against them. I'd never been one to judge anyone on appearance alone; there was more to a man than just a handsome face and strong physique. But right now, I needed help, and my instincts were telling me to reach out to Zane.

Since his image was already in the forefront of my mind, it took almost no effort to find him. Relief swept over me when I saw the door to his mind was wide open.

I stepped through the door into Zane's mind more tentatively than I had with Daisey's, feeling far more apprehensive about what I might find here than I had with my little sister.

The moment I entered the dream, I was transported to an unfamiliar and dimly lit room with a fire blazing in an open hearth. A study, perhaps? Or a private library?

The room was full of dark wood and decorated in shades of red and orange, reminding me of the changing leaves in the Fall

Court. The smells of cinnamon and orange peels filled my nostrils, wrapping around me like a comforting blanket.

Deep laughter reached my ears, and I spun to find Zane lounging on a sofa chair with three other unfamiliar males seated on a long couch next to him. They all had defining features that set them apart, yet they were similar enough to make it easy to recognize them as related.

His brothers—could these be the other Ethereum lords?

Zane hadn't yet noticed me. I was standing off to the side, hidden in the shadows, as the flicker of the firelight danced over him and the other fae. Isolde's note had told me that all the lords were brothers and had even included a brief description of each. Glancing at the men with Zane, I determined this had to be them.

I allowed myself a few moments to eavesdrop on Zane's interaction with his brothers, wanting to observe how they related to one another. Within minutes, it was easy to see that Zane had a deep fondness and affection for each of them, even the scarred, serious-looking one who didn't smile as easily or frequently as the others.

I found myself smiling as I listened to them rib each other good-naturedly, getting sucked into the dream more than I intended. It wasn't until there was a knock on the door that I came back to myself, remembering my purpose. I was just about to make myself known when the door to the study opened, and Dawn, Isolde, and Aribella poured into the room.

My heart gave an excited thump at the sight of my fellow Faerie princesses.

The brothers all rose from their seats as the women entered, Zane included. One by one, each of the princesses paired off with one of the lords. Dawn practically plowed into the mischievous-looking brother, throwing her arms around his neck and pulling him down for a quick kiss.

The scarred and serious fae's face split into a giant smile, softening all his hard features as he laid eyes on Aribella. He scooped her into his arms and swiftly left the room with her cradled against his chest.

Even Isolde rushed toward the brother with the longer, sun-streaked hair and teal eyes. Just as she was about to launch into his embrace, he bent over and hefted her over his shoulder. She laughed and playfully swatted at him from her upside-down position, telling him to put her down. Ignoring her protests, he followed his brother out of the room.

I could still hear her laughter echoing down the hall as Dawn and her lord left hand-in-hand, leaving Zane alone. It was the most wonderful feeling seeing them, and all so happy. It was what I needed in my worried state. Then I looked at the Ethereum lord still left here.

Zane gazed at the door his brothers and the princesses had just exited with a smile on his lips, but an aching longing in his gaze pinched my heart. He heaved a sigh and turned toward the window to look out into the dark night.

I sucked in a breath and gathered my courage. I'd already wasted enough time. I needed to make my presence known.

"Zane?" I said his name softly as I stepped forward into the firelight.

Zane's shoulders tensed, and he spun, his gaze fastening on me immediately, sending a trail of warmth down my spine.

"Lorelei?" He said my name like a prayer, then took a hesitant step forward.

I twisted my hands in front of me, suddenly shy and nervous, and gave him what was probably a wobbly smile. "Hello."

"But . . ." Zane glanced around the room, taking in his surroundings. "How are you here in the Western Kingdom? Aren't you in Faerie?"

"I am," I told him. "But so are you."

Zane looked around again, confusion creasing his brow. "This isn't Faerie. This is my study."

"I know it looks like your study, but it's not."

His eyebrows bunched in confusion, and I hurried to explain, realizing why he was so perplexed.

"You and I are real, but this place isn't. Physically, we're both in Faerie, but mentally, we're in your mind right now." I was explaining this all wrong. I bit my bottom lip in frustration, and his gaze dropped to my mouth. The confusion in his eyes morphed into something else. Heat.

Heat that was as delicious as it was dangerous.

"We're in a dream," I blurted out. His gaze snapped back up to mine.

"A dream?"

I nodded. "Yes. *Your* dream, specifically."

He sighed deeply, his shoulders sagging. Running a hand through the long strands of hair on top of his head, he began to turn away. "So, you aren't real, after all."

Without thinking, I stepped forward and grabbed his arm. The muscles of his forearm bunched under my touch, and he froze, looking over at me.

I swallowed, overwhelmed by our proximity. "I'm sorry. I'm not explaining this well at all."

Dropping my hand from his arm, I shifted back a half-step. He frowned at the distance.

"I'm a dream walker, and I wouldn't be able to enter your dream unless you were in my realm. That's how I know you're in Faerie."

Zane looked around again, his eyes widening. "You've somehow entered my dream?"

"Yes," I said, relieved that he seemed to finally be catching on. "And I reached out to you because I need your help."

At those words, Zane turned toward me, closing the space I'd put between us. Grabbing both of my arms firmly but gently, he held me in place.

"You're in trouble? What's wrong? Are you hurt?"

His gaze traveled up and down my body, searching for injuries he wouldn't even be able to see if they were there. I could appear however I wanted in dreams, so I knew I looked perfectly healthy and unharmed to him right now, which was mostly true. The pain Queen Liliana had inflicted on me so far hadn't left visible marks. But I'd already tasted some of her cruelty, and I didn't doubt she'd inflict more harm if she thought it would suit her ultimate purpose.

"I'm okay," I told him, worried that if I confessed I was injured, he wouldn't be able to focus on anything else. "But I do need your help. Queen Liliana has kidnapped me. She wants to try—"

A sudden, familiar tugging sensation pulled at my gut, and I gasped. I was waking up.

"What? What's wrong?" Zane asked, his gaze wild.

"I have to go. I'm waking up," I said, ripping myself from his grasp. The dreamscape wasn't dissolving around us like it had with my sister, but I had to get back to my void before I fully woke.

Turning from him, I rushed back through the door, cursing myself for wasting so much time watching him interact with his brothers instead of getting to the point. I had to hope he'd be asleep again tomorrow so I could tell him everything.

"Wait," I heard him call just as I fled from his dream.

Even as I started to blink my eyes open, I could still hear the echoes of his shouted plea for me to stay.

Chapter Five

ZANE

I awoke with a start, panting and covered in a thin sheen of sweat, as I frantically scanned the space to get my bearings. I wasn't sliding down a mountain of oil, nor was I in my study in the Western Kingdom. I was in Faerie, in the cottage at Orange Hills, with a sleeping redheaded child beside me.

Releasing a shaky breath, I glanced outside to see that it wasn't yet light. Then again, Nellie had told me it never got very bright here, so I had no clue what time of day it might be.

That dream . . . it felt so real. Lorelei's presence, her telling me she was in trouble, and then her sudden departure had turned the dream into a nightmare.

But was it real? Did she really need my help, or was I just imagining things out of some savior complex?

Already, the details of the dream were hazy. She'd referred to herself as something . . . a dream maker? A night visitor? I shook my head, trying to dredge up the memory from the depths of my mind. But as I grasped for the details, they slipped through my fingers like fine grains of sand.

It didn't help that after she left, the dream had morphed into something nonsensical. I was on a quest with a talking raccoon and bear, searching for marshmallow snowballs, when suddenly, the black oil from the Harvest Mountains swept us away. I was certain *that* wasn't real, so did that mean I'd simply conjured Lorelei as well?

She'd been on my mind constantly, so it made sense that she would appear in my dreams. I'd never heard of anyone having the power to visit someone in their dreams. The most logical explanation was that the dream was just that: a figment of my unconscious imagination.

But what if it wasn't?

I rubbed my forehead, the knot in my gut tightening with worry for Lorelei. My instincts told me she needed me right now. Then again, my instincts had been screaming at me to protect her since the moment I first laid eyes on her. That didn't necessarily mean she was in any more danger now than she had been before. Right?

A rustling beside me broke through my spiraling thoughts. Nellie stirred awake and peered up at me with sleepy eyes, pulling my attention.

"Hey, good morning," I whispered softly.

"Mmm," she grunted, still groggy.

I stood, guilt prickling in my chest, as I noticed the dark smudges under her eyes. She looked so tired. If given the chance, I knew she would roll over and fall back asleep. She probably needed the rest. But the best thing I could do for Lorelei was to get to her as quickly as possible. We didn't have the luxury of wasting time.

"Come on, we need to get a move on," I said gently.

With a groan, she sat up, rubbing the sleep from her eyes. Then she crossed her arms and leveled a defiant look at me. "Not until I've had a proper breakfast and thanked Evander and Elida."

I growled in frustration. If it were just me, I'd chew on some jerky while walking, but she was right. We should thank Evander and his wife for their hospitality.

An hour later, we were all seated at the table, eating flatbread and jarred fruit jam.

When Evander hacked up a powdery cough for the fifth time, I couldn't take it anymore. He and his wife had been so kind and generous to us, a couple of strangers, and it didn't sit right with me to just leave them here to continue to get worse.

"Come with us," I blurted out.

I was on an urgent mission to save Lorelei, but I couldn't let this old couple die.

Elida shared a look with her husband.

"This is our home," he said, but I could hear the defeat in his voice and the rattling in his lungs.

"We heard Princess Isolde went to Ethereum to end the curse. Maybe if we just wait another week—" Elida started, but a violent cough racked her body, cutting her off mid-sentence.

Her cough was even worse than her husband's, and that worried me.

Evander rubbed his wife's back as she tried to compose herself, then gave me a solemn look. "We would just slow you down."

It was true. They might not be as fast as Nellie or me, but the fae couple was still fit enough to walk. If I left them here, there was no doubt in my mind they'd die. I couldn't, in good conscience, let that happen when it was in my power to prevent it.

"I'll get us all to the Spring Court safely," I told them firmly. "You have my word."

Elida peered at her husband, her expression filled with silent pleading. Evander looked around their small home with misty eyes, clearly reluctant to leave. "Okay," he finally said quietly.

And with that, my party of two was now four.

Evander had a wheelbarrow that he'd filled with his most precious belongings, along with a walking stick for Elida. Though both were suffering from the effects of powder lung, they managed to stay steady on their feet for the most part and kept a decent pace. The only thing that slowed us down was their frequent coughing fits. We'd only been walking for an hour and had already stopped four times for both Elida and Evander to hack up powder. Sometimes, the fits were so bad we had to take a small break to let them recover.

The good news was that the further we got from the village of Orange Hills, the less gray dust there was coating everything. I made sure to shake out Nellie's clothes and dust her hair, not wanting any of the powder to cling to her.

We headed west for the next two hours until we stopped for lunch. After chewing on some dried meats and fruits, Elida sat in the wheelbarrow on top of their trunks of belongings while I pushed her. Wheezing and looking ashen, it was clear that the strain was wearing her down.

Nellie, who had been nervously watching Elida, stepped closer to me. "Is she gonna be okay?" she whispered.

I flicked a glance at Evander, who seemed as sturdy as a tough workhorse. He pushed on without complaint, though his face was sullen and void of emotion.

"Yeah," I lied, unsure what age kids should be told hard truths. But I also knew that Nellie had had to deal with so much already, and I didn't want her to have even more weight to carry on her young shoulders.

Elida twisted toward me, asking if I needed a break from pushing her. That's when I noticed her lips were tinged blue.

I shook my head, telling her I was fine, and started walking faster. The truth was, if we didn't find a healer for her soon, she probably wouldn't survive the journey.

The further we got from Orange Hills, the better the landscape became. There were trees with green foliage, albeit dusted with a thin layer of powder. The sun even seemed to be trying to peek through the gray cloud coverage every now and then. We found a stream to fill our canteens, and while the water wasn't crystal clear, it was relatively clean, with only a few oil-covered rocks at the bottom.

"Where is the nearest town? One that might have a healer?" I asked Evander.

He looked at me in shock. "Haven't you been to Spring Court before?"

I flicked a glance at Nellie, who was grinning. I had told her that if she kept my secret about being from Ethereum, I'd buy her some sweets when we found a decent town.

"No," I said smoothly. "Grew up poor. Never been past the Harvest Mountains."

I racked my brain, trying to recall the towns I'd seen on the map before it was destroyed.

Evander nodded, seemingly satisfied with my answer. "Buttercup Village is coming up. It's just across the border. The second biggest town in Spring Court. Plenty of healers there, if you've got the coin for them. I certainly don't."

Coin. Right.

"I'll figure that out," I told him.

I was more of a "figure it out as I go" type of person. There was no sense in worrying about something I didn't have. Maybe I could convince the healer to help by offering a trade of some sort.

Evander glanced at me and then at his wife, who was now sleeping in the wheelbarrow, her chest rattling with each labored breath.

"You'd do that? For us?" Evander asked, his voice heavy with disbelief.

I was taken aback by his question. I would have wanted to help them anyway, but after the kindness they had already shown us, I certainly wouldn't let his wife die over a lack of coin.

"Of course. You helped us, and now I'm going to make sure you're both taken care of."

I just hoped Lorelei could hang on a little longer.

When we reached Buttercup Village, I was taken aback by its beauty. Gone were the dust and oil-covered rocks. This area of Faerie was thriving, and I'd never seen so many beautiful flowers in my life. The entire road into the city was lined with thick, bluish-purple lavender bushes, their scent alone making me sigh in contentment. Each house within the white stone gates of the town was painted a pastel color. Fae of all ages ran to and fro, dressed in bright dresses and suits, including the men. A man tipped a light green top hat to me as we walked.

"It's like a dream," Nellie said, her eyes wide. "And I'll bet they have a sweets shop."

Right. I'd need coin for that, too.

I glanced down at Elida, still asleep in front of me, and felt a pang of worry. The blue hue of her lips had darkened.

"Excuse me, milady," I said, stopping a redheaded fae wearing a vibrant green dress. "Where is your most talented healer?"

She glanced at Elida in the wheelbarrow and then at Evander, her expression softening. "The best in the village is Percival Pennyweather."

She pointed toward the end of the lane where a bright blue shop bore the sign *Healer*. Then she hesitated, scanning our dust-covered secondhand clothes. "But the cheapest is Kelsie. She's in the hot-pink-and-white-striped house across from the sweet shop."

It was a veiled insult, but she meant well, I knew.

"Thank you." I tipped my head to her and started toward Percival Pennyweather's shop.

Evander grabbed my arm, stopping me. "Hang on. Should we try Kelsie first?"

I glanced at Elida and was almost certain she wasn't merely asleep but had lost consciousness. "If it were my wife, I'd want the best."

Evander rubbed a hand over his mouth but nodded. If we tried Kelsie and failed, I'd never forgive myself.

As we walked through the busy lane, I was dismayed to see a long line of fae stretching from the healer's front door all the way around the corner. Some clutched broken arms; others were bleeding or leaning on loved ones. This would take all day. I maneuvered Elida to the end of the line and told Evander to stay with her.

Nellie remained at my side as I bypassed the line and stepped up to the healer's door.

"Hey, no cutting," someone spat from the line.

"I'm only asking a question about price," I assured the male fae, who was holding a sickly looking child.

He grunted but said nothing, so I stepped inside. A bell chimed overhead as I glanced around the warm space. To the right was a waiting area of six hollowed-out logs, and a desk stood in front of me, manned by a stern-looking fae in a green apron and a blue bonnet. Above her, hundreds of potted flowers hung from the glass ceiling. The place smelled earthy and wonderfully fragrant. Behind the woman, a brightly painted hallway led to rooms where more helpers, dressed similarly, bustled about.

"Checking in? Payment upfront. Give me your name, and I'll put you on the list," the stern fae said without looking up from her parchment.

"I'm just inquiring about price," I explained. "We're at the back of the line, and my friend is gravely ill."

She glanced up, glaring at me. "So is everyone who comes here. But Percy is the best. No one leaves unhealed."

I sighed. "I'm here for my friends. We just traveled from the Fall Court. They're in their fifties and coughing up gray dust."

Her eyebrows shot up. "Middle-aged fae with powder lung?" She let out a low whistle. "That's gonna cost you."

"How much?" Nellie demanded, her voice tinged with sass.

I elbowed her lightly to calm her down.

"Five gold coins," the fae said flatly.

"Five golds! Are you insane?" Nellie shrieked, earning her another nudge from me.

The fae's eyes narrowed at Nellie's outburst.

"Five for the female, and I'm assuming another five for her husband?" I clarified.

She nodded.

"Is there a rush fee? Could I pay extra to move to the front of the line?" I asked.

She leaned forward, lowering her voice. "For ten gold coins each, you can use our side entrance and get immediate service."

"Ten golds," Nellie grumbled, and I nudged her again.

My heart sank. I had plenty of money back in Ethereum, but I hadn't thought to bring any with me. And anyway, it was useless here.

"And what if I were on a secret mission for the Spring princess, a close friend?" I asked, grasping at straws. "Could you bill her?"

The fae glared. "Are you wasting my time?"

"No," I promised. "I have the backing of Princess Lorelei."

She rolled her eyes. "Then where's your official summons?"

This wasn't going well.

"Okay," I said, desperation creeping into my voice. "If someone in this town wanted to make money fast, where would they go?"

"The treasury," she said as though it were obvious.

Right. The treasury.

"If you have collateral, they can loan you coin."

A loan? The Ethereum lord of the Western Kingdom getting a loan was unheard of. I had enough gold to buy this entire town.

"Next," she called over my shoulder, and someone scurried forward to take my place.

Defeated, Nellie and I left the healer's shop and headed for the treasury.

I wasn't a quitter. I would see Elida and Evander healed, and Nellie would get her sweets. I just needed to make some quick coin first.

The treasury master, a Mr. Donahue, stared down his crooked fae nose at me. "Let me get this straight. You have no deed to any land, no witness of character, and no job, yet you want a loan for thirty gold coins?"

I'd spent the last ten minutes trying to convince him that giving me the money was a good idea, that Princess Lorelei would pay it back. But the way he looked at me now, with such disgust, told me I was wasting my time.

"Yes," I said firmly.

Donahue tipped his head back and laughed, the smell of alcohol wafting over me. I glanced at Nellie to see if she noticed. She scrunched up her nose and scowled at the man.

"I'm not leaving without the money," I said, standing tall and towering over him as he sat at his fancy burgundy desk. Nellie stood as well, mirroring my movements. "Can you send a messenger to the Spring Court? Princess Lorelei will vouch for me."

At least, I hoped she would.

He sized me up, his beady-eyed gaze traveling up and down my body. "You've mentioned Princess Lorelei thrice now, and yet you do not wear the Spring Court armor, nor do you have a letter with her signet."

I growled softly. "My clothes got ruined by the river of black oil back in the Fall Court. Send a letter to Princess Lorelei, and I promise you she will vouch for me."

"I could," Donahue said, standing and tapping his long, crooked fingernails on his desk. "But that could take days, and I'm guessing you need this money fast?"

The sly glint in his eye put me on alert. He was about to offer me something I couldn't refuse. I could feel it. "I do."

"How tall are you?"

"Why?" I ground out through clenched teeth. The more he spoke, the less I liked him.

"Ever fought in hand-to-hand combat?" he asked.

That was unexpected.

My powers negated the need to fight in hand-to-hand combat, but I enjoyed the workout, so I'd trained in boxing and wrestling for years as part of my regular exercise.

"I've been known to win a few fights," I told him, thinking back to when Stryker and I used to spar as kids. We had a no-magic rule, which made things particularly fun.

The fae grinned, ear to ear. "Tomorrow night, there's a little competition. Each business owner sponsors one champion in an underground fighting ring. The prize is two hundred gold coins to be split with the fighter."

Two hundred gold coins. One hundred for me. That was decent. It would be enough to pay the healer. With what was left over, I could probably buy us a horse to get to the Spring Court faster. And Nellie would get those sweets I promised her.

Next to me, Nellie shifted from one foot to the other anxiously. "You want him to fight for you?"

Donahue nodded. "My current champion is decent but not nearly as big as Master Zane here."

Master Zane. He was already fluffing my ego.

A thought struck me. One that would make it impossible for me to fight and keep my identity secret.

"Is this a magicless fight?" I asked. If I used my magic, everyone would know I was from Ethereum. Nellie, a twelve-year-old child, had figured it out within seconds of meeting me.

His eyes lit up, and he leaned forward. "Of course. Why? Do you have magic? What kind?"

His eagerness made me wary. Perhaps magic was rare here, so I didn't want to give anything away.

"No. Just making sure I know the rules before I agree."

He nodded. "It's five fights. No magic, no rules. Occasionally champions die, but—"

"Die!" Nellie gasped. "No way. He's not doing that."

She reached for my hand and tried to yank me out of the office, but I stood strong. I caught her gaze. Her eyes were filled with tears, and something tender tightened in my chest. She'd lost her nana, and even though she barely knew me, I was now her lifeline. It felt like a lot of responsibility and not something I wanted to mess up. I crouched down to her level.

"Trust me," I whispered. "Death will not come easily for me."

She frowned and crossed her arms over her chest, clearly unconvinced. "You're too confident. You're probably not as strong as you think."

I smiled. "And you're a lot cheekier than you think."

"Cheekier," she said.

Straightening, I turned to face Donahue and extended my hand. "I will fight as your champion for a fifty-percent cut of the winnings, but I want twenty gold coins in advance to heal my sick friends."

Elida didn't have until tomorrow night.

The fae scowled at my hand. "How do I know you won't take my money and leave town?"

He was right to be cautious. "I could leave you with something valuable as collateral."

He glanced at Nellie, and the look he gave her sent chills down my spine.

"Not her," I growled and noticed Nellie take a half-step back so that she was a little behind me. I wanted to rip the fae's head off for the way he looked at the little girl. But I tamped down the desire.

Reaching into my pack, I pulled out Isolde's faestone dagger and laid it on his table. The blue kyanite stone embedded in the hilt glinted as it caught a beam of light.

His eyes widened, and he gasped as he stared down at the deadly weapon. "You've had this in your pack the entire time? There's no need for you to fight as my champion. I'll buy this off you—"

"It's not for sale," I told him, and he snapped his head up to glare at me.

He studied me with suspicion. "How did you get this?"

"Does that matter? Do we have a deal or not?"

He glanced between me, Nellie, and the dagger, weighing his options.

"Fine. Twenty gold coins, but if you lose the fight, I keep the dagger." He held out his hand.

"That's not fair," Nellie said, outraged, but I held up my hand to stop her.

The dagger was worth far more than a hundred gold coins, let alone the twenty I was asking for. But I didn't plan on losing any of the fights, so I nodded and shook his hand.

Nellie huffed beside me, clearly unhappy, but it didn't matter. The deal was done.

With one last look, I handed the faestone dagger over to Mr. Donahue, and Nellie and I left. We went straight back to the healer. After handing over the twenty golds to the fae at the front desk, she led Evander and Elida through the side entrance.

Within ten minutes, Percy, a flamboyantly dressed fae with a flair for theatrics, entered the room. He had them chew on some flowers, then placed his hands over their chests.

Nothing happened for a couple of minutes, but then they both coughed out the flowers and expelled more than a cupful of dust from their lungs. It was grotesque to watch, and Nellie looked positively green by the end of it.

"I can breathe," Elida said as we walked toward an inn on the main row of shops.

Evander grinned, holding his wife's hand. "I haven't felt this good since before the curse."

They both looked ten years younger, and their pace was noticeably faster as well.

"Thank you," Evander said as I pushed their cart filled with their belongings.

"You're welcome," I told him, matching his grin. It felt good to see the two of them well again.

Evander stopped and grasped my upper arm, forcing me to look at him. There was a tenderness in his gaze that made my chest tighten.

"I mean it, son. Thank you."

At his words, a lump formed in my throat. I hadn't been called "son" in so many years. Not since my father died. It reopened an old wound inside of me, but I managed a nod.

"You're welcome. And I'm out of coin now, so I hope you've got money for the inn," I joked, trying to lighten the mood.

Everyone burst out laughing. "Now that I can manage," Evander assured me, and we made our way to a little yellow building with a bustling tavern beneath it.

It had been a long day, and I was weary. With an even longer day ahead of me tomorrow, when I planned to win those fights, all I could think about now was getting some sleep.

Chapter Six

LORELEI

"We're going to have to take this slower than I intended," Queen Liliana said as she stood, looking down her nose at me with an expression that was both haughty and annoyed.

I lifted my chin in defiance. It didn't matter that her hair was perfectly coiffed, and she was dressed in an elegant red silk gown, while my dress was soiled and in tatters, and my hair dull and knotted from spending days in her dungeon. I was still the Spring princess, and I wouldn't let her make me feel less than.

We were back in the room with the mirror portal, and no matter how hard I searched the ground beneath me for magic, for a single shred of life, there was none. It was just a cold, hard floor, and that filled me a little with terror.

"Where are we?" I asked, knowing she wouldn't give me a straight answer but hoping she might accidentally reveal something.

She grinned at me, and it made my stomach churn. "Can't feel any flowers nearby?" she asked mockingly, then rolled her eyes. "How stupid do you think I am? I know better than to do this in the middle of a garden."

I clenched my fists, promising myself I would fight back, even though my instincts had never been to harm another.

She noticed my balled hands and barked out a laugh. "Oh, Lorelei. Try it, honey. Try to overtake me by force."

I did. With a battle cry, I burst from where I stood, my hand raised in front of me, ready to strike. But when I got within range, Queen Liliana lashed out with her fist and punched me square in the nose.

Pain exploded between my eyes as I reeled back, a wail ripping from my throat. Something wet and warm gushed from my nostrils, dripping onto my lips as I sank to my knees in shock.

The coppery tang of blood hit my tongue, and I peered up at the Summer queen in disbelief.

She'd hit me. Hard.

"Do you think I enjoy this?" she asked, frustration etched across her face. "I assure you, I don't."

Reaching into her shirt, she pulled out the locket that held the heart of an Ethereum lord, letting it dangle in the air. "I'm not doing this for myself. I'm doing this for all of us. All of Faerie depends on this magic to stop the curse. Already, three of our courts have been overtaken. Would you sit by as the Spring Court is eaten alive? Every tree, every flower, every blade of grass will turn black," she seethed. "And every fae still alive will die of starvation or illness. All because the princesses of Faerie were too stupid and too weak to do what needed to be done to protect their people and their land."

I whimpered as tears spilled down my cheeks. I wanted to tell her that Dawn had a plan, that she was alive and had sent Zane to help me, but I knew better than to divulge anything. Anything I told the queen would only be used against me. She was single-minded in her purpose, and I knew no amount of begging or reasoning would change her mind.

She cocked her head to the side, studying me as if reading my thoughts. "You think the Ethereum lord they are sending will save us all? You think my Dawn will save us?"

Gathering my strength, I rose to my feet and faced the queen, even as blood continued to drip from my nose. "She might. And then you'll be ashamed of how you're acting."

She rolled her eyes. "Dawn is weak. She fell in love and left her people to die. She's running her wheels so she doesn't have to live with the guilt of the genocide she's contributed to. So at the end of this, she'll be able to say she tried."

"You're wrong," I gritted out.

She stalked toward me then, brandishing the faestone dagger. My dagger.

With the dagger in her left fist, she grabbed my throat with her right hand and squeezed. It wasn't hard enough to completely cut off my oxygen, but enough to send a clear and dangerous message.

"I'm willing to do whatever it takes to restore Faerie. They will write about me in history books, and you can say you played your part," she sneered.

A ripping sensation started behind my navel and worked its way up to my chest, sharp and agonizing. I gasped, whimpering as the dagger flared to life, glowing with a rosy-pink magic.

"You . . . can't . . . go through the portal . . . until it opens," I managed to huff between stabs of pain. "By then . . . it might be too late."

The Spring Court had never sent a champion and never would. By the time the portal opened, the curse might have already overtaken my court.

"I have a plan for that, too," she said with a chilling smile.

That sadistic look on her face was the last thing I saw before blackness claimed me.

I became aware again in my void—my dreamscape. Without thinking, I rushed to find Zane's door first, bypassing my mother, father, and sisters because they couldn't help me right now.

I knew in my gut that only Zane could stop this.

When I stepped into his dream, I expected to find myself in his study again. Some people had a recurring dream space, but today, he was in a crowded tavern. There was a little girl, about eleven or twelve years old, standing next to him. The men around them were leering at her. One of them reached for her, clamping his hand around her wrist, and Zane exploded with rage. He punched and kicked at them, fighting like an animal, as the little girl screamed for him.

Oh no.

I realized I was in a nightmare.

This had happened before, and I hated it because it made it so much harder to reach the person. Zane wouldn't see reason while he was stuck in a nightmare, and I needed him to. The only way to gain his trust in this situation was to join him. Even though we were not enemies in real life, in a nightmare, he might attack me, and I'd get nowhere.

I ran forward, pulling the girl into my arms and twisting her out of the way just as one of the men lunged for her. I moved in front of her and kicked the man between the legs. He went down, moaning.

"Nellie!" Zane bellowed, several men now between us.

Clutching the girl tightly, I crossed the room to get to him, twisting out of the men's grasps as I went. Zane fought to reach us, and when he did, I passed the girl off to him. He picked her up, and she clung to his neck, nuzzling her face into his chest. My heart melted.

Who was this girl?

Zane held her close, his protective instincts palpable, and stared at me wide-eyed. "You're here again."

I nodded. "Zane, you're dreaming. You can stop all of this. You can think them away." I gestured to the angry men, who were now trying to stand up and go for a second round.

Zane's brows bunched together, and even in a dream, I couldn't help but be struck by his handsomeness.

"Zane," I urged him. "I need you. Please, will them to be gone."

At my words, he closed his eyes. One by one, the angry men faded from the tavern. The girl, Nellie, was still tucked tightly in his arms, now sound asleep. The speed with which he'd done all of that amazed me. Most fae would not be able to control their dreams or nightmares with such clarity, and it made me feel even more attracted to him. So capable as well as handsome. And then I shook myself. We had other things to discuss.

When he opened his eyes and noticed the men were gone, he staggered backward in shock.

"Zane, I don't have much time," I told him, and his gaze snapped back to me.

"Dream drifter," he whispered.

"Dream walker," I corrected him.

He rubbed his forehead, clearly trying to recall our last dream.

"Yes. This is real," I assured him. "I'm really contacting you, and I need your help."

He nodded and walked over to one of the couches at the back of the tavern. Gently, he laid the sleeping Nellie down and covered her with his coat.

When he strode back over to me, I couldn't help it. I had to ask.

"Who is she?"

He glanced back at the girl, his expression softening into something like adoration. "A kid I met in the Harvest Mountains. She's had some rough luck. I'm traveling with her to the Spring Court to reunite her with her aunt, and to see you."

Hearing that he'd found this girl in the Harvest Mountains and was helping her made my heart flutter. But I couldn't focus on that right now.

"Listen to me. I'm not in the Spring Court. Or at least I don't think I am. Queen Liliana has kidnapped me—"

"What?" he bellowed, and then suddenly, he was inches from me, scanning my body as if searching for injuries. "Are you hurt?" he asked.

Oh, stars. I lost all train of thought then and had to take a half-step away from him to regain my wits.

"Not right this second," I hedged. "But the queen is draining my power. She has some sick plan to go through the Spring Court mirror portal and . . ." I hesitated. His brothers were the Ethereum lords, so I couldn't say the next words lightly. "Carve out the heart of one of your brothers."

Grim determination settled over his features. "How long do I have?"

I shrugged. "I don't know . . . Every time she siphons my power, I black out—"

"Does it hurt you?"

His concern was sweet. "Not really," I lied.

"Where are you? I'm coming to get you right now."

I shook my head. "I'm not sure. But I'm afraid if you come to me, then she'll kill you. That's what she really wants. Going through the portal is just her backup plan."

"Lorelei," Zane growled. "There's no way I'm just going to leave you with that monster. If she's draining—"

I lifted my fingers to his mouth to stop him. As touched as I was by his concern, we were running out of time. At any moment, one of us could wake.

The instant my fingertips brushed his lips, Zane fell silent, and his pupils dilated. I meant to speak, but as I stared into his blue-and-brown gaze, my heart skipped a beat, and my throat suddenly went dry.

Zane slowly reached up and took my hand. I licked my lips, and his gaze dropped to my mouth, heating with emotion.

Finding my words, I forced myself to slip my hand from his. "You need to get to the Spring Palace and rally with my mother. They think I'm just training with Queen Liliana. They don't even know I've been kidnapped. My mother will bring in the royal guard, and once I'm free, we can destroy the curse."

He nodded and ran a hand through his hair, clearly agitated. "Okay. I will. I'm coming for you, Lorelei."

The way he said it, with such confident conviction, made me

believe him. I relaxed a little, freeing up my mind for other things. "So, what's the plan?"

He cocked his head in confusion.

"You know, the big plan to destroy the curse. The reason you're in Faerie. There's something we're supposed to do together, right?"

"Oh, well, that's . . . we're not really sure," he began, looking around the room as if searching for something.

I placed my hand on his arm, forcing him to meet my gaze. "I'm sorry, what? You aren't sure? So there's no plan?"

The shock of it made me feel sick. I'd hung everything on the belief that there was a way to destroy this curse.

"There is a plan. I have a note for you. It's just not here."

A note. From Dawn? Isolde? Of course, it wasn't here. This wasn't real. We were in a dream.

The tavern around us started to go hazy, alerting me that Zane was waking up.

"I have to go," I said, beginning to back out of the room. But this time, Zane ran after me.

"No, not yet," he begged as I stepped out of the door.

Trying to follow me, he slammed against an invisible barrier, wincing in pain. Only a dream walker could cross through there.

I wanted to stay and study the lines of his concerned face, but even as I watched, the dream around him started to dissolve until Zane disappeared as well.

Chapter Seven

ZANE

I bolted upright, my heart hammering in my chest like a war drum, a thin sheen of sweat coating my skin.

The dream. Lorelei. It was real.

The dream, as well as the one I'd struggled to remember the night before, came back to me with full clarity. Lorelei was a dream walker, and she'd been kidnapped by Dawn's delusional mother. I had to rescue her.

I leaped out of bed and turned on the kerosene lamp, scouring the dark space for my boots. The sun had yet to rise, but that didn't matter. I couldn't stay here. I had to get to Lorelei.

A groan came from the other side of the room, and I glanced over to see Nellie asleep on the cot. I'd momentarily forgotten about her. Of course, I couldn't just leave her here.

I went over to where she lay and shook her gently until her eyes opened to slits, and she stared up at me groggily.

"Grab your stuff. We're leaving," I told her, then started packing my own belongings.

Lorelei. Lorelei. Lorelei. Her name was a frantic call in my mind. From the moment I'd laid eyes on her in the vision with Isolde, all I'd wanted to do was protect her. And now, after seeing her in my dreams twice and knowing she was in danger . . . it caused my protective instincts to flare to unimaginable levels.

I'd kill Queen Liliana for this. And burn down whoever got in my way.

"You're scaring me." Nellie's voice was small, and I froze.

I hadn't realized I'd been aggressively shoving things into my bag and growling to myself in anger.

I took a second to breathe deeply and looked over at her.

"I'm sorry. It's just that someone I care about has been taken. Princess Lorelei. I have to rescue her."

Nellie sat up, looking concerned. "Okay . . . where is she?" she asked, her red hair mussed from sleep.

Now that I'd calmed down enough to think, I realized I didn't have an answer to her question. "I don't know, but I can get help from someone at the Spring Palace. And then I can return you to your aunt."

She made a face. "Right. My aunt. Well, you can't leave without that pretty dagger, right?"

I ground my teeth in frustration. Moving to her side of the room, I started stuffing her things into her small pack. She was right. I did need that dagger. It was far too valuable to leave behind.

"I'll steal it back," I told her. I wasn't above breaking the law if it meant getting to Lorelei sooner.

Nellie frowned. "Then we go on foot to the Spring Palace with Mr. Donahue looking for us with his goons?"

Why was a twelve-year-old making more sense than my own thoughts right now?

Lorelei, Lorelei, Lorelei.

Her soft brown hair and those sharp purple eyes pierced into my very soul. I had to get to her. But was I being too hasty?

I stopped what I was doing, clutching Nellie's small boot in my hand. If I stayed another day and participated in that fight, I could win enough money to buy a horse. That would cut our travel time to the palace at least in half, making up for the day I'd lose here.

I let out a shaky breath, and Nellie laid her small hand on my arm, startling me. I hadn't even noticed she'd padded over to me. She stared up at me with understanding in her eyes.

"I get scared a lot, too. I was really scared when my nana left," she said, voicing what I hadn't yet admitted. That I was terrified of losing Lorelei before I'd even had a chance to get to know her. "How about you just leave the dagger with Mr. Donahue? Then we can set out on foot right now and save the princess. I can even help."

My gaze dropped to the hole in the bottom of her boot I was still holding, and a weight settled on my chest. She couldn't last another day on foot.

"You need new shoes, kiddo," I told her, inspecting the boot closer.

"It's fine," she snapped, her sassy personality coming back out to play.

"Hey, don't worry. It's not just about your shoes. I need that dagger. It might be important."

"So you gotta compete in the fights?" she asked, and I could see the fear in her eyes.

I didn't want to fight for this money. I wanted to forget about the dagger and leave town right now. But I didn't even know where Lorelei was, and even though I had no idea how, these daggers might be important to ending the curse. I couldn't just leave one here.

Nellie needed new shoes, the sweets I'd promised her, and we had to get a horse to make the best time. According to what Evander had told me, we could reach the Spring Palace in twenty-four hours if we rode all day and night. That was more than twice as fast as it would take us on foot.

It was obvious what needed to be done.

"You ever ridden a horse?" I asked her, and her eyes lit up.

"It's only my favorite thing in the world."

"Good. Tonight, after I win the fights, we'll ride all night and day to make up for lost time. Okay?"

She nodded enthusiastically, but then her face fell. "What if you don't win? What if you . . . die?" Her bottom lip started to quiver, and I reached out to squeeze her hand.

"Remember my shadow magic? The secret magic you're not supposed to tell anyone about?"

She nodded as a tear welled in her eye, and she batted it away.

"Well, that makes me *really* hard to kill."

She frowned. "But you're not allowed to use magic in the fight."

"Right. And I won't. Unless I think my life is in danger. Then it's okay to break the rules."

I was confident I wouldn't need my magic, but I wouldn't hesitate to use it if the fight turned dirty, which something told me it might. Rules tended to get broken in these kinds of fights, leaving you to rely on whatever you had at your disposal. I hoped it wouldn't come to that, but I'd do what I had to. Most importantly, I wanted Nellie to feel safe. For the time being, I was all she had.

She nodded. "And if it comes to that, I'll use my magic to protect you." She crossed her arms over her chest and tipped her chin high.

Did I have that much confidence at her age? No, I didn't.

This kid had grown on me. Beneath her tough exterior was something soft and vulnerable, and I wanted to protect that.

"I need to get a message to someone in the Spring Palace. Do you know where I could do that here?" I asked her.

If I wasn't going to head out immediately, I at least wanted to warn Lorelei's parents and let them know I was coming to help.

"I do," she told me, then pointed to her stomach. "But I need to fill this first."

Despite the situation, I grinned. "Oh, is that a fact?"

The kid could be bribed to do anything for food, which was a little scary. She was also very bony, and that made me wonder what she'd been living off of until I found her.

I glanced out the window and noticed the sun was finally starting to rise. "Come on," I said. "Get dressed, and we'll go find Evander and Elida to see about breakfast."

At breakfast, I told Evander about a friend I needed to help and explained that I had to procure a horse and supplies to get to the Spring Palace. I mentioned that I wouldn't have the money to pay until later this evening. Evander offered to help, reaching for his coin purse, but I waved him off. Evander and Elida had just lost their home and livelihood. They needed that money for themselves, and besides, it might not even be enough.

I explained to them that I planned to win a fight to get the funds I needed. Elida raised an eyebrow when I told her but said nothing. Evander nodded with respect and then gave me some pointers on keeping my arms up high and protecting my head.

After Evander and Elida graciously paid for our meal, Nellie and I set off to the messenger's barn to send a note to the Spring queen. Once we arrived, I found someone willing to send a message via raven for me on loan. He was a fan of the fights and said word had spread all morning that the exceptionally tall outsider was Mr. Donahue's new champion.

I sent a brief letter to Queen Gloriana explaining that Lorelei had contacted me in a dream and that I was coming to help rescue her. I also mentioned that I had a plan to end the curse, though I didn't elaborate. I avoided saying I was from Ethereum and instead claimed I was a powerful fae from the Fall Court and a friend of Lorelei's.

I didn't know if the Spring queen would believe me. I was a stranger, after all. But if Lorelei hadn't visited her parents in a dream yet, they needed to know what was going on. I hoped my message would spur them to ready their troops for a rescue.

Once I got to the Spring Palace and dropped Nellie off with her aunt, I was going to find Lorelei, and nothing would stand in my way. But having an army of troops at my back wouldn't hurt.

"Now what?" Nellie asked as we walked through the shops.

I ran my hand through the longer strands of my hair for the hundredth time that day. I hated waiting. Sitting around and doing nothing was my least favorite thing to do. But the first fight wasn't until sundown, several hours from now.

I glanced at the sweets shop we were about to pass, then down at Nellie. She grinned up at me, her expression softening something inside me in a way I hadn't expected. I found myself wondering if Lorelei wanted kids, and if so, how many. I'd always wanted a big family. At least five children.

With those thoughts, a burning ache flared in my chest. I had to find something to occupy my mind, or I'd go crazy, so I stepped into the sweets shop.

Twenty minutes later, after a lot of charm-filled wooing, I convinced Britana to give Nellie a free bag of sweets in exchange for coming back just before closing in a couple of hours to sweep the entire shop and wipe down all the counters.

As we walked down the lane, Nellie fisting chocolates and shoving sours into her mouth, she glanced up at me with bright eyes. "I could get used to this," she mumbled over a mouthful of candy.

I chuckled, though my smile didn't quite reach my eyes. I could only enjoy her happiness a little, knowing that Lorelei was hurt and counting on me. The fight wasn't for another eight hours, and waiting that long before doing anything to rescue the woman I was pretty sure was my mate was going to be one of the greatest challenges of my life.

Fate help me.

Chapter Eight

LORELEI

I'd come to terms with the fact that I couldn't physically overpower Queen Liliana, at least not without using my magic. But I didn't have access to the part of my magic that could help me. Giving life and healing ailments were useless when you were kidnapped in a barren wasteland devoid of life. Instead, I used a rusted nail I'd pried from the cell door and worked at the lock.

Lock-picking was not a skill a princess should possess, but our parents had taken to locking up the sweets in the larder. When I was ten, I decided to ask one of the stable hands, who was known to have a colorful past, to teach me. For two years, my parents couldn't figure out how the sweets kept disappearing until my mother caught me with a hairpin mid-lock-pick. I thought she'd be furious, but instead, she grinned, called me resourceful, and told me not to do it again.

Now, this nail was five times thicker than my trusty hairpin, but it fit in the lock, and I was determined to keep trying until my fingers bled. My arms were shoved through the bars at an awkward angle, my hands cramping, but I wasn't going to give up. Every time Queen Liliana fed on my magic, I grew weaker and weaker. If I didn't escape, and soon, she was going to kill me. I couldn't let that happen. I had to find Zane and destroy this curse.

I was extra nervous because I hadn't been able to reach my parents. Either they'd discovered I'd been taken and were sick with worry, or there was some other reason they weren't sleeping much, leaving me unable to reach them.

I hoped my little sister had delivered the message I'd given her, but I just didn't know. Daisey was so young. Who knew if she even remembered my visit, or if anyone would believe her?

The only thing keeping me sane right now was Zane. Seeing him in his dreams and knowing he was looking for me gave me the strength to keep fighting.

I was on my hundredth attempt at picking the lock when it finally clicked open. The telltale sound rang out, and I wasted no time pulling my arms back through the bars, shaking them to get the feeling back.

When had Queen Liliana been here last? How much time did I have to escape?

When I'd tried to overpower her before, I'd failed miserably. She was ruthless, and I'd never been taught to fight. She told me that if I resisted again, she'd blind me with her sunlight magic, and I knew she was capable of it.

My heart pounded frantically in my chest as I yanked the old steel door open and bolted out of the cell. She always took me left to the study where she kept the mirror portal, so I went right instead.

As my bare feet padded soundlessly on the stone floor, I

prayed to every star in the sky that I wouldn't run into her. I nearly wept with relief when I found a staircase leading upward. I hadn't seen the sun in days, and I wondered if that was another reason why I was growing so weak. I wasn't meant to be cooped up. I needed sun, fresh air, and earth to thrive. It was always sunny in the Spring Court, with light rain and a cool breeze at night, the perfect growing weather.

Oh, how I longed to feel the warm rays of the sun on my skin again, to reach down and touch the cool, damp earth. Being in the garden was my life, and without it, I felt . . . like I was dying.

At the top of the stairs was a closed door. I slowed my pace, hoping it wasn't locked. If it was, I'd have to turn around and search for another way out. Picking the lock would take too long, and I couldn't risk being caught.

When I reached the door, I twisted the handle, and to my immense relief, it turned.

I sighed quietly and began to push the door open, freezing when I heard voices. "She wants her soup warm but not hot, but also not cold," a female voice grumbled to another as they passed by.

Peeking through the crack in the door, I saw two women walking down the hallway. One looked to be around my age, and the other was a gray-haired elderly woman. Both were wearing maid uniforms.

"When you serve royalty, you get used to these requests. Make two bowls at different temperatures and let her choose," the elder maid said in a matter-of-fact tone.

The younger one groaned but didn't argue as they turned a corner and disappeared out of sight.

I don't know why, but I had thought I was alone here with the queen. Part of me wanted to run to the maids and beg for their help, but if they were employed by Queen Liliana, even if her demands frustrated them, they were most likely loyal to her. If she convinced them she was saving all of Faerie, they might just let her get away with anything, maybe even murder.

I had to get out of here.

Gently pushing the door open wider, I padded into the hallway and tiptoed toward another corridor lit dimly by a soft glow. I stopped at the threshold, carefully peeked around the corner, and then rushed down the hall toward a giant set of double doors.

My freedom.

Quiet muttering voices sounded behind me, but instead of stopping to look, I broke into a full run, my heart pounding in my chest.

Reaching the door, I yanked it open and slipped outside, shutting it quietly behind me. I stood there, panting, my heart slamming against my ribs as the panic of fleeing washed over me.

But there was no time to dwell on it.

As I surveyed my surroundings, my stomach dropped.

Spread out in front of me was a barren wasteland, worse than I had imagined. Dry, cracked earth stretched as far as the eye could see. Small black ash rained from the sky in an endless, suffocating drizzle. There wasn't a single tree or bush anywhere in sight.

A world devoid of life.

It was my worst nightmare, but I had no choice. I had to run through it to escape.

Breaking into a sprint, I aimed for what looked like hills in the distance. The raining ash was so thick it blurred the landscape, making it hard to pinpoint any landmarks.

I scanned the horizon desperately, trying to get my bearings. It was daytime, but the sun was hidden behind thick clouds, its rays muted and weak.

Behind me, the large estate loomed, crumbling and decrepit, with a dilapidated barn sagging off to the side.

Where was I? Which way was the Spring Court?

I felt a wave of helplessness as I ran, pulling the bodice of my loose dress up to cover my mouth from the ash trying to invade my lungs. My feet pounded over sharp rocks, a jagged edge splitting a gash between my toes, but I ignored the pain.

As I neared the hilly range, the clouds parted for a brief moment, and I could finally see the shapes and details of the rounded peaks. They resembled a row of turtles laid out in formation.

The Turtle Mountains!

I was on the desolate side of the Turtle Mountains in the Summer Court. That meant I was—

A bolt of light shot past my head, barely missing my ear. I spun around in shock.

Queen Liliana was stalking toward me, flanked by three armed guards.

She shook her head, clicking her tongue. Her face was eerily calm, but fury burned in her eyes. "I told you what I'd do if you defied me again."

Before I could respond or move, a beam of light so bright it instantly brought tears to my eyes ripped through the air toward me.

Falling to my knees, I screamed as pain engulfed me. Clutching at my face, I cried out.

She'd blinded me.

Chapter Nine

ZANE

I walked the entire town with Nellie. She followed me like a little duckling, never complaining about her feet hurting as she ate her bag of sweets. I had pre-negotiated a price for a nice mare to get us to the Spring Palace, along with some supplies, including new boots for Nellie. A fae named Jasper, at the east end of the city where his farm shop was located, was holding everything for me.

Now, I was waiting outside the sweets shop while Nellie swept and cleaned to pay back her debt to the owner. I rolled my neck, stretched my arms, and did some basic warm-ups in front of the shop as the sun began to set. A part of me wanted to fall asleep just so I could see Lorelei again. Even in my dream state, she was irresistible. Her full, red, heart-shaped mouth. Her soft, creamy skin that I was dying to press my lips against. Even her scent was enticing.

I had no idea how I could remember a fragrance from a dream, but I did. Even now, as I closed my eyes and drew in a deep breath,

I could almost smell the sweet notes of floral honeysuckle and vanilla carried on the wind.

But it wasn't just Lorelei's physical beauty that drew me to her. The way Isolde had talked about the Spring princess had made her seem delicate, almost fragile. Isolde hadn't said it in so many words, but I got the distinct impression that she, along with the other princesses, thought Lorelei was too soft for this world. With her gentle demeanor and kind heart, I could understand why they thought that. But I'd seen the fire in Lorelei's eyes when she came to me in my dream.

The way she protected Nellie against a room full of hostile males. How she didn't just beg me to save her but cautioned me against coming until I had the support of her court to protect me. Even now, she was standing up to Queen Liliana and enduring who knows what kind of torture in order to do the right thing rather than the easy thing. She was fierce, with an inner strength that most overlooked. Sweet and kind didn't mean weak.

Movement on my left caught my attention. A hulking male fae with short-cropped black hair approached, walking with purpose. He was tall but still at least three inches shorter than me and very muscular. I tensed as he stopped directly in front of me, but then he smiled, and I relaxed a little.

"Are you Zane? Mr. Donahue's new champion fighter?" he asked, his voice gruff and low.

Maybe Donahue was looking for me. Was I late?

"Yes," I answered.

He moved blindingly fast. Reaching behind him, he grabbed what looked like a metal rod and swung it at me. I lifted my arm to protect myself, and the rod connected with my wrist.

Hot, sharp pain exploded at the point of impact and reverberated down my arm. I buckled forward, dropping to my knees. I barely had time to process what had happened before the guy took off running, and the door to the shop flew open.

Nellie rushed out, wide-eyed, holding a broom and still wearing her apron.

"Zane," she cried, hurrying over and peering down at me. "What happened?"

Kneeling on the ground, I held my arm to my chest, wincing in pain. I glanced up just in time to see the male who had attacked me round the corner. It took effort to stop myself from lashing out with my magic and alerting the whole town to who I was.

"A fellow fighter trying to take out the competition," I told her as I ran a hand carefully over my wrist.

Her eyes went wide as she gripped the handle of her broom and shook it at the empty street. "You better run away, you coward!" she yelled at the fae, who was no longer in sight.

She turned back to me, frowning as she examined my wrist. There wasn't any blood, but it was already starting to swell. Holding it in front of me, I gingerly tried to bend my wrist. Pain shot up my arm, and I sucked in a sharp breath.

"You can't even bend it?" she asked.

I shook my head.

"If you can't bend it, then you certainly can't throw a punch. And if you can't throw a punch, you can't fight."

I glanced up at her concerned little face. "I have powers you don't know about," I told her. "One of which is fast self-healing. I'll be fine. I just need several hours."

She sighed exasperatedly. "You don't have several hours." She chewed on her lip. "I'll be right back."

After stepping inside, she returned without her apron and

broom and helped me over to a bench on the other side of the street. By this time, my wrist had swelled to twice its size, and I was panting through the pain. I could move it a little, but was there any possibility it wasn't broken? I didn't think so.

Nellie was right. I couldn't fight like this, at least not without my magic. But I needed that prize money.

Nellie grasped both sides of my face. I looked into her deep green eyes and was captivated by the compassion I found there. She was such a good kid, a loving kid, whom I'd somehow become the temporary guardian of, and I had no complaints.

"Remember when I threatened to kill you with my power?" she asked.

I chuckled despite the discomfort. "I'm assuming you don't have power? Which is okay. There's nothing wrong with—"

I sucked in a sharp breath as the pain in my wrist flared tenfold and then disappeared. Dropping my face, Nellie broke into sobs, clutching her arm to her chest.

"It hurts," she cried.

I sat there in shock, wide-eyed, as I watched her rocking back and forth on the bench in agony.

"Nellie. What did you do?" I asked, suddenly becoming frantic with worry when my gaze landed on her now-swollen wrist.

She looked up at me with tears streaming down her face. "I'm a healer, Zane. But the worst kind. I have to take someone's injury into my own body in order to heal it. My mother was a Spring fae, but my father was from Fall, so my powers work differently than full Spring fae who have healing magic. My nana said there were ways to help lessen the side effects, but she never got around to showing me how. I was too scared to try it on Elida for fear I'd die."

I grabbed her shoulders, held her steady, and found that my wrist was totally healed. No more pain. No more swelling.

"Give it back. Give me back the injury." I'd take that and more to never see her sweet face full of tears.

She shook her head defiantly. "We gotta go now. You're gonna win those fights, and then we can help the princess."

"Nellie. I command you to give me back the injury. Now." I tried the stern voice my father had used on me and my brothers when he meant business, but she just shook her head.

"My magic doesn't work like that. It's mine now. It'll heal in a few days."

A few days!

A knot tightened in my chest. I picked her up, being careful not to jostle her wrist. Cradling her against me, I walked toward the inn we were staying at. I'd leave her with Evander and Elida and then collect her after the fights. A brutal underground fighting ring was no place for a young girl like her, especially with a painful wrist injury.

Anger swirled inside me at what she'd done without my permission. She was just a sweet kid. She shouldn't have to live with that kind of agony, even if only for a few days.

"The second I win this fight, I'm tracking down Percy and paying him to heal you. And if you ever do something like that again, I'll—" I let the threat hang in the air because I didn't know what to say. "Don't ever do that again."

"Okay. Geez," she muttered but rested her head against my chest.

I walked a few minutes before I said, "And thank you."

I felt Nellie nestle into my chest just a little bit more.

When we reached the inn, I left Nellie in Elida and Evander's care after making sure her wrist was bound. Even injured, she'd put up a fight about staying behind that night. But injured or not, I wasn't about to bring her to an underground fighting match. I'd grown to care deeply for that child, and Evander and Elida were about the only people I trusted to watch her while I fought.

We didn't tell them that Nellie's injury came from healing me. Instead, we said she'd tripped and fallen on it. By the time we got back to the inn, she could bend her wrist a little, but it was red and swollen. Elida, who seemed to know at least something about these things, didn't think her wrist was broken, but she couldn't be sure. I hoped she was right.

I already felt bad enough leaving Nellie with them instead of taking her to the healer immediately, but there was nothing I could do until I won the prize money to pay for his services. Nellie had smiled bravely at me before I left, saying her wrist hardly hurt at all, but I saw in her eyes the pain that she was trying to conceal. It made my chest feel like it was caving in.

That injury was meant for me, not her.

After leaving the inn, I made my way quickly to the treasury, where Mr. Donahue was waiting outside for me with a muscular fae I didn't recognize who was holding an ornate wooden box. The unfamiliar man had black hair, pale skin, and ice-blue eyes. Donahue introduced him as Malek.

I glanced at the box in his hands, but neither of them offered an explanation. The prize winnings, perhaps? I'd learned that

Donahue was one of the fight's sponsors as well as the town treasurer, so it made sense that he was the one handling the prize money.

Donahue looked me up and down. "You look good. Feeling ready?"

I nodded. "Let's get this over with."

The pointy-nosed fae frowned at that but turned and walked down the street toward a side alley, beckoning me to follow.

"Aside from the prize money, there are a lot of side bets going on," he warned. "Everyone saw how large you are while you walked around town today, and a lot of bets were placed on you. If you don't win, a lot of fae are going to be angry."

I chuckled. "Trust me. I'm going to win."

There were clusters of fae loitering around the mouth of the alley, mostly men. They stared and whispered as we passed.

Ducking between an alterations shop and a shoe repair store, we turned the corner to find a long line that snaked further down the alley. We walked to the front of the line, where a burly male stood at a red door, checking tickets before letting anyone enter.

The large fae took one look at Donahue, then at me, and nodded, stepping aside to let us pass. We entered the building and immediately started descending a long set of dark stone steps.

Red-and-black damask wallpaper covered the walls, and a velvet carpet runner lined the center of the stairs. Despite its entrance being in an alleyway, the place was clearly well-maintained, likely because it brought in a lot of money for the owners.

"Because you're new, you'll have to work your way to the top. Your first few fights will be easy, but after that, you'll be up against Buttercup's finest," Donahue informed me.

"Watch out for Brunok," Malek said, walking a few steps behind us.

Donahue nodded. "Brunok has been known to break the rules."

"Break the rules, how?" I asked, wondering if Brunok was the same guy who had tried to shatter my wrist earlier. Because of that attack, Nellie was back at the inn, lying in pain. If it was Brunok, I'd make sure he paid.

"He likes to use his magic on his opponents," Donahue replied. "But his magic is concealed, so no one can really tell when he's doing it."

That got my attention. "What's his magic?"

We were nearing the bottom of the long staircase, and the noise of a bustling, lively crowd reached my ears.

"He can heat up your internal organs just enough to make you uncomfortable so you slip up," Donahue explained. "Not enough that the Enforcer notices."

Boil my organs? That was definitely something to watch out for.

"The Enforcer?" I asked, unfamiliar with the term.

Donahue nodded. "Judge, announcer, and rule maker all rolled into one. What he says goes down here."

We reached the base of the stairs, and the space immediately opened into a massive circular room with a high, domed ceiling. At the very top was a circular glass window, perfectly framing the moon.

"What is this place?" I asked.

Donahue's gaze cut to mine. "Used to be an underground dance hall and tavern. Years ago, one of the former Spring queens got it in her head to outlaw wine and spirits. Fae didn't take too well to that, so they built this place to have somewhere to enjoy themselves away from prying eyes. In that sense, it's still being used for the same purpose today."

I scanned the room. There was a giant barred cage in the center of the space with an open top. The sides rose about eight feet, something I could easily scale and jump over if I had to.

Fae of all class levels pushed against the bars, jockeying for a good vantage point. Some were dressed in fine silks and velvet top hats, while others wore rugged clothing half-marred in soot.

There were quite a few females down here, something I hadn't expected. They were dressed nicely, too. Wives of some of the other attendees? Or just ladies who enjoyed a good brawl?

As I looked around, I noticed that everyone had a red ticket clutched in their hand.

"Their betting cards," Donahue told me as he strode forward, passing a makeshift bar where drinks were being served.

"I bet a lot of money on you, handsome," a female fae said as I passed. She held up her red ticket, and I saw my name on it with the words *five gold* written below. "Make me proud." She blew me a kiss.

Donahue grinned. "Win tonight, and you can have your pick of the ladies."

"Not interested. Is that the prize money?" I asked, glancing over my shoulder at the ornate box in Malek's hands as he followed closely behind us.

Donahue raised an eyebrow at me. "Yes."

"And what about my dagger?" I asked.

"In the box as well," Donahue said. "And my associate will be heavily guarding both the prize money and the dagger until a winner is declared."

I looked back at Malek again, and transferring the box to one hand, he raised the other. Razor-sharp icicles ending in deadly points formed on his fingertips, showcasing his magic.

A Winter fae? I wondered. His magic reminded me of Isolde.

"I'm not going to steal it," I said with a roll of my eyes. "I just have plans after this, and I need to get on the road quickly."

Donahue nodded just as we reached the door. "Very well. If you win, we will split the winnings, and you can be on your way."

"When I win," I corrected him.

Stryker was probably the best among my brothers in hand-to-hand combat. He loved bare-knuckle fights the most, saying it made him feel alive, but I was second to him in skill. Growing up with four brothers, and as an Ethereum lord, I'd learned a thing or two about fighting.

Donahue grinned. "I like that confidence. You'll need it."

Opening the door, he motioned for me to enter ahead of him. A few other fighters were sitting on benches, getting their hands wrapped.

A male attendant with shaggy brown hair who looked barely sixteen approached and introduced himself as Bucky. He smiled at me and his large front two teeth stuck out over his lip, giving me a hint as to how he got his name. He insisted on wrapping my hands for me, even though I told him it wasn't necessary. I was glad I didn't argue, though. His wrapping technique was excellent.

As Bucky finished my second hand, my gaze flicked over to the other fighters. Their attendants were rubbing oil on their faces so that punches would slide off. The other fighters were at least a head shorter than me and much leaner. I almost felt bad that we'd be paired up.

Bucky was applying oil to my face when a hulking male stepped into the room.

His shaved head sat atop a wide, meaty neck lined with thickly corded veins. He scanned the room until his black-eyed gaze landed on me and held.

Just then, I felt a rush of heat flood through my body, and my eyes widened.

Is this Brunok? Is he using his power on me? But as soon as I thought it, the heat vanished.

"Brunok!" One of the scrawny fighters ran over to fawn over the larger male, showering him with compliments.

I eyed Brunok. He wasn't the one who had tried to break my wrist, but there was something decidedly evil in his gaze as he continued to glare at me.

According to my brother Stryker, half of the fight was mental. So, I grinned maniacally back at Brunok and slowly stood.

His expression faltered as I stretched to my full height, my overly cheery grin seeming to unsettle him.

"What's so funny?" he called out to me.

Bucky finished applying the oil to my face and moved back as I took a step toward Brunok, crossing my arms over my chest. "I think it's cute that you're so insecure about fighting that you break the rules and use your power."

"Did you just call me cute?" Brunok roared and lunged for me, but Donahue, who had been standing off to the side, jumped between us.

"One hit before the fight and you're disqualified. You know the rules, Brunok. Save the fighting for the ring," he snapped. Then he glanced over his shoulder at me. "Come on, Zane. You're up first."

I laughed then, an evil, unhinged laugh that caused Brunok to shift warily on his feet and look at me like I was sick in the head. I didn't enjoy playing this role, but I'd do whatever it took to win. And a guy who could boil my organs was not someone I wanted to piss off without a plan. I'd have to take him by surprise and knock him out before he could even throw the first punch. The only way to do that was to mess with his head first.

"See you soon." I winked and left the room.

Donahue trailed out after me. "That was either extremely stupid or very smart," he told me as I made my way through the throng of fae toward the cage in the center of the room.

Inside the cage stood a large, bald fae with bright blue eyes I assumed was the Enforcer Donahue had mentioned before. He had a weathered look to him like he'd lived a rough life and a scar through one of his eyebrows that just narrowly missed his eye. Next to him was a scrawny little fighter, barely the size of a teenage boy but sporting a full-grown beard.

"I'm hoping for the latter," I replied to Donahue and stepped into the cage as the amassed crowd roared with excitement.

Win the fights. Get the money.

Heal Nellie. Find Lorelei.

I was on a mission, and I wasn't going to let anything stand in my way.

Chapter Ten

ZANE

I'd won my first two fights within seconds. One punch to the side of their head or an uppercut to their jaw, and the scrawny fae had dropped like a stack of old books.

The crowd had cheered for the first two knockouts, but now they just looked bored. Donahue was probably annoyed that I wasn't giving them more of a show, but I didn't care. I was consumed with getting to Lorelei, and each fae I faced was just another obstacle I needed to defeat to reach her.

After defeating my third opponent almost as quickly as the first two, I was beginning to think I'd be out of here in less than a half hour. Then, the next fae entered the ring.

One I recognized.

The bastard who broke my wrist.

The crowd roared their approval as the large, muscular fae with short black hair sneered at me. He flexed his pec muscles, making them jump from left to right like some kind of ridiculous showman.

As much as I wanted to knock this fool out the second the bell rang, I needed to make him pay for what he did to me and, ultimately, to Nellie. That sweet girl was lying in pain back at the inn because of him.

"Our next fight," the Enforcer announced from his seat just outside the metal cage, his voice booming magically throughout the space, "is between the newcomer, Zane, and the legendary Hammer."

Hammer?

I rolled my eyes. What a stupid name for a coward who tried to take me out of the fight rather than face me head-on.

"Feeling better, I see," he growled, flicking his gaze toward my forearm.

"Oh, you have no idea how good I'm about to feel," I shot back just as the bell rang.

Instead of going for my usual uppercut knockout, I kicked out my foot and landed a solid hit squarely in his chest.

He grunted, spittle flying from his mouth as he staggered backward. The crowd roared their approval.

"It looks like our newcomer is finally going to give us a show," the Enforcer's voice boomed around us as Hammer ran at me, eyes feral and hands up. He was ready to box, and I reminded myself how fast he could be.

Bring it, you slimy coward.

He might have bested me once, but I wasn't about to let it happen again.

When he got within striking range, I clipped his jaw with an uppercut. My hits were fast and hard. Even though it was a light hit since he shifted left at the last moment, it still rattled him. He shook his head as if trying to clear the ringing in his ears.

He tried to counterattack, but his punches were sloppy. They had weight, but I was able to block every blow.

After only a few minutes of fighting, Hammer was already winded. He swung at me, a move I saw coming from a mile away, and I easily dodged. His punch missed entirely, and his momentum carried him forward, slamming him into the bars.

I couldn't help but grin as I watched him stumble before regaining his footing. I moved to the other side of the cage, and he twisted back toward me with a growl.

To think I thought these fights would be a challenge. I mean, I was an Ethereum lord, but since I wasn't using my magic, I'd expected to at least work for my wins.

With a roar of fury, Hammer charged at me with renewed energy. He faked left, and I should have seen it coming, but I'd gotten cocky. He landed a solid blow to my right ear that sent me staggering to the side. As I steadied myself, I felt wetness trickling down my cheek.

Wetness.

Blood.

Black blood.

No.

Panic seized me as I realized my huge oversight. I'd been so careful not to use my magic since I saved Nellie, but I'd completely forgotten that my magic wasn't the only thing that set me apart from the seelie in Faerie.

Reaching up, I quickly covered my ear with my right hand. The lighting in the cavernous room wasn't great. Maybe no one had noticed the color of my blood yet. If I could get through this fight, I could clean up and bandage my ear. As long as I avoided another hit, I might still have a chance to continue in the tournament and win the prize money.

But with my ear covered, I'd have to fight one-handed.

Hammer came for me again. I jabbed out with my weaker left hand, landing three quick blows to the side of his head. The hits opened a gash over his eye, and crimson blood trickled down his face. He staggered back but didn't go down like I'd hoped.

"Both fighters look hurt. Zane appears to be protecting an injury on the side of his head," the Enforcer announced as the crowd roared.

"Knock him out!" a familiar voice ripped through the noise, and my blood ran cold.

Nellie.

No. She wouldn't.

I flicked my gaze toward the voice and saw her pressed up against the bars, cradling her injured arm to her chest.

My heart skipped a beat.

I barely had time to process the fact that she'd snuck out and found her way here before Hammer lunged at me again. Twisting away, I stuck my foot out at the last moment and tripped him. He went down hard.

As he lay on the ground at my feet, I punched him in the back of the head four times until he went limp—knocked out cold.

The crowd went wild as the bell rang, and my heart hammered in my chest.

Think. Think.

The second I took my hand off my ear, it would expose my black blood.

Hammer regained consciousness quickly and rolled onto his

back. His eyes were unfocused, and his face was covered in red blood from the damage I'd inflicted with my fists.

Reaching down with my free hand, I grasped his face, smearing blood all over my palm and fingers.

"That beating was for my wrist," I growled at him before pulling away.

I swapped hands quickly to cover my bleeding ear, hoping that Hammer's blood, now smeared over my hand and the side of my face, would hide my own incriminating black blood.

My heart raced as Bucky leaped into the ring with a small patch-up kit, probably intending to stitch up my ear.

I glanced at Nellie, who chewed her lip worriedly, and shook my head lightly. I couldn't believe she was here. But on the other hand, the girl had more spunk than anyone I'd ever met. Should I really be surprised she'd found her way to the fights?

"Let me take a look so I can get you patched up," Bucky said.

I cast him a wary glance before slowly removing my hand, praying I'd smeared enough of Hammer's blood on my face to make it look like I bled red like everyone else.

At least the corner where we sat was dark, but even so, I avoided throwing Bucky nervous looks as he worked.

"It's not too bad. I think the bleeding has stopped," he said, and I sagged in relief. "You only need a stitch or two."

"Great," I muttered, swallowing a curse as he stuck the needle into my ear and began stitching me up.

Glancing down, I noticed my black, oil-like blood covering my fingers and palm. I quickly began unwrapping my hand to destroy the evidence.

"Can you rewrap me, too?" I asked.

"Sure thing," Bucky said. I felt the warmth of a washcloth against my neck and face as he cleaned me up.

Nellie's little face suddenly swam into view between the bars, and the little brat had the audacity to grin.

"That was awesome," she told me.

"How long have you been here?" I asked, searching behind her for Evander or Elida, though I was certain they wouldn't have let her come. She'd likely snuck out while they slept.

"Since the second fight," she said. "I wasn't going to miss this. You might need me."

I glanced at her injured wrist and shook my head. "Nellie, go back. Please."

She tipped her chin high. "No."

I growled in frustration as Bucky took the wadded-up cloth from my old wraps and tossed them into the trash. I peered down at the rag he'd wiped my face with, relieved to see it was mostly dark red, with only faint streaks of black.

Now I had to get through the next fight without bleeding, and I'd be in the clear. It was the final match, and I was up against Brunok. This one was going to be brutal. But could I get through it without taking a hit to the face?

I'd have to try. The easiest way to avoid a punch was to knock him out cold right away. No more messing around like I had with Hammer.

Once Bucky finished rewrapping my hand, I thanked him and kneeled down to where Nellie was still pressed against the bars. Many in the crowd had refilled their drinks during the break and were now making their way back.

"Nellie, things might go bad. I need you to go back out to the alley and wait for me in front of the alterations shop on the corner."

She frowned, glaring up at me. "No way, Zane. I'm not leaving."

Heaving a sigh, I tilted my head back and spotted the moon through the skylight above. Why was this child so difficult?

Taking a deep breath, I glanced back down and into her eyes.

"I'm trying to get you to your aunt in one piece," I snapped, my patience wearing thin.

"And I'm trying to watch your back, too. We're a team," she snarled, and something inside me softened.

She had the disposition of a feral lion cub sometimes, and I adored that about her. I'd grown up with brothers, so I never had a sister, though I imagined if I did, she'd have been like Nellie.

Fierce. Loyal. Loving on the inside with a hard outer shell.

"Fine." I lowered my voice. "Stay close, but be ready to flee at any moment."

Her eyes widened slightly at that, as if surprised I'd relented, but she nodded dutifully.

"And now for our main event," the Enforcer's voice boomed, and the crowd erupted with applause.

I turned just as Brunok stepped into the ring, his eyes locked on me like I was prey.

Movement on the other side of the cage caught my attention. I saw Malek, Donahue's associate, standing beside the Enforcer. His black hair and ice-blue eyes reminded me so much of Isolde. Still holding the wooden box with the winnings and the faestone dagger, he stood like a sentinel, guarding the prize.

"The winner of this fight walks away with one hundred gold coins," the Enforcer roared, and the crowd cheered their approval.

"Not to mention the bragging rights," he added with a chuckle as Brunok beat his chest like a wild animal.

I rolled my shoulders, trying to push aside the thoughts of my black blood and Nellie's face pressed against the bars. I needed to get into Brunok's head before the bell rang and—

The bell rang.

Brunok exploded forward, charging at me like a bear.

I steeled myself, raising my wrapped hands as he threw a strong left hook. I ducked, dodging the blow aimed at my temple, and took a step back to get out of range.

I needed to focus, but my mind swam with concerns: being exposed, Nellie watching, the stakes of this fight.

Brunok's fist slammed into my stomach, forcing bile up my throat and the breath from my lungs.

I stumbled back, coughing, struggling to catch my breath.

I'd barely seen him move.

"Well, folks, it looks like Zane is finally getting tired. Brunok has the upper hand," the Enforcer's voice boomed as the crowd cheered.

Focus, Zane, I chastised myself. Then an image of sweet Lorelei rose in my mind, and an eerie calm washed over me.

Win the fight. Get the money. Find Lorelei.

I rolled my shoulders again, meeting Brunok's gaze. He smiled, smug, as if he'd already won.

He hadn't won.

We were just getting started.

I went berserk, snapping out rapid-fire jabs to Brunok's left cheek, chin, and right temple. He tried to back out of range, but I moved with him, hammering him over and over with my fists.

"Oh, and Zane is back in the fight," the Enforcer shouted as the crowd roared.

Brunok finally broke my onslaught by kicking out at me, forcing some space between us. He glared, his expression dark. Just as I was about to move in again, I felt it. My insides started to warm.

The fiend was using his power.

"You coward," I spat. "Using your power because you can't take me like a man."

I saw the exact moment he snapped. His already-black eyes went cold and emotionless, and he came at me like a man possessed. Then, he broke the one unspoken rule between every man alive.

He kicked me hard, right between the legs.

Pain and nausea exploded through me as I dropped to the ground.

Before I could react, Brunok delivered three brutal blows to the side of my head. The pain there was nothing compared to the deep, throbbing ache between my legs.

My stomach threatened to revolt, but I fought it.

This bastard is going to die.

Summoning strength I didn't know I had, I shoved myself to my feet and attacked Brunok with every ounce of fury I possessed.

I kicked, punched, elbowed. He fell to the ground, and I was on top of him, pulverizing his face, until I realized he'd gone limp.

The bell had already rung.

It wasn't until I was being pulled off him that my rage finally began to subside.

Standing half-dazed in the middle of the cage, I barely registered the Enforcer's grin as he grabbed my right hand and raised it into the air.

"And our winner is—"

Before he could finish his sentence, the smile fell from his face. His brow furrowed, and his grip on my hand clamped down like a vise. His gaze turned murderous.

I didn't understand what caused the change until I felt a warm trickle slide from my forehead over my temple and down my cheek.

"Black blood," he snarled, his thin lips peeling back from his teeth in revulsion. "He's got black blood," he roared, using magic to project his voice throughout the room.

That's when I snapped out of it and exploded into action.

Nellie was my first concern. I yanked my wrist out of his grasp, shoved him against the bars, and bolted for the open cage door. Nellie was already waiting for me. The second I stepped out, I held out my hand. Grasping it, she leaped onto my back, locking her legs around my hips and holding onto my neck with her good arm.

"Black bleeder! Ethereum demon!" someone spat.

Terror surged through me as I imagined them ripping Nellie off my back. I reached for my power, intending to clear a path, but horror swept over me when I found only a trickle of it.

My worst fears were confirmed. The time on the mountain wasn't just a fluke. This realm was draining my powers or at least limiting them somehow.

As a fae lunged at us, I aimed my hand at him. A small black lightning bolt shot from my palm, striking his face. It wasn't nearly as powerful as I'd hoped, but it was enough to make the crowd shrink back in shock and fear.

"He's an Ethereum lord! Who else would have magic like that?" someone shouted, and half the crowd began to flee.

We had to get out of here, but I couldn't leave without the prize.

Glancing over my shoulder, I spotted Malek on the other side of the fighting cage. He was still standing like a sentinel, holding the wooden box as chaos erupted around him.

I shoved through the remaining spectators, skirting the cage to reach Malek.

"We need to bring him to Queen Gloriana to take his heart!" a male shouted.

"He can stop the curse!" someone else yelled.

Fae began crowding around us again, but by then, I'd reached Malek.

"I earned that," I said, nodding at the box in his hands.

Malek sneered, and sharp icicles began forming on the ends of his fingers. "Ethereum monsters earn nothing here," he spat. With a flick of his wrist, one of the icicles shot from his hand and impaled me in the thigh.

Pain sliced through my leg as the crowd turned hostile.

It all happened so fast. One second, there was no one close by, and the next, we were swarmed. Hands grabbed at me, trying to pull me to the ground.

"Zane!" Nellie screamed as I felt her slipping off my back.

Praying to my ancestors, I gathered what little power I could and let it explode outward.

Like a bomb, black electric zaps erupted in every direction, stunning the mob and dropping them to their knees in pain.

It wasn't deadly. I didn't have enough power for that, but it was enough. Anyone struck by the blast was momentarily incapacitated, including Malek, who dropped the winnings.

Without wasting another second, I grabbed the box from the ground. Shoving it under my arm, I reached back to secure Nellie and ran for the exit, mowing down anyone in my path.

When I reached the stairs, I took them two at a time.

"Tell me you're okay," I asked Nellie as she bounced up and down on my back, clinging tightly.

"I'm okay," she whimpered, but I knew the jostling must have been hurting her.

At the top of the stairs, no one tried to stop us. We burst into the alley, and I sprinted at top speed.

When we reached the treasurer's door, I made a split-second decision. Sliding Nellie off my back, I dropped the wooden box at the door and smashed the top. Reaching inside, I grabbed the faestone dagger and my winnings, leaving the rest behind. I didn't want to give Donahue an excuse to come after us, at least not another one.

"Ethereum lord?" Nellie asked, her voice small beside me.

I glanced down to see her staring at me wide-eyed.

Right. Nellie knew I was from Ethereum, but she didn't know I was a lord.

I nodded, hoping what I saw in her eyes wasn't fear. "It's still me. I'm the same fae you've been traveling with these days. I won't hurt you, I promise."

"I know," she said. "I'm just . . . impressed."

Laughter burst out of me unexpectedly, but then a shout from down the street reminded me we had to move. They were already looking for me.

"Can you run?" I asked her.

She clutched her injured wrist to her chest and nodded.

Shoving the coins into my pocket, I clutched the dagger in one hand and grabbed Nellie's uninjured hand with the other. Together, we bolted for the barn a few blocks away.

I hated that we wouldn't get to say a proper goodbye to Evander and Elida, but there was no way we could spend another second in this town.

When we reached the barn, Nellie made me stay outside.

"You're bleeding everywhere," she told me, pointing to my thigh and face.

I glanced down, realizing I'd forgotten about the icicle wound. The shard had melted and fallen off somewhere, leaving a sizable gash that soaked the thigh of my pants with black blood.

Nodding, I handed her the amount of gold coins I'd negotiated with Jasper earlier in the day. It wasn't more than five minutes before she emerged from the barn, leading a mare already saddled with the supplies we needed.

I silently thanked the fates I'd made arrangements earlier in the day.

Nellie handed me the reins, her concerned gaze fixed on my thigh. "Let me patch you up first," she said, starting to reach for me.

I sidestepped her, shaking my head.

There was no way I was letting her take on my injury again. Never again. I told her I could bandage myself on the way. The most important thing was putting distance between us and the mob of angry people who wanted to carve my heart from my chest.

Grabbing Nellie, I hoisted her onto the horse before leaping into the saddle behind her. With a click of my tongue and a kick of my heels, the horse took off north, heading toward the Spring Palace.

While Nellie slept against my chest, I wrapped a tourniquet around my thigh as best as I could. Without stitches, the wound would leave a nasty scar, but it wasn't bleeding enough to be fatal. My fae healing would close the wound soon enough.

Gripping the reins, I spurred the horse on, the throbbing in my thigh forgotten as my mind focused on one thing and one thing alone.

Getting to Lorelei.

Chapter Eleven

LORELEI

I'd been pacing in the darkness of my dream void all night, searching for a door to anywhere. Were Mother and Father not sleeping? I'd tried to reach them time and time again, to no avail. Even my eldest sister wasn't available.

It hit me then. Maybe I couldn't reach anyone because I wasn't sleeping during normal hours. I was imprisoned and now blinded, although thankfully, that didn't extend to my dream state. But I had no idea what time of day or night it was. If I wasn't sleeping when anyone else was, I'd never be able to reach them.

Panic began to swell in my gut just as one of the dream doors I was monitoring popped up in front of me. Without hesitation, I rushed through it, not even knowing who it belonged to, and was relieved to see Zane.

He was in a saloon, holding a hot bowl of soup and looking out at a band playing. As I sat down at the table next to him, he turned and looked over.

"Lorelei?"

I quickly reminded him that I was a dream walker and that this was real. He shook his head slightly, as if to clear it, then nodded.

"Right. I don't know that I'm ever going to get used to this, but I'm glad you have this magic." Turning in his seat, he faced me fully, sincerity filling his eyes. "I'm on my way to the Spring Palace. I sent a message ahead to your parents so they know I'm coming. I'm going to find you."

"Did you tell them who you are?" I asked, a knot forming in my gut. The last thing I needed was for Zane to show up at the Spring Palace and for my mother to kill him on sight.

"Not exactly," he said. "I told them I was a friend, but I didn't tell them I was an Ethereum lord."

I chewed on my lip but nodded. I didn't know if that was the right decision or not, but now I really needed to reach my parents. I had to explain about Zane before he showed up at their door. Still, I could deal with that later. Right now, I needed to get some information to him before he woke.

Without thinking, I reached out and grasped his hand. "I tried to escape yesterday. I was captured again, but I got a look at where I am. They're holding me somewhere east of the Turtle Mountains. My mother will know the general direction. Make sure you tell her."

He nodded. "I will. I promise. I won't stop until I find you."

He squeezed my fingers to emphasize his point, and I blushed, realizing I was still clutching his hand tightly. Embarrassed, I pulled my hand free and reached up to tuck a strand of hair behind my ear. He was very sweet, but I reminded myself that

Zane was still very much a stranger. I shouldn't have been so forward.

"I'm . . . not sure how much time I have left," I said, forcing myself to look into his blue-and-brown speckled eyes. "I made Queen Liliana mad, and she . . ." I hesitated, chewing my bottom lip, unsure if I should tell Zane about my blindness.

I looked down, but Zane placed two fingers under my chin and gently tipped my face up.

"She did what?" he asked.

I opened my mouth to answer him honestly when the saloon around us began to dissolve.

No. I'd only just gotten here. But I needed to leave before he woke.

"Just hurry," I said, bolting from the chair and running for the door.

"Lorelei!" he cried out.

I ran through his dream door, but his growled words followed me before it shut behind me.

"If Queen Liliana hurt a hair on your head, I'll kill her."

Relief and joy swept through me at his words. I was counting on that. Because if I'd come to realize anything during these days of captivity, it was that Queen Liliana had to be stopped. And I didn't think I had the strength to do it myself.

I waited in the darkness for what felt like forever, praying that my mother's or father's door would appear. Just as I was about to give up hope, my mother's door materialized. I bounded through it without hesitation.

My mother was well-versed in my dream walking, so the moment I burst into her dream, she grasped me and pulled me into her arms. We were in her bedroom, at the makeup vanity, where she got ready every morning.

"Lorelei, I've been worried sick." She held me tightly. "Daisey said you visited her and that you've been taken by Queen Liliana. She told us she was taking you for training. I'm so sorry we believed her lies. We've been looking all over for you, but we don't know where you are."

I pulled away, and I saw her face was wet with tears. Her grief and sorrow made my heart ache.

"It's not your fault," I said. "She deceived us all."

Her face started to fade in and out, and I realized I was on the verge of wakefulness. But through sheer willpower alone, I forced myself to remain in the dream. There were things I had to tell her. My life and Zane's life depended on it. I knew I had only moments left, if that.

"I don't have much time," I said quickly. "Queen Liliana is draining my magic so she can go through the mirror portal herself—"

"What?"

"Mother, listen. A man named Zane is coming to you. I know he sent you a message, but you need to know that he's an Ethereum lord."

Her mouth fell open. "An Ethereum lord? But . . . they're evil."

I shook my head, desperate for her to believe me. "He's not. I promise. You have to believe me. Zane is on our side. You need to trust him, and you can't hurt him."

The thought of something happening to Zane caused a stab of

pain in my chest, but I pushed forward. If I didn't leave before I fully woke, I might be lost in my dream void for days.

"Zane will help you find me, and together, he and I will destroy the curse."

I felt myself waking. The pull was stronger now.

"Check my nightstand drawer for a letter from Dawn," I said urgently. "It's all been a lie. Don't hurt him, Mother. I . . ."

I love him didn't feel right. I barely knew him.

"He's good."

A tug at my navel told me I was out of time. I pulled myself from her grasp and ran for the door just as my feet began to disappear. A moment later, I was yanked from sleep.

I heard the sound of scraping metal and sat up screaming. My heart pounded frantically against my chest as I blinked rapidly, to no avail.

I was blind.

I clawed at my eyes, desperately trying to summon my magic to heal the loss of vision, but nothing happened. I was drained, and this place was barren. There was no life force for me to pull from.

I started to hyperventilate. It was terrible knowing that Queen Liliana was capable of causing so much injury and that, right now, I was helpless from stopping her from doing anything to others and myself. But I reminded myself this was only temporary. As a royal, I would naturally heal. It might take days, but my sight would return. Even a short time without vision was terrifying, but I had to try to keep calm.

"I told you not to disobey me," Queen Liliana said from somewhere in front of me.

"You're insane," I spat, kicking out but connecting with nothing. "I wonder how Dawn would feel if she knew just how deranged you've become."

There was a whooshing of air, and then her hand gripped the back of my hair firmly. I whimpered as she forced me into a standing position.

Her hot breath spread over my neck as she said, "One of my spies sent me a raven. Your little Ethereum lord is here in Faerie, seemingly making his way to the Spring Palace, and then I'm sure he's going to come look for you. I do hope he arrives swiftly, so I can carve his heart from his chest."

Zane. Panic spiked through me at her threat.

"This is perfect," Queen Liliana went on, "because by now, the curse will have taken effect on his magic."

"What do you mean?" I asked, confused. What would Zane's magic have to do with the curse?

Queen Liliana chuckled, a dark sound that sent shivers down my spine.

"I've been learning all sorts of new things about the curse," she said, her voice dripping with malice. "Not just how to use your dagger to get to Ethereum, but I also uncovered an interesting tidbit of information buried in an old scroll."

She paused, as if savoring the moment before delivering her next words.

"If an Ethereum lord were ever to venture to Faerie, the curse would begin to pull on the magic of his black beating heart, weakening him. By the time Zane arrives, he may be completely depleted of his magic, making him all the easier to target."

I gasped. If he were to face off against Queen Liliana, Zane was going to need his magic. Fear for Zane squeezed my heart painfully.

"If you hurt him," I warned, but I knew the threat was baseless, and so did she.

"You'll do nothing," she sneered. "And if Zane doesn't make his way here, I'll just go to Ethereum and cut out the heart of a different Ethereum lord. I'm not picky."

I growled, bucking and kicking against her until her fingers wrapped around my throat, cutting off my airway. I went limp, submitting to her grip.

"If I were you, I would think long and hard about the decisions that got you to this point," she spat.

"You don't have to do this," I choked out, struggling to speak with her hand still wrapped around my throat.

But my words seemed to fall on deaf ears as she threw me to the ground, and I landed hard, my head slamming painfully against the unforgiving stones. I lay there stunned as she left the cell, the sound of the lock engaging echoing in the silence. Her footsteps retreated down the corridor.

Zane.

I needed to talk to him, to tell him that not only his life was in danger but possibly his brothers' as well.

The only problem was, sleep wasn't something you could force, and at that moment, I was wide awake.

Chapter Twelve

ZANE

Biscuit was a good girl. She stayed on the trail and rode through the night. Just before the morning light, we stopped at a creek beside a field of beautiful tulips to let her rest.

Exhausted from the fight and fleeing, I accidentally fell asleep for a few minutes, leaning against the trunk of a tree. That's when Lorelei visited my dream.

If only I could have stayed asleep longer. But Nellie shook me awake, thinking she'd heard something nearby. It turned out to be nothing, but by then, it was too late. The dream was gone, and so was Lorelei.

Even in those few short minutes, I'd gained something I hadn't had before: a place to start looking.

The Turtle Mountains.

But Lorelei was clear. She wanted me to go to her mother, the queen, first. I just hoped her parents would receive my message before I arrived. I didn't want to waste time convincing them that Lorelei was in danger and that I was there to help.

"How's your arm?" I asked Nellie as she used the creek water to rinse out her mouth.

"I'll live," she said, but her demeanor was less cheery. She winced whenever she moved too much. She'd dozed a bit while I held her on the horse, but the dark circles under her eyes told me she wasn't well-rested.

Having responsibility for this child, even temporarily, was something I took seriously. I needed to do a better job.

"The second we get to the Spring Palace, I'm getting you a healer," I promised.

"What about saving Princess Lorelei?" she asked.

"I'll do that. But getting you healed is also a priority."

She smiled faintly at that.

"And I'll bet your aunt will be glad to see you, too. Is she a Spring fae?" I asked.

I wasn't sure how all of that worked here. Could different fae live in different places? I guessed so, considering all the refugees. We'd even passed several camps along the road last night. Seeing them had renewed my determination to end this curse. So many lives had been affected in both realms. This had to stop.

"Mmhmm," she murmured, sipping some water. Then she pointed to her belly and said, "Feed me, please."

I grinned. The girl was easy to please. Keep her belly full and give her some sweets now and then, and she was agreeable.

I handed her a hunk of smoked meat, some soft herb bread, and a little surprise I'd been saving.

"Chocolate!" she gasped when I pulled out a huge bar.

I'd negotiated it as part of my travel package with Jasper back in Buttercup Village. Nellie had a sweet tooth.

"With dried fruits, yes. But you only get one square a day," I said, breaking off a piece and handing it to her.

Grinning from ear to ear, and before touching the rest of her breakfast, Nellie snatched the small square from my hand and popped it into her mouth.

I laughed, folding the paper around the remainder of the bar and stashing it away. "Now finish your breakfast."

She did so dutifully, but soon began to eye the road with concern.

"What's wrong?" I asked.

She shook her head. "We're almost there. That means we'll be parting ways soon, right?"

I wasn't expecting to feel pain in my chest at her words. A pang of it ripped through my chest. I didn't want to part ways with the child, but I wasn't her family. It was best that she be with her aunt.

"We will have all day to ride, but yes. You need to go with your aunt, and I have to rescue Lorelei."

Her eyes welled with tears, and she turned away from me.

"Nellie." I reached for her, but she stood, brushing the tears off her cheeks.

"Let's ride. I can eat on the way," she snapped, giving me the cold shoulder.

I remembered the wild little girl in the cabin and how far we'd come, and a sad smile came to my face. I would miss her.

I quickly packed up our things and loaded everything into Biscuit's saddlebags. Once we were on the road again, Nellie was silent for hours.

I tried to engage her in conversation or songs, but she wasn't biting. The closer we drew to the Spring Palace, the more I dreaded leaving Nellie. The kid had grown on me, and I hoped her aunt had the means to take care of her. If not, I'd give her all the gold coins I had left to make sure Nellie was provided for.

Biscuit required little rest and rode beautifully through the day. It wasn't until the sun hung low in the sky and the Spring Palace appeared far off in the distance that Biscuit began to show signs of fatigue.

"How about an early dinner before we reach the Spring Palace?" I asked Nellie.

"Our last dinner together," she pouted.

It was. A sad reality, but reality nonetheless. Nellie was a child, and she had no idea that there would be no more dinners at all if I didn't find Princess Lorelei and end this curse.

Biscuit munched on grass and rested while Nellie and I prepared and ate our dinner.

"I'm glad you found me," she said softly. "I didn't have enough supplies to last much longer there before you came along."

The thought of what might have happened if I hadn't found her made a knot tighten in my chest.

"I'm glad I found you, too. I didn't know how much fun life could be with a sassy eleven-year-old in it."

"I'm twelve," she yelled, correcting me.

I'd called her eleven on purpose. Bursting into laughter, I rolled onto my side as she jumped on my back and started to playfully pound my ribs with her good hand.

I was just about to throw a weed at her when a twig snapped behind us.

In one swift move, I tucked Nellie beneath me and sprang to

my feet, ready to draw on what little magic I still had access to in order to protect her. But whoever was there was already retreating, a blur of movement through the trees.

"Who was that?" Nellie's voice trembled with fear.

"I'm not sure. Maybe a scout," I told her. "Come on. We should go."

Was it a scout from Buttercup Village? Or someone else?

I'd left Donahue his share of the prize money in the hopes it would deter him from coming after me, but maybe he didn't care. Maybe the villagers just wanted the very heart that beat in my chest.

I quickly gathered our things, threw Nellie onto Biscuit, and settled behind her. Then we rode fast and hard toward the palace and surrounding city on the horizon.

Tents of what I assumed were refugees from the other courts were scattered about around the main city walls. I understood why this would be, having seen how much of the land here had been ruined by the curse already, but it still made me sad to see so much upheaval for these fae. It also made me feel more resolved to do everything I could to destroy the curse. I steered Biscuit to the south, where there weren't as many fae loitering about.

The sun was setting, and I feared if we didn't make it there by dark . . .

The ground shook with the sound of heavy hoofbeats behind us.

I turned and saw at least two dozen men riding hard on our tail. I recognized one of them, Malek from Buttercup Village. Even from this distance, his icy blue gaze was filled with loathing as he gained on us.

"Don't look behind us," I told Nellie.

Of course, she did exactly that.

A shriek tore from her lungs when she saw the advancing horde.

"We're gonna die!" she screamed.

"No, we're not," I said, urging Biscuit to go even faster. I felt bad for the loyal mare. She'd been riding nonstop for almost a full day, but I needed her to go a bit farther.

"Come on, girl," I muttered, stroking her neck as Nellie and I jostled up and down with the speed of her gait.

The entrance to the city and the Spring Palace beyond was in sight, along with half a dozen guards. If we could make it there, we'd have a chance.

If I was honest with myself, though, I wasn't sure I had enough magic left to fend off the advancing fae. I was running on a fraction of my usual power, and I feared that the longer I stayed in Faerie, the more it drained from me. I only wish I knew why. The princesses' magic hadn't waned when they traveled to Ethereum, so why was my power failing me here?

In the distance, I saw the guards at the gate suddenly scramble. At first, I thought they were coming to our aid, but that hope was dashed when they began to close the gate.

"No!" Nellie wailed. "What are we gonna do?"

I thought fast, my gaze taking in the closed gate and the guards now moving into position in front of it.

"When we near the gate, we're going to stop and dismount. Then you're going to run behind those guards," I yelled over the pounding of Biscuit's hooves. "I'm going to fight with whatever strength I have left."

"I'll fight, too," she yelled back. At that moment, I wanted to meet her grandmother, to see what kind of woman had raised such a ferocious young lady.

"No. You run behind the guards and try to convince them to help. Tell them I'm a friend of the queen."

That was stretching the truth, but my hope was if they believed Nellie, it would buy us some time.

As we neared the city gate, the guards didn't draw their blades. Instead, they held their hands out in front of them, which told me they had powerful magic.

I yanked back on Biscuit's reins, and she skidded to a stop. I leaped off her back and then pulled Nellie down as well.

Turning toward the guards, I lifted my hands in the air in a display of surrender.

One of them stepped forward. "Who are you, and why are you being pursued?" he asked as the fae chasing us closed in.

I opened my mouth to respond, but Nellie beat me to it.

"He's the best friend of Queen Gloriana, and if you let him get hurt, she'll kill you all."

It was a life-or-death situation, and now was the worst possible time to smile, but I couldn't help it.

This kid.

"Well, not exactly," I said with a nervous laugh.

The riders reached us, and I realized it wasn't just Malek chasing us. Brunok and the Enforcer were with him as well.

"He's got black blood," Brunok shouted at the guards.

"And shadow powers," Malek added.

"He nearly killed us all in Buttercup Village," the Enforcer said. "We're here to cut out his heart and stop the curse." He held up a small, nondescript dagger, his gaze dropping to my chest.

"Black blood?" one of the guards repeated.

Movement at my feet drew my attention downward. Vines had grown up from the ground and were now tightly winding around my ankles. They were strong and I could tell it would be difficult to get out of their grasp.

"Hurt him, and I'll kill you all. I have very scary powers," Nellie cried, holding her uninjured hand out as if she were about to unleash magic I knew she didn't have.

"Nellie, please don't. They could hurt you," I told her as the vines climbed my thighs. I tested their strength by moving my foot slightly, but they only cinched tighter.

Dread sank like a stone in my stomach. I wasn't sure from where the danger was worse. The guards or those from Buttercup Village.

"Take the child," one of the guards ordered.

Another guard moved to grab Nellie, but she twisted out of reach. "Stay back, or I'll curse you!"

The guard faltered. "Is she a witch?"

I shook my head as the vines twisted up my torso, trapping my arms against my sides. This was not good. How could I protect Nellie? Suddenly, that felt like the most important thing to me. "She's scared. Don't touch her. Just tell me where you want her to stand."

If they hurt Nellie, I'd use every last shred of power I had to destroy them all.

"Stand facing the gate," the guard ordered.

Nellie looked at me with wide, scared eyes.

"It's okay. I promise," I lied. "Just do as they say."

She scrunched her nose, and for a moment, I thought she was going to argue. But then she nodded and turned toward the gate, her back to me.

Good. This way, she won't have to watch when they carve my heart out, I thought grimly.

I struggled hopelessly against the vines, but they were too strong, winding even tighter around me. I tried to pull on my magic, hoping to cut through the vines with my lightning, but it was like trying to carry water in my hands. As soon as I thought I'd grabbed hold of my power, it slipped right through my fingers.

The Enforcer approached, blade raised and hate blazing in his blue eyes.

I steeled myself.

Lorelei.

I pulled up her image in my mind: her purple eyes and soft lips curved into a sweet smile, her brown hair blowing in a gentle breeze. That was the last thing I wanted to see before I died. Not this.

"I have the cure for the curse," I said, trying to buy time as I continued to hopelessly reach for my power, only to feel it drain away.

"Yeah. In your chest," the Enforcer sneered, moving blindingly fast.

Nellie screamed a hair-raising sound that I knew would haunt my dreams forever, but I kept my eyes forward just as the Enforcer's blade swung toward my chest. I saw it coming toward me, could almost feel the sharp edge carving into me when—

A vine shot up from the ground and wrapped around his wrist, yanking it back with such force that I heard the bone snap. He screamed and fell to his knees. I let out a breath I hadn't realized I was holding.

Dozens of shouts and grunts erupted around me. I looked up

to see that every one of the fae who'd pursued us was now bound by vines wrapped around their wrists.

Did Nellie—?

"You have no authority over this man," a strong female voice boomed behind me. "He is mine."

The vines holding me in place fell away all at once. Around me, every person dropped to their knees and bowed.

Now freed, I spun around, coming face-to-face with a radiant older woman. She was probably in her mid-forties. Her long, light brown hair cascaded in curls over one shoulder, and she wore a purple dress that matched her eyes. Lorelei's eyes.

"Queen Gloriana." I bowed my head, and despite everything that was happening, I managed to bring a respectful tone to my voice.

When I looked back up, I couldn't read her expression.

"So, you're the Ethereum lord?" she mused. She walked through the now-open gates, past Nellie, and toward me. Although I was now free of the vines and the Enforcer no longer had a blade coming at me, I suddenly felt that I was in more trouble. If the queen had heard all that had been said about me, she would see me as a threat. She was royalty and would think that my heart was the way to end the curse. I couldn't bear it. She had power and guards, and I was a goner for sure. I was so close. Should I say anything?

She looked me up and down. I swallowed. Then she turned her gaze to the fae from Buttercup Village, still on their knees.

"You fools think you can carve out his heart with just any dagger?" She clicked her tongue. "No. It takes one of the four faestone daggers. Unless you have one of those, all you'd be doing is killing an Ethereum lord."

I thought about Isolde's faestone dagger in the pack still slung over my shoulder, as well as the faestones that remained from the other two daggers. Now was definitely not the time to bring them up.

I cleared my throat, and the queen's gaze shifted back to me. Her expression wasn't outright hostile, but it wasn't warm either.

"Did you get my message?" I asked her. "I'm friends with Lorelei and—"

"I know exactly who and what you are," she interrupted matter-of-factly. "If I'd met you yesterday, I would have killed you where you stood. But my daughter has spoken on your behalf. So . . ."

I held my breath, unsure of what she would say next.

"I welcome you into Spring Palace."

A wave of relief rushed through me.

The queen turned to the fae from Buttercup Village, and with a flick of her wrist, the vines binding their hands fell away. "You are welcome to rest before returning home, but Lord Zane is my guest and will not be harmed."

With that, she turned back toward the open gate, gesturing for us to follow.

Grabbing Biscuit's reins, I quickly went over to Nellie and brought her to my side before catching up with the queen and a contingent of her guards as they led us into the city.

The queen glanced down at Nellie, then up at me, a question in her eyes. "Your sister?"

I shook my head. "This is Nellie, a Fall fae. She's a travel companion who is very important to me and has helped me on my journey to meet you. She was stranded in the Fall Court when I arrived, and as with many of the subjects from her court and the others, she has lost much at the hands of the curse. I'm returning her to her aunt, who lives here."

She gave me a look as though I were an enigma but nodded. "Well, it's late. You both can spend the night at the palace, and we'll call for her aunt in the morning. What's her aunt's name? I'll send someone to find her."

I glanced down at Nellie, noticing her wide eyes and pressed lips. I'd never seen her like this before. She looked . . . afraid? Shocked?

She'd probably never met royalty before, besides me, though that was different, so perhaps she was overwhelmed.

"I think you intimidate her," I told the queen.

She laughed, a warm yet commanding sound. "I do have that effect sometimes. It helps keep my husband, Thalion, in line."

I smiled at her comment. I was not expecting humor from her, especially in such a strange situation. I liked her. A lot.

"I have much to tell you," I said, and she nodded. But then her gaze flicked warily to her guards. I got the impression she didn't want us to talk out in the open, and I understood that completely.

"And I have many questions as well," she replied. "Let's get Nellie settled in, and then we can go somewhere more private to talk."

An hour later, after being seen by the queen's healer and having her wrist attended to, Nellie was bathed and tucked into a bed in the guest wing of the Spring Palace. At my request, I'd been given the room next to hers so we could stay close.

The queen was waiting for me in the study, and I was eager to plan Lorelei's rescue. But first, I wanted to make sure Nellie was settled.

"You'll be here when I wake up in the morning, right?" Nellie asked, chewing her lip.

I nodded. "I'll see that you're brought to your aunt first thing in the morning, and then I'll leave right after."

She chewed her lip harder, her expression pained. "About that . . . my aunt. I gotta tell you something, but you're going to be mad." She pulled the covers up to her chin, as if preparing to hide under them.

Mad? About her aunt?

"I won't be mad," I promised.

"Yes, you will." Her eyes filled with tears.

I frowned. "Nellie, what is it?"

She pulled the blanket over her face, and my chest squeezed. "If you just tell me whatever it is, I'm sure we can work it out."

There was a long moment of silence before she ripped off the blanket, fat tears streaming down her face.

"I don't have an aunt, okay? All I had was my nana, and now all I have is you." A sob tore from her throat, and she yanked the blanket back over her face.

My heart shredded into a hundred pieces. She lied? For a moment I wondered why.

But the answer became obvious almost immediately. She knew I wouldn't have taken her all this way if I'd known she was an orphan. I might have left her in Buttercup Village with Elida and Evander, if they would have taken her.

All I have is you.

Her words caused my chest to constrict painfully. I thought

carefully about what I should say to her to not cause any further pain.

"Nellie, I'm going on a dangerous mission to rescue someone, and I can't bring you along."

"I know," she wailed under the blanket, her muffled sobs racking her chest.

I'd never felt like this before, like someone had ripped my heart out of my chest. She was not a relation or even someone I knew well, but I had grown so fond of her that I couldn't bear to see her so distraught.

Reaching forward, I gently pulled the blanket down, and her red, teary-eyed gaze met mine.

"But I promise to come back for you," I told her, and I meant it.

She sniffled. "You promise?"

I nodded. Reaching into my pocket, I pulled out the rest of my gold coins and set them on the bed next to her.

"I'll ask the queen if you can stay here while I'm gone, but just in case, I want you to have money for food or lodging."

She peered down at the small bag of gold coins next to her, her eyes wide. "I can't take that. It's yours."

I shook my head. "It's yours now. Don't spend it all on sweets."

She grinned at that, and I leaned over to give her a hug.

If someone had told me a week ago that I'd bond so closely with a young Fall fae girl, I'd have thought they were mad. But in such a short time, Nellie felt like family, and now I had a hard time imagining her not being here.

In truth, I felt a sense of relief knowing I wouldn't be dropping her off with a relative and saying goodbye forever. I'd have to figure out what to do with her long term. I didn't know what the future held, but for now, she'd be safe here.

After wishing her goodnight, I grabbed my satchel. Inside was the broken Shadow Heart, a note for Lorelei attached to the vial, and the three faestones: Isolde's intact dagger, as well as the remains of Aribella's and Dawn's, which Stryker had melted down.

Straight from Nellie's room, I headed for the queen's study. When I arrived, there were two guards flanking the door. They patted me down before letting me enter and checked my bag. When they spotted Isolde's dagger, they insisted on taking it in themselves.

I reluctantly handed over the satchel but made sure to keep it in my sight.

When we entered the room, the guards pulled all the contents out and placed them before the queen before leaving.

"Will the Fall and Winter Court rulers be joining us?" I asked. I'd learned that the monarchs of the Fall and Winter Courts, along with their families, were also taking refuge in the Spring Palace. Yet, I hadn't encountered any of them.

Queen Gloriana shook her head. "No. They're busy enough supporting their displaced subjects. I'm sure you noticed the tents outside the city gates as well as how crowded the city is right now."

I nodded. Seeing the hopeless looks on so many faes' faces since entering the city had definitely hardened my already steely resolve to find Lorelei and end this once and for all.

"Besides," Queen Gloriana went on, "I didn't think it wise to let them know there was an Ethereum lord in the palace." She arched a brow at me, her gaze dropping to my chest, where my black heart beat. "I didn't want to risk it. That heart of yours is far too tempting."

Right. As far as they knew, I was still the enemy. "In that case, I appreciate your discretion."

"Hmm," was all she said, giving me a look that seemed to mean I'd better be worthy of her trust.

As I stood before her large oak desk, her gaze dropped from my face and settled on Isolde's dagger and the faestones from Dawn's and Aribella's daggers.

"Please tell me you did not kill the princesses for these," she said, her voice shaky.

I frowned. "What? No. The princesses are now my sisters-in-law. I would never."

At that, her wide-eyed gaze snapped back up to meet mine. "So it's true, then? Mates?"

I nodded. "Dawn married my brother Zander first. Then Aribella married Stryker, and Isolde has just wed my brother Adrien."

The queen looked genuinely mystified. "So they're all safe and . . . married in your world?"

I nodded again. "They are. Though my realm is also under the curse, and they worry about you here."

She looked down at her hands, silent for a long time before finally meeting my gaze again.

"Are you telling me that my daughter Lorelei is your . . . mate?"

I swallowed hard. "I think so, yes."

I'd waited so long for my mate, my wife. Father used to tell us stories of what it was like to meet your mate, to kiss them for the first time. I longed for those magical feelings, and I thought that, in a way, I had already felt them a little myself. But in the dream, when I had met Lorelei, the pull that she had on me felt too distant because the memories were hazy. I was also realistic enough to know that things needed to unfold somewhat naturally.

I had no idea how Lorelei felt about us being mates or if she even believed it. She'd only read about the concept in Isolde's letter to her. At some point, each of my brothers and their wives had denied their mate bonds existed before finally embracing the truth.

I'd had more time than Lorelei to learn about and accept the idea of mates, so the last thing I wanted to do was pressure her. That would only push her away. If she needed time, I would give it to her, no matter how hard it might be for me.

"And what's all this?" Queen Gloriana gestured to the items on her desk.

"Part of what I need to bring to Lorelei to help her end the curse."

The queen perked up at that. "So you have a plan to end the curse?"

"One that doesn't involve my heart, yes. But first, I need to save Lorelei from Queen Liliana."

I then told her about the dreams Lorelei had visited me in and where she thought she was: the Turtle Mountains.

"The Turtle Mountains," the queen mused, standing suddenly.

I nodded. "She said she was east of them somewhere. I'd like to leave immediately to look for her, but Nellie just confessed to me that she doesn't actually have an aunt here. Apparently, she only told me that to get me to take her here with me."

The queen appeared deep in thought, as if working through a hundred different scenarios in her mind.

"Could Nellie stay here while I go look for Lorelei?" I asked. "I've left her what little coin I have—"

"Yes, of course she can," she said, waving me off. "Thalion will stay back and look after the children. I have three other daughters besides Lorelei. You and I, along with my royal soldiers, will leave at first light. I must go now and prepare."

She gestured to her desk and the items the guards had taken from me. "You can have this back."

I noticed her hand was shaking, and her eyes welling with tears. Reaching out, I gently grasped her fingers.

"Queen Gloriana, I vow to bring your daughter to safety."

I met her gaze, and she seemed to relax a little.

"Please, call me Glori. There's no need to be so formal. Not if what you are telling me about you and my daughter is true."

I nodded, pleased to find the queen was warming up to me.

"Lorelei is one of the sweetest souls you will ever meet. The thought of her—" Glori's voice broke.

I nodded. I believed her. I hadn't had the chance to get to know Lorelei well yet, but I wanted to. I knew that when I did, I'd probably fall madly in love.

Chapter Thirteen

LORELEI

I could only sleep in snippets, and I had no idea what time of day it was. Not because I could not see. My eyesight was mercifully almost fully restored, thanks to my rapid healing ability as a royal.

Queen Liliana hadn't been to see me in some time. Maybe she'd already accomplished her task and opened the portal into Ethereum early? I was torn about what that meant. That would be awful for Dawn, but it might mean I would actually survive this.

Just as I had that thought, the door scraped open.

I spun from my place in the corner of my cell as two large fae stepped in, both clutching swords in their hands. I'd never seen them before, but with their fair features and tanned skin, they looked like Summer fae. Loyal to Queen Liliana, no doubt.

"What's going on?"

Without a word, they grabbed me by the arm and dragged me out of the room. I tried to fight, but the tip of one of their swords pressed against my throat, and I relented.

"Where is Queen Liliana?" I asked.

They said nothing.

"I can break the curse. Destroy it forever. Just let me go, and—"

The blade returned to my throat. I gasped at the sharp sting and felt a warm trickle slide down my neck.

No talking. Message received.

My heart hammered in my chest as they hauled me down the familiar corridor toward the room where the queen kept the mirror portal.

When we reached the door, I steeled myself.

Inside, it was the same scene as always. Queen Liliana stood in front of the mirror portal, holding my faestone dagger. Books, papers, and diagrams were strewn all around her in a chaotic mess. But this time, she wasn't frantic or unhinged like before. Instead, she was deadly calm.

The men deposited me at her feet, and I peered up at her.

"We will be right outside the door, Your Majesty," one of them said. She nodded, and they left.

I knew better than to fight her, so I just kneeled before her, waiting for whatever torture she intended to inflict.

"I've just received some interesting news about your handsome lord," she said, her tone cold and deliberate. "I did not expect him to join forces with your mother and her army. Bold move."

A sliver of relief worked its way into my chest.

Then it had worked. Zane had made it to the Spring Palace and teamed up with my mother. That meant there was hope.

Reading the excitement in my gaze, the queen clicked her tongue. "But don't you realize this is bad news for you, my dear?"

I stayed silent. The cunning look in her eyes made my stomach churn.

What was she up to now?

"You see," she continued without needing any prompting, "I had intended to use the last of your magic to open the portal early, but only if I couldn't get the heart of the dark lord who is coming to rescue you."

My blood ran cold. *The last of my magic.* That would probably kill me.

"I am a powerful fae," she admitted, "but your mother and her entire army, along with an Ethereum lord, are not odds I want to face right now. Faerie has a better chance if I go through the portal and take one of the three lords' hearts. They won't be expecting me."

My stomach dropped out.

Dawn. Aribella. Isolde. Their mates.

I clasped my hands in front of me. "Don't do this," I pleaded, my voice trembling. It was my last resort. "There is another way. If you would just try to work with us. Zane is bringing another way to end the curse once and for all."

She raised an eyebrow, her expression unimpressed. "So you've said. But tell me, what do you need to do to end the curse?"

I swallowed hard. "Well, I don't fully know yet, but—"

"Lies," she snarled, cutting me off. "These deceptive lords open their mouths and spew their lies, and you girls just fall in love with them? How stupid are you? There is no way to destroy the curse, only to delay it for another hundred years."

I opened my mouth to respond, but she clamped her hand down on my shoulder. Pain sliced through my chest.

"Please, no," I whimpered, reaching up to fight her off.

A sudden wave of weakness overtook me as my magic drained faster than ever before.

"It took me a while," she said, her voice sounding distant and far off, "but I finally figured out how this works."

She held up my dagger. The moonstone embedded in its hilt glowed a bright, searing pink.

With her daggered hand, she reached out and began dragging the tip of the blade across the surface of the mirror portal.

It cut through the hard glass like it was butter.

I gasped as a wave of dizziness overtook me, and Queen Liliana glanced down at me with a frown.

"I really hoped it wouldn't have to come to this. But your people, and their children's children, will thank me. I'm saving us all."

The cut she'd made in the mirrored surface began to peel open, like window shutters. She hacked at it some more, and then suddenly, I was staring into another world.

A cobblestone pathway stretched ahead of us, leading to a bustling street beyond.

She still had a hold of me and as my magic left me, black dots danced at the edges of my vision as the queen stared down at me.

"Thank you for your sacrifice, Princess Lorelei. I won't let it be in vain," she said, tightening her grip on my shoulder.

It felt like my soul was being ripped from my body.

Horrific pain flared from my navel to my nose as I struggled to breathe. My eyelids grew heavy, and I couldn't keep them open as the last vestiges of my magic were siphoned away.

Then Queen Liliana released me.

I slumped to the ground, my vision flickering in and out.

This was the end. I was dying. I thought about my parents and my wonderful sisters. And Zane. He appeared in my thoughts, too. Those blue eyes with the fleck of brown.

But Zane hadn't come soon enough, and now I would never get the chance to end the curse. I only hoped Zane could find a way to do it for me.

Zane.

The thought of him again and a phantom spike drove straight into my heart. Oh, how I wished I'd had more time to know him.

As my eyesight dimmed, I watched helplessly as Queen Liliana stepped through the portal and into Ethereum, her mind set on murder.

Then the darkness took me into its sweet embrace, and there was pain no more.

Chapter Fourteen

ZANE

That night, I slept soundly, but I had no dreams of Lorelei, which scared me. Was she hurt? Is that why she hadn't visited me? Or was it simply because we'd been asleep at different times?

In the early morning hours, before the sun had risen, Nellie and I ate a quick breakfast with Glori, Thalion, and their three daughters: Octavia, Fawn, and Daisey. They were beautiful young ladies ranging in age from about three to thirteen. It was hard to look at them because of their resemblance to Lorelei, but I loved that they were trying to talk to Nellie. So far they had asked her about the games that she loved to play and whether she liked to sing. But poor Nellie.

I glanced over and saw Nellie staring at her oatmeal instead of eating it. No one in Lorelei's family seemed to have eaten more than a bite or two of their own meals, either. A melancholy hung over the table. We were leaving on a dangerous mission, and no one knew when, or if, we'd return.

"Did she visit you in your dreams last night?" Glori asked me.

I shook my head. "You?"

"No." She looked at her daughters and her husband, who all frowned and shook their heads.

I wanted to tell myself it didn't mean anything, but my gut told me something wasn't right.

Hold on, Lorelei. Just a little longer.

After breakfast, we went out to the stables to ready our horses. Even the king and the girls, who were staying behind, joined us. As I attended to Biscuit, I caught Lorelei's sisters playing some game I didn't recognize. One person stood in the center, and the others bopped them on the head before being chased.

Nellie was participating, but her smile didn't reach her eyes.

Glori called me over.

"You will not truly be able to help save my daughter without something to defend yourself with." At first I was not sure what she meant, but then she looked at a guard who brought over a sword.

"This is for you," she said. "Use it well."

I was grateful. I usually relied on my magic to protect myself, but with how unreliable my powers had been since arriving in Faerie, I felt better having a weapon at my disposal. I thanked her and assured her that I would do everything I could and that I intended to save Lorelei from whatever happened.

"I'm counting on it," she said.

By the time the sun was fully up, the queen and I, along with her troops, were ready to leave. The queen's children stood in a line by the stalls, heads hung low as their mother kissed them goodbye.

When she was done, Thalion stepped forward and pulled her

into his arms. The king looked to be almost twice as big as his petite wife and almost swallowed her in his embrace.

I glanced away to give them a moment of privacy, and anyway, I had my own goodbye to make. I went over to Nellie. She wouldn't meet my gaze, so I got down on one knee in front of her.

"If you find the princess and ride off into the sunset and forget about me, I won't blame you," she said, still refusing to look at me. But I caught the telltale sheen of tears in her eyes.

The walls this little one had built around her heart to protect herself were high.

I gently grasped her chin and forced her to look down at me.

"I won't forget you. I will be back. It's a promise," I told her.

She nodded, chewing on her lip.

She sucked in a shaky breath and then, bursting forward, wrapped her arms around me. "Don't get killed."

"I told you once before," I whispered into her hair as she clung to me, "I'm very difficult to kill."

Letting me go, she stepped back and rubbed her hand over her eyes before saying, "You better be."

Some of her usual spunk returned, making me smile.

I noticed she was wearing a necklace I hadn't seen before. Hanging on a delicate gold chain was an orange jewel set in a teardrop pendant.

"That's nice," I said, pointing to it.

Nellie's face brightened, and it made my heart lighter to see her smile. "Thanks. It was my nana's."

When she said that, I remembered how she'd taken it with her before leaving her house. I wished I had something to give her as well, but I hoped that her nana's necklace would give her comfort while I was gone.

Standing, I watched as the king gathered his children and Nellie, and they all began to return to the palace.

I turned to face the queen, who was watching me with a warm smile. "You must have really made an impression on her. I can tell she's not one to trust easily. She's bonded to you."

I nodded, not trusting myself to speak.

With that, I climbed into Biscuit's saddle, and we rode toward the Turtle Mountains.

The journey started out pleasant enough, with a crisp, westerly breeze and a partially sunny sky. But the farther east we traveled, the more the clouds disappeared and the hotter it got until the ride became grueling.

We had to stop the horses more than once to water and rest them. Even the Spring queen looked red-faced.

I glanced at the sky, the sun beating down relentlessly. "Any chance you could bring clouds or something?" I asked Glori.

She shook her head. "I don't have that type of control over the weather. That would be the Summer queen's power. The Turtle Mountains mark the barrier between the Spring and Summer Courts. Beyond them is only dry, scorched earth and unrelenting sun. It will get worse."

She wiped her brow and gestured to some nearby soldiers, who I now noticed were carrying potted plants and flowers.

"The plants will help me replenish my power, if needed."

I nodded. That made sense. Spring fae drew their magic from life itself. If the ground didn't hold life, she had to bring some with her as reserves.

We pressed on, and sure enough, the lush green landscape gradually turned barren. Instead of riding straight over the Turtle

Mountains, we skirted them to stay hidden from Queen Liliana as we approached.

We wanted to find where she was hiding before she knew we were coming for her.

We rode until the sky was streaked with orange from the setting sun as it began to drop lower.

"We're going to have to stay another night unless we get a lead on where the Summer queen is hiding," Glori told her soldiers.

They fanned out, and we all scanned the horizon for any sign of life: a house, a tree, a castle, anything. But the land stretched flat and empty.

It had been too long since anyone had heard from Lorelei in her dreams. Something wasn't right. I truly feared for her life and whether she would make it another night, but I couldn't say so aloud.

"I fear Lorelei is in too much danger to delay," I said, tactfully voicing my concerns.

Glori nodded, still scanning the horizon. "Let's split into four groups," she said to me before turning to her troops and shouting names, pointing in different directions.

"Zane, you go northeast with Captain Lace," she said, gesturing to a stout fae on his horse.

I gave a sharp nod and maneuvered Biscuit to ride next to the captain. Anything to get to Lorelei faster.

After Glori divided her troops, we spread out with the Turtle Mountains at our backs, all on a mission to find Lorelei.

It reminded me of bird hunting back home, when we had to fan out to find the downed bird. But this bird was Lorelei, and darkness was approaching, with a vast landscape still to cover.

The queen and her group headed southeast as I rode northeast. We moved fast and hard, praying to the fates I'd find Lorelei in time.

The horizon felt endless. Every time I thought I'd reached it, the line kept moving, signaling an unending expanse of dry, scorched earth. There wasn't a tree or bush in sight, just a few hills, a mountain, and a jagged rock cropping.

The sun had already set, and it was getting harder to see. I lightly nudged Biscuit, urging her forward as panic rose inside me. Searching for Lorelei in the dark would be nearly impossible, but I knew I couldn't wait another night to find her. To rescue her.

She hadn't given me specific details about what Queen Liliana was doing to her, but I knew it was some form of torture.

"We should make camp," Captain Lace called from behind me.

I ignored him, spurring Biscuit toward the jagged rock cropping in the distance.

As I neared, my stomach clenched. What I'd thought was a rock cropping wasn't that at all. It was a large stone manor house.

"I see a house," I yelled back to Captain Lace, then pushed Biscuit harder than ever. Her muscles shook as she pounded the ground, no doubt picking up on the urgency in my voice. Horses were intuitive like that.

"Good girl." I stroked her neck as we neared the stone manor, the night continuing to darken.

The moment we arrived in front of the manor entrance, I leaped off Biscuit, not bothering to tie her up. I risked a glance behind me to see if Captain Lace and the others were close, but in the darkness, I couldn't see or hear them.

They might still be on their way, but it didn't matter. I wasn't going to waste time waiting for them. Each heartbeat banged against my ribs like a clock counting down. I had to get to Lorelei now.

Pulling the sword Glori had given me, I raced up the front steps and tried the door handle. It pushed open without resistance, which made me wary.

Where were the guards?

I slipped inside the manor, pausing when I was met with complete silence.

Allowing my hearing to sharpen, I picked up faint clanking noises, like pots and pans, coming from the right. Perhaps someone was in the kitchen?

Whatever operation Queen Liliana was running here, it appeared to be lightly staffed. Probably because most fae wouldn't agree with kidnapping the Spring Court princess. At least, I hoped that was the reason and not because they'd already left or this wasn't the right place.

Moving quietly through the manor, I checked a few bedrooms, but they were empty. If Lorelei was being held prisoner here, Queen Liliana was probably keeping her somewhere more secure, like a cellar or dungeon. I just needed to find the—

A door to my left opened, and someone stepped out directly in front of me.

We both startled.

It was a guard. A large fae with a sword on his hip.

Before he could reach for it, I cracked the handle of my sword against the side of his head. He crumpled to the ground.

I had no qualms about killing someone who had helped abduct Lorelei, but I still wasn't entirely certain this was the right house. Some innocent lord or lady could live here, and I didn't want to kill anyone until I knew for sure.

Peering into the open door the guard had just come through, I sagged in relief when I saw a set of stairs leading down. If Queen Liliana was holding Lorelei here, she was most likely below.

I started down the stairs, sword aloft, taking the steps two at a time. When I reached the bottom, I was horrified that some of my fears had been correct. In front of me were barred cells, not a larder or wine cellar, as most estates might have. No, this was clearly a dungeon.

I began running past each cell, looking inside, only to find them all empty. My chest felt like it was caving in.

Where was she?

"Lorelei?" I yelled, not caring if my voice drew every one of Queen Liliana's guards. Let whoever was here come for me. I'd cut them down.

At the end of the row of cells, I spotted a door ajar.

Slipping inside, I scanned the messy space. Books, maps, papers, a huge mirror . . .

Lorelei.

I sheathed my sword and ran to her. She was crumpled on the ground in front of a full-length mirror, and as I reached for her, movement caught my eye. I glanced up and froze.

In the mirror's reflection, I saw not only myself but a gash in its surface, revealing another realm.

My realm.

I recognized it instantly. The town with the clock tower in the distance. It was my home. Westeria in the Western Kingdom of Ethereum.

For a moment, I was stunned. But I pushed the thought from my mind and dropped to my knees, pulling Lorelei into my arms.

She was so pale and still, her skin cold to the touch. Terror gripped me as I feared she was dead, and my heart felt like it stopped. Then she let out a soft moan.

"Lorelei." I shook her gently, but she remained limp. Only the slow, steady rise and fall of her chest assured me she was alive.

My fates, she was even more beautiful in real life than in my dreams. The lamplight cast soft shadows across her upturned nose and full lips. Her long brown hair cascaded over my shoulder in silky waves.

I didn't know what was wrong with her, but I knew I had to get her out of there and to her mother, who might know how to wake her.

Lifting her delicately, I carried her out of the room. I kept a sharp eye and ear as I moved through the dungeon corridor, passing the empty cells.

"Lorelei. You're safe now," I whispered, but her head just flopped back and forth against my chest.

Reaching the stairs, I began to ascend, pausing at the door at the top of the landing.

Aside from the guard I'd knocked out, I hadn't seen anyone else since entering the manor. But that didn't mean no one else was there. And the guard could have regained consciousness.

I needed to be prepared.

Reaching for my power, I readied myself. I might not have full access to my magic, but I'd rather use what little I had left than set Lorelei down to grab my blade.

I didn't ever want to let her go again.

As I reached for my magic, panic rose inside me. This time, I didn't even feel it at all.

Why? How?

Brushing the questions from my mind, I dug deeper than ever

before into the reservoirs of my power until I felt a spark flare to life. There was only a tiny grain of magic left, but it was enough. I'd make sure of it.

Steeling myself, I burst through the opening at the top of the stairs, and sure enough, not one but two guards were headed my way.

"He's got her," one shouted.

"What are our orders? Can we kill him?" the other asked.

They were clearly confused, and I used that to my advantage. Shifting Lorelei's slight weight to one arm, I freed my other hand and blasted the first guard with a black lightning bolt. He fell to the ground, twitching.

I turned to the second guard, aiming my hand and forcing my magic outward.

But nothing happened.

I'd used what little I had left. There was nothing else for me to pull from.

The second guard lunged for Lorelei, reaching as if to take her from me, and I went berserk.

Snapping my head forward, I headbutted him, and he stumbled back with a cry. Lifting my right boot, I kicked him squarely in the chest, sending him backward into the wall. He cracked his head against the stone and slumped to the ground.

I didn't stop to assess the damage. Running for the front door, I shoved it open with my shoulder, holding Lorelei tightly to my chest the entire time.

Biscuit was waiting for me, loyally standing right where I'd left her.

Carefully, I draped Lorelei over Biscuit before climbing up behind her. Once in the saddle, I pulled her back into my arms.

Throughout the whole ordeal, Lorelei remained limp and unconscious.

Fear clawed at my chest. What if she never woke up?

The terrifying thought spurred me on. I squeezed my heels into Biscuit's sides, urging her forward by the faint moonlight in the direction where I'd last seen Captain Lace.

Pushing Biscuit as fast as she could go, I kept glancing over my shoulder, worried someone from the manor might give chase and catch us before I could meet back up with the Spring Court troops.

When I finally spotted a fire on the horizon, relief threatened to weaken my muscles. But I tightened my grip on Lorelei and the reins, urging Biscuit to go faster.

As we reached the fire, I saw over a dozen fae surrounding it and many more setting up tents in the surrounding area.

"I have her," I called out, and the men erupted into a flurry of activity.

"Get word to the queen," Captain Lace snapped at one of his men.

"It's dark. I don't know where she camped—"

"Go!" Lace roared.

The messenger nodded, mounting his horse and riding off into the darkness. As I scanned the horizon, I spotted three faint fires in the distance. He'd have to check each one to find Lorelei's mother.

"Is she alive?" Captain Lace appeared before me, his arms outstretched as he looked at Lorelei with a mix of adoration and awe.

I growled slightly, disguising it with a cough. I felt possessive of her and didn't want to hand her over. But I reminded myself this was his princess, his charge to protect.

"Yes, but she's weak," I said, reluctantly letting him take her from my arms. "Something's wrong. She should have woken by now."

When he took her, it felt like he'd taken all the warmth from my soul, leaving me hollow. Between leaving Nellie behind and now this, I felt utterly empty.

The captain gently laid Lorelei on her back in front of the fire. Her soft hair fanned out around her as he spread her arms, palms up. She looked as though she were peacefully sleeping, but the soft whimpers escaping her lips told a different story.

"Get the plants," Captain Lace ordered, and the men began moving quickly around the princess.

"What's happening?" I demanded. "Is she okay?"

Captain Lace glanced at me, his expression grim. "Our princess has a unique magic. It requires her to be near living plants, flowers, weeds, even trees. This is the worst place for her to sustain an injury."

Injury?

My gaze flew over her body, scanning her pale purple dress for blood or any visible wounds. But I saw nothing. No visible wounds anywhere.

"Where is she injured?" I demanded as the captain hovered his hand over her body, slowly running it from her head to her feet.

He glanced up at me, his expression grim, and a pit formed in my gut. "I'm no healer, but I have a touch of healing magic. Most Spring fae do. She's . . . It's hard to explain. It's like she's . . . empty."

Empty.

That didn't sound good. I couldn't bear what that might mean for Lorelei.

One by one, the soldiers brought over the potted plants they'd carried from the Spring Court, setting them around their princess. Captain Lace gently removed the plants from their pots, spreading the rich soil across her hands, legs, and chest.

Lorelei lay on the ground, her body covered in dirt and vegetation.

It was strange to watch, but I reminded myself that she was a Spring fae. She must need the life of her court to heal.

"Now what?" I asked.

The captain stared at Lorelei, his brow furrowed in concern. It was as though he expected something to happen, but it wasn't.

I was about to repeat my question when I noticed the purple flowers in her right hand begin to shrivel.

I gasped at the same time Captain Lace let out a sigh of relief.

The flower withered completely, and then the one in her left hand followed.

One moment, the flowers were vibrant and colorful in the fire-light. The next, they crumbled into powdered ash.

Suddenly, Lorelei gasped, her body jolting as she sat bolt upright.

Her purple eyes locked onto mine, and it was like taking a lightning strike straight to the chest.

At that moment, I knew I would never be the same again.

Chapter Fifteen

LORELEI

I'd gone to a terrifying place when the queen took my magic, an endless void with no dream doors. I was near death, but then Zane found me. I remembered calling his name into the void.

And then I regained consciousness.

When I opened my eyes, he was there, standing in front of me with a look of raw awe mixed with desire on his face. The intensity of it sent a rush of awareness through me.

Of course, we'd already met in his dreams, but seeing him in real life was entirely different. I found myself staring at him across the firelight as Captain Lace peppered me with questions, his voice fading into the background.

Zane was everything I remembered from my dreams: tall, handsome, and striking blue eyes. But he was also so much more. His shoulders seemed broader. His gaze was more intense. And his sheer presence left me breathless.

It was as if the dream version of Zane had been only a pale imitation of the man standing before me.

Now that I was seeing him in the flesh, I couldn't stop the questions that had lingered in the back of my mind.

Was Zane truly my mate?

And if he was, what did that mean?

Was he expecting me to live with him in Ethereum, like the other princesses? Would he want to stay here in Faerie instead?

Did I even want a mate at all?

Before he'd appeared, I'd been content, expecting to live out my life in my court. Of course, I'd known that someday I would find a partner and marry. But I'd always assumed that fae would be my choice, not someone thrust upon me by fate.

Yet the pull I felt toward Zane, from just one glance, was undeniable.

It was all so overwhelming that I couldn't even sort out my own thoughts. So, I did what I had done before and pushed it to the back of my mind.

I held a hand out to Captain Lace, and he helped me to my feet.

I curtsied to Lord Zane. "Thank you for rescuing me."

"Yes, you're wel . . . come." He fumbled over his words, then cleared his throat.

I didn't miss the slight color that rose high on his cheekbones, and I blushed as well.

We had both been so confident in his dreams, yet now, standing before each other, it felt as if we were starting anew.

"Are you still hurt?" Captain Lace asked, breaking a little of the awkward tension.

I shook my head, glancing at the withered plants around me. They had been smart to bring them. My mother's idea, no doubt.

"Where's my mother?" I asked.

It was crucial I spoke with both her and Zane. They needed to know that Queen Liliana had taken my faestone dagger to Ethereum so we could form a plan for what to do next.

"She's—"

"I'm here."

My mother's voice boomed behind me, and I spun toward her. It was dark, but the firelight illuminated her as she dismounted her stallion and ran to me.

Even though I was a full-grown adult, when she opened her arms, I fell into them, just as I had when I was a child.

"Did she hurt you?" Her voice was a low growl.

"I'm okay now," I replied, not wanting to lie. Queen Liliana had hurt me, but I was safe now, and that's what truly mattered.

"I need to speak privately with you," I whispered to her, "and Zane."

She nodded and called Zane over, then barked orders at her guards to enforce a perimeter around us. A large canvas tent had been set up nearby, with an oil lamp already lit inside.

We stepped through the flaps, and I took a shaky breath, trying to gather my thoughts.

"Please tell me you killed Queen Liliana," my mother asked Zane.

A dark look crossed his face, making him appear fierce. "I would have loved nothing more, but I didn't have the chance. She wasn't there. But I saw something. I'm not sure what it was, but it looked like some sort of portal to my world. I didn't stay to investigate. My priority was getting Lorelei to safety."

His gaze shifted to me, and I read the panic in his eyes.

I chewed my lip. “The Summer queen figured out a way to drain my magic using my dagger and then used it to open the mirror portal to Ethereum early. I didn’t even know that was possible.”

I took a breath, looking Zane straight in the eyes. “I’m so sorry, Zane. After opening the portal, she escaped into your world.”

My mother gasped, and Zane began pacing the small tent.

“How is that possible?” my mother asked. “The portal isn’t supposed to open until the Spring Equinox.”

I wrung my hands, my heart aching for Zane. Queen Liliana was targeting his loved ones, and I wasn’t sure there was anything we could do to stop her. “She had all these books about the princesses’ daggers. The faestones are special. They hold far more power than we were ever taught.”

Anger flashed across my mother’s face. “Oh, I feel like such a fool for giving her that mirror. I had no idea. She said she was training you, and by the time I realized—”

“It’s okay. You couldn’t have known,” I said, grasping her hands and squeezing them.

Zane went deadly still, his gaze locking onto me. “She’s going to kill one of my brothers, isn’t she?”

I had already told him about her plans in one of his dreams, but I could see on his face that he wanted me to tell him it wasn’t true.

“She’s going to try,” I told him honestly. “She took the faestone dagger with her.”

Zane resumed pacing, rubbing his jaw as he got lost in thought. Despite everything, I found myself distracted by how handsome he looked. Wholly inappropriate thoughts considering the circumstances, but I couldn't help it.

"What are you thinking?" my mother asked him. She was the smartest strategist I knew, and I hoped she could help him process this.

"I'm thinking that mirror portal is still open back at that manor house. I could go through it, warn my brothers, and kill the Summer queen."

My mother nodded. "You could. But what if the portal is only one way? What if, after you kill her, you can't get back? Or what if, rather than you killing Liliana, she manages to kill you? It could take days or weeks to find her, and in that time, you might miss your opportunity to end the curse forever. Isn't that why you're here in the first place?"

Zane stopped walking, his gaze flicking to me for a brief second. That look said so much. He'd traveled to Faerie not just to destroy the curse but also for me, maybe even more for me.

That realization sent warmth spreading through me in a way that was not entirely unwelcome.

Returning his attention to my mother, Zane nodded slowly. "I've thought about all of that, too."

Oh, my heart ached for him. It was an impossible choice. I didn't want him to have to choose at all.

"Zane?" I asked, drawing his attention. "Aren't your brothers really powerful?"

"They are," he replied. "As are their wives. But if they don't know the threat is coming . . ."

I nodded, understanding. If they weren't on guard, even their power might not be enough.

"I understand." I held out my hand, gesturing to the bag slung over his shoulder. "If you give me the note and all the items you brought from Ethereum, I'll journey alone and destroy the curse while you go after your brothers."

My mother's mouth opened in protest, but I shut her down with a sharp glare. This was my life, my purpose. I couldn't live with myself if something happened to Zane's brothers, my fellow princesses' husbands, because we hadn't acted when we could have.

Instead of handing me the bag, Zane placed his hand in my outstretched one and squeezed gently. A wave of heat swept through me at the contact, and my breath hitched.

"A valiant offer," he said softly, his eyes fixed on mine. "One I will not forget. But leaving you to face this mission on your own is not something I am capable of."

My legs felt weak, and I inwardly swooned at his words. Out of the corner of my eye, I caught my mother grinning.

Zane squeezed my hand once more before letting it go, but even after, I could still feel the imprint of his palm against mine.

"You are right," he continued, a look of determination sliding over his features. "My brothers are ten times more powerful than Queen Liliana. They can take care of themselves. The best way to help them is to stop this curse once and for all."

"Wonderful," my mother said, approval clear in her tone. That alone was impressive. She didn't give her approval lightly. Protective of my sisters and me, she rarely deemed anyone good enough. Yet somehow, Zane had managed to earn her respect, and that meant something to me.

"I will prepare my troops," she added. "We'll join you on your quest in the morning."

Zane and I both nodded. Reaching into his bag, he pulled out a small rolled note attached to a glowing blue vial and handed it to me.

"I have some other items we might need to end this curse," he said, tapping the bag. "But this note, I've been waiting to give it to you, and you alone."

I glanced down at the tiny scroll. My name was written on the side.

Lorelei Maebry, Princess of Spring.

"May I have some time to read it alone?" I asked, sensing that this was something I needed to experience privately.

Both Zane and my mother nodded, leaving the tent.

Stepping closer to the lantern, I peeled the tiny wax seal from the scroll and unrolled the letter. My gaze swept over the note as I began to read.

Princess Lorelei Maebry,
The curse that has plagued your land for thousands of years ends with you. To destroy it, you must journey alone with your mate, Zane Warrick, to the Tree of Transformation—the place where the curse began, and the only place where it can end.

I stopped. My throat tightened as I processed the words: *Journey alone with your mate, Zane Warrick.*

Seeing it written on the scroll in front of me made it real. Zane was my mate. I took a whole couple of breaths before I carried on reading.

When you arrive, place the pieces of the Shadow Heart within the tree and drink the contents of the vial. Then, place your hand upon the trunk and surrender yourself to the curse. Only through this act can it be healed forever.

Before you begin this task, there are two vital truths you must understand:

First, the curse will not relinquish its hold without a fight. As you undertake your journey with the intent of ending it, the curse will rise against you with all its might, seeking to hinder your progress at every turn. Come for the curse and the curse will come for you.

Second, when you drink the contents of the vial, your life force will be the price paid to end the curse. This is the ultimate sacrifice.

We honor your courage and selflessness, sweet princess of Spring.

With deepest respect,
The Wise Ones

But I didn't have time to dwell on that, if I even truly knew how I felt about it, because the letter also said I'd have to give up my life to end the curse.

A single tear slipped down my cheek, and I quickly wiped it away.

End my life before it truly began? No marriage, no children, none of the dreams I'd always hoped for would come to pass. Not seeing my sisters grow or ever seeing Dawn, Aribella, and Isolde again or watching how their lives would flourish once the curse was over. I would miss all of that.

But I'd save hundreds of thousands of lives in the process. As much as it felt like my heart was breaking, I knew this sacrifice was worth it.

I nodded to myself, rolling up the note. I couldn't show it to anyone. If my mother or Zane realized what I'd have to do, they'd try to stop me. But my life wasn't worth more than anyone else's.

I'd simply have to make the most of the time I had left. Yes, that's what I'd do. And I'd take comfort in knowing that the curse would no longer threaten my people or their descendants because of the choice I was making.

I wiped my cheeks again, ensuring there was no trace of tears, and stepped out of the tent where my mother and Zane were waiting. Their gazes shifted to me, and I forced a smile, pretending everything was fine.

"The note was from the Wise Ones," I said, and Zane's eyebrows shot up.

"The Wise Ones?" he asked.

I nodded. "Do you know who they are?"

"I do," he replied. "The Wise Ones are unseelie fae who reside in my world. They're the oldest among us and can foresee the future. They've guided my brothers and the princesses this far. We only have the Shadow Heart and what was hidden within it because of their direction. They're the ones who told me I needed to come to Faerie to help you destroy the curse."

I sucked in a silent breath. Foresight was a gift I'd only read about in books. I couldn't fathom having that kind of power. If what Zane said was true, that meant they'd seen my fate and knew I'd have to die to end the curse.

Another wave of sadness crashed into me, and I swayed on my feet.

Zane quickly reached out to steady me. His gaze filled with concern. "Are you all right?"

I took a deep breath and forced another smile. "Yes, I'm sorry. This is just a lot to take in."

He nodded like he understood, but the concern didn't leave his eyes.

"What did the note say?" my mother asked, breaking her silence.

"Zane and I must venture alone to the Tree of Transformation."

My mother's face tightened with worry. "The Tree of Transformation? Alone? That's dangerous."

She had no idea how dangerous. The note warned that the curse would try to stop us the moment we began our journey.

The Tree of Transformation was located in the dead center of our realm, within the uninhabited lands between all four courts, an area we called the Savage Lands. Our courts were like spokes on a wheel, and in the center of those spokes lay wild terrain that no court claimed. It snowed one second, only to turn scorching hot the next. Droughts would last for months before the sky opened, and torrential rain flooded the land for days on end. It was as if the curse itself lived there permanently, never straying outside its boundaries. We'd always suspected that's where the curse began, in such an inhospitable place. It was also rumored to be where the curse was born.

"What do we do once we get to the Tree of Transformation?" Zane asked.

I swallowed hard. "We use the black crystal you brought, place it in the tree," I said, tapping the vial in my pocket along with the note. "And then I use my power to heal the tree and the curse," I lied.

It was a plausible answer. I did possess rare healing and rejuvenation magic, after all.

My mother nodded, seemingly satisfied with my explanation, but Zane had a look about him, a look that said he wasn't entirely convinced, and I wondered whether he would ask for more information later. We might be mates, but I didn't know him well enough to predict how he would act. And now I would not have time to find out. My heart ached at the thought.

"And you're sure we can't come?" my mother asked, gesturing behind her to her guards.

I shook my head. "Not according to the note."

Her brow pinched, and I could tell she wanted to argue, but before she could, Zane spoke up. "I promise I'll make sure nothing happens to her." He placed a hand over his heart. "I'll protect her with my life."

My mother stared at Zane, her gaze assessing him. Minutes seemed to stretch into hours before she finally nodded, albeit reluctantly.

"Very well. But I'll hold you to that."

Zane gave a sharp nod, and my mother released a weary sigh that turned into a yawn. “I’m exhausted. Lorelei, I’ll have the men put some bedding in the tent for us so we can sleep. You and Zane can leave at first light.”

“Thank you,” I said, meaning not only for the tent but also for trusting Zane and me to complete our task.

She gave me a warm smile, then turned to speak with her men. Before leaving, she told Zane that Captain Lace would have a bedroll ready for him.

Zane stepped closer, lowering his voice. “What is the vial of liquid for?”

I cleared my throat, searching for an answer he would accept. “It boosts my power.”

“And what am I needed for?” he asked. “Did the letter mention me?”

It did. It said he was my mate. A mate I would never have a long, happy life with. And I knew it anyway, I had felt a connection between us and I wanted to say it, but I didn’t.

“I think you’re meant to protect me as I travel to the tree,” I replied instead. “It said the curse will . . . try to deter us. *Come for the curse and the curse will come for you*.”

His brows furrowed, and his gaze bore into mine, making my stomach do flip-flops. “I can do that. I will protect you.” There wasn’t a hint of fear or hesitation in his voice.

Why did life have to be so cruel? As I stared at him, I had a sudden urge to run my fingers through his brown hair, to feel its texture, to press my lips to his and discover if they were as soft as they looked.

But I forced myself to look away. What was the point?

I cleared my throat, and Zane shook himself, as if coming out of a trance. "I'm tired. I think I'll go see if that tent is ready yet."

"Right. I'll be here in the morning," he said, pointing to a spot in front of the tent's entrance.

That night, when I fell asleep, all of the doors appeared before me: Father's, Mother's, my sisters', and Zane's.

I walked over to Zane's door and laid a hand against it, tempted to spend more time with him. But I decided to stay in the darkness, alone. There was no point in deepening our relationship. It would only hurt more when he lost me.

Chapter Sixteen

DAWN

Zander hovered over me, one hand resting gently on my swollen belly and the other stroking my cheek. His eyes were full of concern as the healer, Eowyn, waved her arms over my midsection.

I'd been woken by cramping pains late last night. There was no blood, but the cramps were coming every hour, radiating painfully to my back. It was far too early to give birth, and I couldn't help but feel nervous.

Eowyn, a woman in her sixties with silver hair and long, pointed ears, had a motherly kindness about her, though she was quiet. Zander had been searching for her ever since I told him I was pregnant. He'd sent messengers throughout the kingdom to track her down. It took months, but she was finally located last week on a refugee train coming up from the Southern Kingdom.

It was rumored that she was the most talented healer in all of Ethereum, but after losing a patient, she had become a recluse.

When Zander finally found her, he'd had to all but beg her to come and attend to me.

"You're in early labor," Eowyn said, her voice heavy with sadness.

My stomach dropped. "No," I whispered, shaking my head.

She pressed her lips together in a stern line, her brows furrowed deeply. "There are too many babies in there to stay put much longer."

I looked up at Zander, who stood rigid like a stone statue next to me, his face void of emotion. He seemed to be in shock.

"How many? Can you tell?"

Eowyn nodded. "I sense four heartbeats."

Four.

My eyes widened. I had known there was more than one, maybe even three, but four?

"Like my mother," Zander breathed, his voice barely audible. He rested his forehead lightly on my stomach, his expression torn between awe and fear.

I turned to Eowyn, seeking her honesty. "You can heal them if they come too early, right? Help them grow until they can survive on their own?"

From what I'd heard, she was skilled at managing complicated births and could even create a bubble of healing energy around premature babies, feeding them strength until they were big enough to survive on their own.

Shadows crossed her face, and she turned away, giving me her back. "I used to be able to."

Zander's head snapped up. "Used to be able to? Are you saying you can't anymore?"

Eowyn remained silent, her shoulders tense. I wondered if this inability had something to do with why she had become a recluse.

I glanced at Zander, worry and fear etched into the lines of his face. Reaching for his hand, I gave it a reassuring squeeze. "Darling, can you give us some time alone to speak?"

He frowned, reluctant, but finally nodded and left the room. I watched him go with a heavy heart, knowing that if anything happened to me or the babies, he might never recover.

The moment the cramping pains had started, Zander had sent a letter to Adrien and Isolde, asking them, along with her sister Seraphina, to join us and Stryker and Aribella here in Zane's castle in the Western Kingdom. We, along with our subjects, had fled here to escape the curse. It was the only remaining kingdom yet untouched by the curse. Zander believed we'd be stronger together, and I agreed.

"Eowyn, you are the only chance my babies have to survive. If they're coming earlier than they should, and you have the magic to keep them alive once they are delivered, I need you to try. No matter what."

She turned back to me, unshed tears glistening in her light teal eyes, her wise, wrinkled face etched with emotion. "Even if they die at my hand?"

Her words were shocking, but I could feel the weight of what I was asking her, to bear the responsibility of four fragile lives.

I nodded, my throat tight. "Even if they die."

Her chest heaved as she glanced from my face to my stomach. "You should know something before you agree to this," she said, her voice trembling.

Here it was. Whatever had caused her anguish and driven her into hiding. I braced myself for the revelation.

"I was in this same situation over ten years ago," she began, her voice shaking. "I was confident I could help the mother deliver her twins early. Confident I could help keep them alive until they were big enough to suckle and survive outside the bubble I created. I'd done it dozens of times before. It was second nature to me, like breathing. I barely had to think about how to conjure such magic."

A tear slid down her cheek, and she batted it away quickly.

My heart pinched for her. Something had gone terribly wrong.

I reached out a hand to her, but she refused to take it. "They all died, Lady Dawn," she whispered. "Both babies . . . and the mother." Her face contorted in agony, and my stomach dropped.

This was why she had gone into hiding. This was why she had stopped healing.

Still, she was my only chance. "Do you know what happened?" I asked gently.

She nodded. "I think so. When I create the bubbles babies need to survive, I tie them to the mother's energy. It's the only way to sustain them. Even though it's my magic, the mother powers it. But I didn't know the mother was sick. She was too weak. I was so focused on the babies that I neglected her, and they all perished."

Relief washed over me at her explanation. I was heartbroken for that mother and her children, but that wasn't going to be my fate.

"Eowyn, look at me."

She lifted her gaze, and the agony in her eyes was nearly unbearable.

"That won't happen with us," I said firmly. "I'm a royal princess of Faerie, and I have self-healing magic. I'm not sick. If I do become sick, my body heals much faster than the average fae.

I'm strong, and if you tie these babies to my energy, I promise you I can support them."

"But it's four babies," she said cautiously. "It could weaken you tremendously, and if you were stressed or injured—"

"I'm strong," I interrupted, my voice resolute. "And I'm not going to let anything happen to my children."

I laid a hand on my enormous belly and held her gaze. Now that I knew their existence was tied to my ability to stay strong, that's exactly what I would do. Stay strong.

"Will you help me?" I asked.

She hesitated but finally nodded, reluctantly. "What choice do I have? This is our only option."

Just as she spoke, another contraction hit, and I buckled to the side, clutching my stomach in pain.

She hurried up behind me and placed a hand on my lower back. "Shhh, breathe through it."

Soothing energy flooded my midsection, and I felt some of the tension ease. I relaxed a little, focusing on breathing through the contraction.

Peering up at her, I offered a weak smile. "Thank you."

She nodded, her expression softening. "You are carrying the future lords of Ethereum. It's a lot of pressure."

I understood that, though part of me hoped there was at least one lady of Ethereum in there, too. But I wasn't sure how that worked. In Faerie, royalty only had girls, while here in Ethereum, it seemed they only had boys.

"I promise. My husband will not blame you if this goes badly."

She swallowed hard, her teal eyes shimmering with emotion. I felt a pang of guilt for the burden she carried, for the fear she clearly held close.

We had a plan now. All that was left was to execute it.

"Hang in there, my loves," I said softly to my belly, resting both hands on its curve. "Mommy's got you."

But as I said the words, my mind wandered to Zane and Lorelei. None of this would truly matter if they didn't succeed in destroying the curse.

Time was running out for all of us, and if they failed, everything, even this, would be lost.

Chapter Seventeen

LORELEI

Saying goodbye to my mother was the hardest. She pulled me into a tight hug, telling me she knew I could do this. I knew it was the last time I'd ever see her, the last hug we'd ever share, but she didn't. When she started to let go, I held on for a few extra moments. Finally, I released her, telling her I loved her. She said the same, her voice warm and steady, and then I turned away and mounted my horse. It was hard not to cry and say more. I had thought about sending messages to my sisters and father, but how could I without giving away the sacrifice I had to make?

Zane and I set out on our quest for the Tree of Transformation at first light, retracing our path back to the Spring Court to approach the Savage Lands from there. Now, the sun was high in the sky, and it was nearly lunchtime.

"The Spring Court is beautiful. You have a lovely home," Zane said as we rode side by side on our horses.

This morning, when I'd stepped out of the tent, I nearly tripped over him. He'd fallen asleep right in front of the entrance, as if standing guard. His protectiveness sent butterflies fluttering in my stomach, but dwelling on it only made my heart ache more, knowing he'd never truly be mine.

Since mounting our horses, I'd barely said more than three words to him, still heartbroken over saying goodbye to my mother and consumed by the contents of the Wise Ones' note. Realizing I was being rude, I forced a smile and turned my gaze toward him.

"Thank you. Did you travel to the Spring Court with the little girl from your dreams? Nellie?"

He nodded. "Your parents were kind enough to let her stay with them until I return. She seemed to get along particularly well with your sisters. Octavia in particular, as they're so close in age."

The mention of my beloved sisters caused the smile to slip from my face. I hadn't been able to say goodbye to them or to my father. Perhaps I'd see them in their dreams, but it wasn't the same. I'd never see any of their faces again in real life.

Zane leaned toward me in his saddle, his expression filled with concern. "Are you okay?"

He was so in tune with my emotions. It was a little unnerving.

I cleared my throat, pushing the bleak thoughts to the far corners of my mind. If I kept acting like this, Zane would start asking questions, and the last thing I wanted was for him to discover the truth about the note. Even though I didn't know him well, I knew enough to be certain he wouldn't let me go through with my plan. And if he stopped me, we'd all die.

"Yes," I said quickly. "Tell me more about Nellie. She seemed very attached to you in your dream."

A full grin lit up his face, making him even more handsome.

Stars, he was everything I wanted in a mate. Kind, respectful, tall, strong. Every step forward felt harder, knowing I'd never get the chance to really get to know him.

"She's sassy, fun, annoying, and loves sweets," he said, his grin widening.

I laughed. "Who doesn't?"

He nodded. "Her grandmother passed away. I found her alone in her house on the Harvest Mountains, trapped. We sort of clicked."

I frowned. "Does she have any other family?"

He shook his head. "No. I'm all she's got. I know it's only been a short while, but she's becoming family already. I won't abandon her too."

"Are you planning to take care of her when this is all over?" I asked, surprised that it might be something he was considering. No other man I knew would. Most would drop her at the nearest orphanage and move on.

"Of course. She has no one."

That stunned me into silence, and my heart swelled. Was Zane for real? He'd stumbled upon a young orphan and decided to take her in and care for her? He was literally perfect.

I glanced over at him to find him watching me. Warmth spread through my chest, making it hard to look away.

Maybe blocking whatever might happen between us was a bad idea. Maybe I shouldn't deny myself the chance to live fully in the few days I had left, to embrace whatever these moments with Zane might bring.

But would that be selfish of me in the long run?

"You're beautiful," he said softly, pulling me from my thoughts.

I looked away, heat rising to my cheeks as I tried not to smile. “Thank you.”

I wanted to say, “you too,” but it felt awkward.

This whole situation was strange. He was my mate, but I barely knew him.

“It’s kind of strange, isn’t it? The mate thing,” he said, breaking the silence. His tone was light, but there was a hint of curiosity in his voice.

I exhaled, relieved. “So strange. We don’t have mates in this realm. At least not in reality. Just in children’s storybooks.”

He nodded. “Well, there’s no need to rush anything. I’ve waited my whole life to find my mate, so I’m in no hurry to force a connection. I just want you to know that.”

Every word he said was exactly what I needed to hear. He was so respectful, so understanding. Part of me almost wished I could find a flaw in him, but I hadn’t, not yet.

“Thank you for saying that,” I replied, smiling. But the smile felt a little hollow.

He didn’t know the truth. We didn’t have all the time in the world like he thought. We only had until we reached the Tree of Transformation, until I drank the vial.

After that, whatever bond we might build would be over. Forever.

I fell silent again, unable to shake the sadness weighing on my heart. The rhythm of the horse beneath me offered some comfort, lulling me into a calmer state.

We ate lunch on the road, keeping our pace steady to reach Meadow Village by nightfall. From there, it would be just a half-day’s ride to the border of the wild terrain where the Tree of Transformation stood.

As we rode, I found myself stealing glances at Zane. His presence was magnetic, and when he started humming a tune to himself, the sound relaxed me.

Everything about him drew me in, making it harder to stay resolute. My heart screamed at me to be reasonable, to remember how this would end. The letter was clear: there was no future for us.

But having Zane here beside me, so alive and real, made my task infinitely harder.

I needed to be strong. To keep my resolve. Yet, riding next to him, my literal dream come true, I couldn't help but wonder what it might be like to have more time. To have a life with him.

Chapter Eighteen

ZANE

Lorelei was quieter than I expected her to be. It didn't bother me, but something seemed to be upsetting her, although she clearly didn't want to talk about it. I couldn't stop sneaking side glances at her, enchanted by her beauty, but I worried I might be overwhelming her. Knowing someone was your mate and then trying to live out that reality naturally felt like two conflicting forces.

Nothing about this situation was natural.

Part of me wanted to pull her down from her horse and kiss her until she was breathless, but the other part knew I had to wait for her to feel comfortable. That meant letting her make the first move. When I'd told her I didn't want to force anything between us, she'd seemed relieved, but then she'd gone quiet again.

I was starting to learn some of Lorelei's personality quirks. When she was nervous, she chewed on her lower lip. She didn't talk just for the sake of it; whenever she spoke, it was with intention. She seemed to enjoy companionable silence but also appreciated it when I initiated conversations.

I was so wrapped up in my thoughts about her and what she might think of me that I barely noticed when we reached Meadow Village. Lorelei pulled up the hood of her soft blue traveling cloak as we passed fae going about their day. I took it as a sign she didn't want to be recognized.

After we navigated through the first crowd and ventured deeper into the village, she moved her horse closer to mine.

"I don't normally travel without an armed guard," she admitted, glancing around nervously.

Her skittish behavior immediately put me on high alert. "Is everything okay? Is there a reason to fear your subjects?" I asked, scanning the streets for any signs of a threat.

She turned to me, keeping her voice low. "They all know about my gift. There are so many with ailments or sickness, especially now that we're housing so many refugees from cursed lands. The last time I went out in public, I was nearly trampled by fae begging for healing. I'm incapable of saying no, so I helped as many as I could until I passed out from exhaustion."

A knot tightened in my chest. She had such a tender heart that I could easily see her giving to the point of endangering herself. And that terrified me.

A surge of protectiveness rose within me. "Trust me, I would die before letting you be trampled."

A pink blush crept up her cheeks, and she ducked her head, smiling softly.

"Even so," I said, "I think keeping your identity hidden is a good idea."

She nodded, then a look crossed her face, as though she'd just remembered something.

"I hope you don't think it rude of me to ask, but have you had any difficulties with your magic since arriving in Faerie?"

The comment startled me. How would she know about that?

"I have, in fact, been having some issues. Ever since I've come to your world, my powers have been . . . unreliable." I hated to sound weak, especially after promising to protect her. "I'm not sure what's been going on, but I can assure you I'm still capable of protecting you."

Her eyes went wide at that, and a blush began to darken her cheeks. "No, no, I'm not questioning you," she said in a rush. "It's just something Queen Liliana said when I was her prisoner."

The mention of the queen immediately blackened my thoughts. What I wouldn't give to have her in front of me right now. Unreliable powers wouldn't stop the retribution that I'd rain down on her for what she did to Lorelei.

"Please, don't be upset," Lorelei said quickly, misinterpreting my anger toward the queen.

I forced a smile, shaking the murderous thoughts from my mind.

"I'm sorry. I'm not upset with you for bringing it up. Only the mention of the queen ignited a spark of my rage. It was nothing you did," I assured her.

She nodded in understanding. "It's just that I think I may know what's going on with your magic."

I raised my eyebrows, twisting a little in my saddle to look at her more fully. "Truly?"

She nodded. "The queen said that she learned if an Ethereum

lord were ever to venture to Faerie, the curse would begin to pull on his magic, weakening him."

So that was what was happening? The curse was taking my magic?

A furrow appeared between Lorelei's brows, concern clear on her face. "She said it would eventually deplete you of your magic entirely."

A rush of alarm shot through me. Was that even something I could survive?

The worry on Lorelei's face deepened, and she looked close to tears. Seeing her so distressed was like a knife to my heart. I forced a fake sense of levity into my voice and a broad smile onto my face. "Well, I can assure you I still have a deep well of magic to tap into. If that is, in fact, the truth, it will still be some time before I have to worry about that."

Relief immediately softened her features, and then her gaze shifted to my hands. "Do you mind me asking what kind of power do you have? I heard the Ethereum lords have—" She stopped herself, biting her lower lip as if unsure whether to continue.

A rush of desire shot through me at the sight, and I shifted in my saddle, clearing my throat. Forcing my gaze away from her mouth and back to her eyes, I urged her gently, my voice a little deeper than usual. "Go on."

She paused for a moment before saying, "Dark powers. Shadow magic."

Ah, yes. I wasn't surprised that's what she thought. The fae in Faerie had been villainizing Ethereum and its lords for hundreds of years, spreading misconceptions and outright lies to justify killing our lords time and time again. From speaking with my brothers' wives, especially Isolde, I knew that many in Faerie believed

Ethereum, and especially the lords' magic, to be dark and evil. It wasn't. It was just different from the magic here, and I believed that, in time, Lorelei would start to see the stories she'd been told about my realm for what they truly were: lies.

I glanced at her and smiled, hoping to put her at ease but feeling a bit nervous that I might scare her. "In relation to your healing magic, yes, mine might seem dark. I can shoot and control black lightning. And I can also manipulate shadows, though not as well as some of my brothers. The lightning is my primary power."

Her eyes widened at that. "Lightning? From your hands?" She didn't seem afraid, more curious, and for that, I was relieved.

I opened my mouth to comment, but before I could, we came across another group of fae stocking a barn with hay bales. I didn't want to speak so openly about my magic in front of other fae, so I kept my mouth shut as we walked our horses past the barn and up to an inn with a sign that read *Meadow's Inn* above the front entrance. The establishment looked small but clean, at least from the outside.

A sturdy man with broad shoulders, shaggy brown hair, and a friendly smile approached us from the barn. "Want to board the horses for the night?"

I nodded. "Yes, do you own the inn as well?"

The man inclined his head. "Adler's the name. And we've got vacancies."

"Good. We'll take two rooms, please."

"One room. Two beds," Lorelei interrupted, and I stopped myself from raising my brows despite my surprise.

Adler grinned and stated his price. I dropped some coins into his outstretched hand. Coins Lorelei's mother had given me before we departed, knowing I'd given all my gold to Nellie. Adler told us to wait where we were while he retrieved the key. He returned swiftly, and after dismounting and handing over the horses, we stepped into the inn, where loud, boisterous music and dancing greeted us.

Lorelei winced. "I'm famished, but—" She glanced at the over-crowded dining hall.

"Say no more," I told her and approached a barmaid. The aroma of stew filled the air, making my mouth water. "Can you send some food and drinks for two up to our room?" I glanced down at the key Adler had given me. "Room six."

The barmaid's eyes flicked to Lorelei behind me, a knowing grin spreading across her face. I resisted the urge to roll my eyes.

"Sure thing, honey," she said with a chuckle, and I paid her.

After arranging the meal, I led Lorelei upstairs to room six. Unlocking the door, I held it open for her, and we stepped inside. The room was surprisingly spacious. Two single beds sat at opposite ends of the room, separated by a privacy curtain. A door on the far wall likely led to the bathroom, and in one corner stood a small two-person table.

Lorelei glanced over her shoulder at me, her cheeks tinged pink. "Are you okay with sharing a room?" she asked shyly. "It's protocol when I travel with only one guard, which rarely happens. And . . . it would make me feel safer to have you here."

Being near me made her feel safe? Pride swelled in my chest, and a goofy grin spread across my face.

"Absolutely," I said quickly, then cleared my throat, embarrassed by my eagerness. "I'll take the bed near the window."

She nodded, mentioning she wanted to freshen up before the food arrived. She disappeared into the bathroom, and shortly after, I heard the sound of water running. When she emerged, she wore fresh clothes: a green-and-pink floral linen skirt with a matching top. Her long hair was tied into a braid over one shoulder, and she smiled when she caught me staring.

"I don't feel normal until I've had my nightly bath," she confessed.

Good to know. I filed that tidbit away, wanting to remember everything about her.

I sat at the small table in the corner and gestured for her to join me. "What else?" I asked as she took the seat across from me. The light cascading through the windows made her silky hair shimmer in a beautifully distracting way. Forcing my gaze to meet her purple eyes, I pressed on. "Tell me more about you."

She seemed to consider the question. "Well, I love flowers, obviously."

"Obviously," I agreed with a smile. "And you like to sing."

Her eyebrows shot up, surprised that I knew that about her.

"The first time we met, when Isolde and I visited you in the palace gardens, you were singing," I reminded her.

She nodded. "Right. That visit was so unexpected, I didn't remember that. It was just so shocking to see you and Isolde suddenly appear in front of me."

"I'm sorry if we frightened you."

"Don't be," she said, reaching forward on instinct to place her hand atop mine in comfort. Just that small touch set my heart racing, but I schooled my features so I wouldn't reveal that truth to her. She lightly squeezed my hand, then pulled back, and I forced myself not to be too disappointed.

"If you hadn't come to me that time, I never would have

known you were in Faerie, and I never would have tried to reach you in our dreams. And if I had never contacted you . . ."

Her sentence trailed off, but I could guess what she was going to say. If she had never dream-walked to me, I wouldn't have known how to find her, and she surely would have died at Queen Liliana's hands.

The look in her eyes was far away, and the sadness on her face made my own heart ache. I would do anything to wipe that sadness away.

"So you do like to sing?" I asked, grasping for something to pull her out of her dark thoughts and back to the present, back to me.

She blinked twice and then refocused on me. The smile that lifted the corners of her mouth looked forced, but it was a start.

"I do," she admitted. "But only to myself. I'm not trained or anything, so I'm not very good."

I shook my head. "That's not true. Your voice is as lovely as a songbird's. I could listen to you sing all day long."

She ducked her head slightly, unsuccessfully trying to hide the blush on her cheeks. "That's kind of you to say," she said shyly.

I leaned forward, wanting to get closer to her in any way I could.

"What else?" I asked again.

I hoped I wasn't overwhelming her, but I couldn't help myself. There wasn't a single detail about her I didn't find completely and utterly fascinating. I wanted to know everything, every small detail, every innermost thought. I was determined to learn her like no one else ever had or ever would.

"Well, I love reading, anything romance. I spend hours in the garden. I hate visiting the Winter Court because snow and cold are dreadful. And I love puppy breath."

My brows furrowed at that last part. "Puppy breath? Is that a flower?"

She burst into laughter, the sound filling the room and causing my heart to thump wildly.

"That's cute," she giggled. "No, like a puppy. A dog. Their breath is amazing."

I barely recovered from her calling me cute. Now I was laughing. "You just go around smelling puppies' breath?"

She nodded, grinning.

"That's weird. I'm going to erase that from my memory."

"It's not weird. We're going to find a puppy after all this is over, and I'm going to make you smell its breath."

I leaned forward, utterly entranced by her. "Promise?"

She smiled, but then her expression fell. I was about to ask what was wrong when a knock came at the door.

The barmaid arrived with two heaping bowls of meat-and-yam stew, fresh bread, and hot cider. The food looked as delicious as it smelled. As we ate, I tried to get Lorelei talking and laughing again, but she'd retreated into one of her quiet moods. Not wanting to press her, I fell silent, too.

I'd wait years if it meant Lorelei would open up to me on her own terms. She was worth it.

Chapter Nineteen

LORELEI

Zane was amazing, funny, strong, patient, and it was killing me to know I had to give up my life to end the curse. I wished I'd never read that stupid letter. It felt like it was burning a hole in my bag, constantly pulling at my attention.

I felt like I was giving Zane whiplash, alternating between engaging in conversation and then falling silent, but I was struggling. Part of me wanted to shut down, to stop getting to know him, while the other part wanted to throw caution to the wind and make whatever time we had left together matter.

I repeatedly found myself staring at his lips when we spoke, wondering what he kissed like. It was torture. A torture of my own making.

We'd had the best time before dinner last night, laughing and joking, but then he'd asked me to promise I'd find a puppy for him to smell. It had reminded me that I wouldn't be alive to do so, and I shut down.

After dinner, he'd gone to the bathroom to wash up, and I used the opportunity to take the coward's way out, pretending to be asleep when he came back. Now, in the early morning light, I lay awake, wondering what to do.

I couldn't keep going hot and cold. It wasn't fair to either of us. I had to stick with a plan. Either lock Zane out or let him in.

"You awake?" his gruff voice whispered from the other side of the privacy curtain.

I chewed my bottom lip before answering, "Yes."

"I've been thinking. There's a very real possibility that one or both of us could die trying to get to this tree."

My heart rate spiked. "I've thought of that, too."

I heard the bed squeak as he shifted. "There's one thing I'd like to do before I die, Lorelei."

My heart was practically in my throat. "What?" I breathed.

"I absolutely must smell a puppy's breath today before we head out."

His statement was so unexpected that a full-body laugh shook me. I tried to stop, but I couldn't. It was just so ridiculous. A dark, scary Ethereum lord insisting he wanted to smell a puppy.

It took me a couple of minutes to compose myself. I hadn't laughed like that since I was a kid. Zane was funny. I loved that about him.

"Well, in that case," I said, sitting up and swinging my legs off the side of the bed, "we'd better get dressed because I think if we head out now, we might have time to fit puppy-smelling into our itinerary."

~

An hour later, after a rushed breakfast of boiled eggs and fruit, Zane and I tracked down a litter of four puppies with help from Adler. Madame Georgette opened her sitting parlor for us early, and when we entered, the cute little balls of fur yipped and yapped at our feet.

"Just born last month," she told us. "Still on the teat, but they should be ready to take home in a few weeks. You can pick them up and play with them if you want." With that, she excused herself and retreated somewhere else in her home.

Zane glanced at me, then picked up one of the black-and-white spotted puppies. "Moment of truth, Lorelei. This better be life-changing."

I grinned, amazed that on a journey to save our dying worlds, Zane had found time to do something I loved.

I reached down and picked up an adorable little female. She wiggled in my grasp, trying to gnaw on my fingers. "Her fur is so soft," I said, my cheeks starting to ache from all the smiling this morning.

Zane lifted his puppy up to his nose, and it licked him, catching him off guard. He reeled back and looked at me with wide eyes. "It's breath. It's sweet."

I nodded, my grin feeling permanent at this point. "Mother's milk."

I snuggled my puppy, nuzzling my nose into her neck and feeling, for a moment, like the weight of the world was lifted from my shoulders.

"Do you have dogs?" he asked.

I shook my head. "My mother doesn't like them."

Zane nodded thoughtfully. "But if it were up to you, would you have one?"

I laughed. "I'd probably have five. Some chickens and goats, too."

Zane rubbed the puppy's back as it tried to bite his shirt collar. "Me too."

Madame Georgette returned to the room, and Zane handed the puppy to her. "Can I prepay and pick them up when they're weaned?"

My mouth popped open in surprise.

"Of course you can, sir. Do you want them both?"

Zane glanced at me and nodded.

I was in shock.

After he paid her, we walked back outside to where we'd left our horses.

I peered over at him, no doubt a look of awe and disbelief on my face. "Zane, did you just buy me a puppy?"

He looked down at me and nodded. "Only if you want her. Otherwise, Nellie won't mind having two, I'm sure."

He'd bought the other for Nellie?

I was suddenly overwhelmed with emotion. It scared me because the heartbreaking truth was that I was falling for Zane. Falling hard and fast for a man I would never be able to make mine.

It took the better part of the day to reach the edge of the uninhabited lands that held the Tree of Transformation, but we were almost there. I could see the black-trunked trees that marked the border of the Savage Lands ahead of us. No one knew why the bark of those trees was the color of charcoal, but they were.

"Have you ever been where we are going?" Zane asked as we eased our horses down the thick, overgrown path.

I shook my head. "No, but my mother has. That's how she was able to pen the map for us. When I was very little, she told me a story about how someone broke the law and ran to hide out in the Savage Lands. She was a young queen at the time and wanted to send a clear message that fleeing justice would not be tolerated."

Zane nodded. "I'd do the same."

"So she went with her guards and ferreted out the criminal herself."

Zane looked impressed. "Has she seen the Tree of Transformation? Does she know what makes it special?"

I nodded. "The tree gets its name because, over the course of a single day, it cycles through all four seasons. Each morning, it's reborn with new leaves."

Awe shone on Zane's face. "That sounds magical."

"I agree." As we approached the first black tree trunk, I glanced at Zane. "Now you tell me something."

He stopped his horse and looked over at me. "Ask me anything."

I squirmed in my saddle. "Isolde said we'd been lied to all our lives, but she didn't give any details. What's your side of the story? How were you told the curse started?"

Zane dipped his chin in understanding. "Balazar Warrick, the Winter king, was offered the hand of the Summer princess in marriage, but he refused. He wanted to marry an unseelie, a nymph, instead."

My eyes widened in alarm. A seelie and an unseelie? Together?

"The Summer queen at the time couldn't handle the rejection and was disgusted by his choice. She started a rebellion against him. They took his throne, killed his unseelie fiancée, and banished him and his brothers, along with all of the unseelie, to Ethereum as punishment."

"No," I gasped. "That's so cruel."

Zane looked at me with compassion. "In retribution for his fallen love, Balazar pulled the magic of Faerie into himself and his brothers, becoming its keepers. The power was so immense that it turned their blood black. In response, the Faerie royals cursed him, but the curse backfired. That's all my father told me."

I was silent for a full minute, trying to process everything.

"Are you okay? What are you thinking?" Zane asked, his voice gentle.

I sighed. "Why is it always the Summer queen who goes evil?"

He chuckled softly at that. "Doesn't matter. We're going to end all that. Right now." He gestured toward the blackened woods we were about to enter.

I knew from past champions' journals that the unseelie were populous in Ethereum, but I had never really stopped to consider why we had none here. I'd been taught they were monsters, evil, like the Ethereum lords who ruled them. But as I looked at Zane riding beside me, I knew I'd been told lies.

There wasn't an evil bone in Zane's body. He was good. Kind, thoughtful, and selfless. And I couldn't help but wonder what other lies I'd been told.

"It's a lot to absorb," Zane said, his gaze fixed on the black trees. "Are you ready for this?"

I forced myself to push aside thoughts of the past. Dwelling on it wouldn't help anyone right now. Ending the curse had to be my only focus. It didn't matter how it started.

"Yes," I answered him firmly.

With that, Zane nudged Biscuit forward, and she cantered into the forest. Suddenly, the sky split open, and a bolt of black lightning struck the ground right in front of Zane's horse.

Zane grunted, leaning forward as Biscuit reared up. He clung to her neck, barely managing to stay on.

"Zane!" I cried, riding up beside him as Biscuit steadied herself. My heart raced as I scanned him for injuries.

Zane sat in his saddle, staring at his hands with a mixture of awe and shock. When he glanced up at me, his eyes flashed yellow for a fleeting moment.

"What just happened?" I asked, my voice trembling.

His chest rose and fell heavily, and wonder filled his expression. "Do you feel that?"

I shook my head, glancing at my hands as if they might give me a clue.

"My magic," he said, his voice almost reverent. "It came back so suddenly, I couldn't contain it. I'm sorry if I scared you."

That was his power? He had mentioned being able to control lightning, but seeing it in action was an entirely different experience.

"But you're okay?" I asked, my voice still laced with concern.

Zane straightened in his saddle, his grin spreading wide. "Better than okay. I have my power back. I can protect you properly now." Relief radiated from his tone.

"Well, I'm just glad you're all right," I said, exhaling a shaky breath. "But why do you think your magic returned now?"

A furrow appeared between his eyebrows, and he shook his head. "I'm not sure. But things feel . . . familiar here."

"Familiar?" I asked, confused.

He nodded. "Like home."

Casting my gaze over the dark forest in front of us, I didn't know how to make sense of that.

"Let's keep going," Zane urged, and I nodded.

We continued through the forest, the blackened trees surrounding us like silent sentinels. After only a few minutes, I noticed Zane's gaze shifting to the forest floor. He seemed fascinated by the flowers, vines, and weeds that tangled together in a colorful tapestry beneath us.

"Huh," he said, pointing to a pale yellow flower with perfectly round petals. "You have luna blossoms here, too?"

I frowned, looking at the unfamiliar bloom. "I've never seen that flower before," I admitted, leaning closer. "Do you have them in your world?"

I let my magic trail along the forest floor, brushing against the plant's energy. It felt new. Bright, effervescent, and undeniably life-giving.

Zane's brow furrowed as he studied me. "Yes, we do. Are you sure you've never seen it before?" He gestured to another patch of the same blossoms.

Rolling my eyes, I let out a small laugh. "Zane, I'm the Spring princess. I know my plant life, and I can assure you this one is new to me."

He nodded, though he still looked thoughtful. Dropping the subject, he led the way forward, our horses trampling over bushes and low ground cover as they forged their own path.

Based on what my mother had told me, I knew we'd have to camp for the night before riding a half day to reach the Tree of Transformation. She had warned me repeatedly that it wasn't safe to travel after dark in the Savage Lands.

And then there was the warning in the Wise Ones' letter—the

curse would "come for us" as soon as we set out for the Tree. I couldn't shake the weight of that ominous prophecy.

A low growl rumbled through the sky, drawing my gaze upward. I peered through the tree canopy, my nerves prickling with unease.

Hmm, looks like rain.

Just as the thought crossed my mind, I heard the pitter-patter of droplets hitting leaves. As a Spring fae, I'd spent many afternoons in the rain gardening. I loved the smell of wet dirt, the cool drops falling on my face, the—

"Cover yourself! It burns!" Zane shouted.

I gasped as the first droplet landed on my uncovered arm. It stung. No, it burned.

The rain picked up, and a dozen more drops struck my skin, each one searing like fire. My horse reared, and before I could process what was happening, she bucked me off. I hit the ground flat on my back, the impact knocking the wind from my lungs. Struggling to catch my breath, I watched helplessly as my horse bolted, galloping back toward the Spring Court.

Two more droplets splattered onto my cheeks, sizzling as they made contact. The pain was excruciating. I screamed, clutching at my face, just as Zane threw himself on top of me. His body shielded me, creating a protective barrier from the sinister rain.

One moment, I was overwhelmed by the burning pain coursing through my exposed skin; the next, my focus shifted entirely. I found myself staring into Zane's piercing blue eyes, the weight of his body grounding me. Suddenly, nothing hurt anymore.

Zane had his cloak pulled up over his head, creating a makeshift shield for us both. His forearms framed my face as he straddled my waist, carefully lifting himself onto his knees to ease his weight. He was, quite literally, a human tent, and I wasn't complaining.

His thumb brushed gently across my cheek, his expression filled with concern. "It got your face," he said softly.

I barely registered his words. My gaze kept drifting to his lips, full and impossibly close.

Kiss him. Kiss him before you die.

"I'm okay," I whispered, my voice breathless. "I lost my horse, though."

Zane's brows furrowed as he nodded. "Me too. They both ran. If this stuff burns through our clothes, we might have to leave. Find another way. Make a new plan."

I nodded, trying to focus on his words. "Thanks for shielding me, oh brave knight."

His lips curved into a grin. "When a princess falls off her horse in burning rain, what else is a gentleman to do?"

I smiled back, warmth blooming in my chest. Were we flirting? Whatever it was, it felt good. He felt good.

The grin slipped from his face, replaced by a more serious expression. "Do you want me to move? My cloak's pretty big. I think we could both sit under it."

I didn't want him to move. Ever. The absurd thought made me giggle, and Zane's frown deepened.

"Sorry," I said quickly, trying to stifle my laughter. "No, I'm rather liking my personal protective tent. Besides, it seems to be letting up."

The sound of droplets hitting the leaves above us was slowing. Zane nodded, lifting a corner of his cloak, and scanning the forest before dropping it back into place.

"Do you think this is what the letter meant? That the curse is attacking us? Or does this kind of thing happen here normally?" he asked.

I chewed on my bottom lip, and his eyes flicked down to my mouth, lingering. "I'm not sure," I admitted. "But I was thinking about what the Wise Ones warned us about, too. My mother did say these lands are strange and volatile. She told me that, once, when she woke up after spending the night here, the trees weren't in the same place as they were before."

Zane's eyes widened, disbelief clear in his expression. "That's not possible."

I shrugged. "I'm not sure what's really possible in these wilds. But she never said anything about burning rain."

The rain had finally stopped, but I didn't want this moment to end. I edged myself a little closer, and as I inhaled, I caught a wonderful scent. Zane smelled like pine, wood bark, and freshly fallen leaves. Something I'd never noticed before, something utterly intoxicating. And then one corner of his mouth twitched up.

Kiss him. Kiss him before you drink the vial and die.

My gaze drifted to his mouth. Why shouldn't I kiss him? He was my mate, after all. He probably wouldn't complain. The way his eyes lingered on my lips right now said he'd definitely kiss me back.

If you fall in love with him, you won't want to drink the potion. And the curse will kill everyone.

The sobering thought crashed through me, snapping me back to reality. I tore my eyes from his lush mouth and cleared my throat. "Rain's stopped," I said softly.

"Right," he mumbled, his voice lower than usual. He sat up, taking his warmth and intoxicating scent with him.

I noticed the red welts where the rain had struck his skin. My own wounds itched, but they were already beginning to heal.

I sat up as well, reaching out instinctively to grasp Zane's face. He froze, his eyes wide as I closed mine, pulling energy from the plants around us and channeling it into him.

"Oh," he breathed, awe filling his voice as he glanced down at his arms.

The red welts had vanished, but the flowers around us were withered, drained of life.

"Thanks," he muttered.

"You're welcome," I said, lowering my hands.

My magic was unique. I could transfer energy from one living form to another, but it always required a sacrifice. That was why I was constantly planting flowers, my quiet penance for taking life from them whenever someone needed healing.

I looked at the withered plants and murmured, "Thank you for your sacrifice."

"You're incredible," Zane said, his voice full of admiration.

I stilled, caught off guard by his sincerity. "Thanks," I replied, feeling sheepish under his gaze.

Zane's eyes shifted to the dense brush where the horses had disappeared. "It'll take longer to get to the Tree of Transformation without them, but maybe we should go on foot. With the thickness of this underbrush, they weren't going to save us as much time anyway, and I'd hate for the horses to get hurt trying to make it through this terrain."

Extra time with Zane before I die?

Yes, please, I thought, though I kept my agreement to a simple nod.

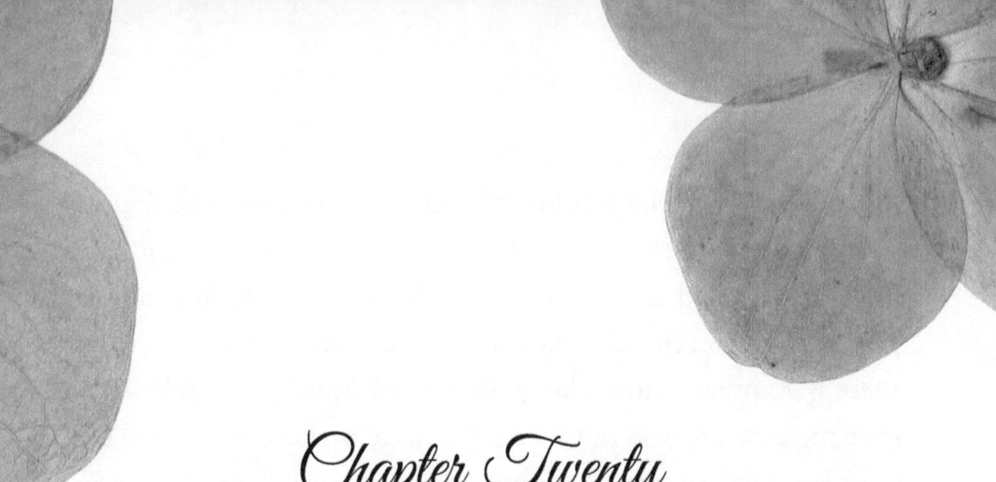

Chapter Twenty

ZANE

I nearly kissed Lorelei when she was lying under me as I shielded her from the burning rain. I'd seen the spark of desire in her eyes, the way she fixated on my lips, and it was physically painful to hold back. But what a first kiss that would have been. Something to tell our future children, I'm sure. *"I kissed your mother after she was nearly melted by poison rain."*

No.

I wanted our first kiss to be perfect, romantic, a moment she would cherish and look back on with as much fondness as I would. Lorelei and I had all the time in the world to fall in love and enjoy each other. If I'd learned anything from watching my brothers fall for their wives, it was to let things develop naturally and to give Lorelei her space.

Right now, we needed to focus on breaking the curse. When we completed our mission, I'd court her properly. Lorelei deserved that much. But it was hard not to think of romance when she was near. She smelled of freshly cut flowers and something sweet that drove me insane. Her healing gift was extraordinary, and the way she cared for even the flowers she drew energy from left me in awe.

What I'd told Lorelei about the Savage Lands feeling familiar was true. Besides the luna blossoms I'd recognized from Ethereum, there were other plants I knew from back home. I was relieved to have my powers back, but it couldn't have been a coincidence that they returned to me the moment we stepped into the Savage Lands.

Was it possible that this part of Faerie was connected to Ethereum in some way? If so, maybe there was an open portal nearby. Or maybe I was stretching, letting my mind invent connections. Either way, having my powers back meant I could protect Lorelei better, and for that, I was grateful. Especially after hearing that the curse was trying to take them from me completely.

It was getting late, and I knew we'd only be able to travel another hour or two before we were forced to make camp for the night. We were hiking through the thick underbrush when Lorelei suddenly screamed. The sound was sharp and full of terror. I barely had time to turn toward her before her body hit the ground, and then she was dragged away, her nails clawing at the earth in desperation.

"Zane!" Her shrill cry pierced the air as she was yanked by an unseen force.

I didn't think; I just started running, forcing myself not to lose sight of her. I couldn't see what had her, but whatever it was pulled her away so fast that I had to sprint at full speed just to keep her in view. Her poor body was dragged over brush and roots, scraping against the ground as she screamed. Rage built inside me like a firestorm, propelling me forward.

There was no monster or beast in sight, and it wasn't until she was pulled out of a dense cropping of trees that I saw what had her: a vine wrapped tightly around her ankle.

Reaching for my magic, I pushed myself to run faster. The vine dragged Lorelei into another densely forested area, and for a terrifying moment, I lost sight of her. Her screams stopped, and dread clawed at my chest. Had she lost consciousness?

I sprinted through the trees, leaping over brush, determined not to lose her. When I caught sight of her again, lying limp as the vine tugged her mercilessly, rage coursed through me like lightning. I aimed my hands at the black, gnarled vine that was trying to steal her from me and let my power surge.

I paused, hesitating before unleashing a stream of black lightning. If I missed, I could sever her ankle. But if I didn't act, the vine could drag her somewhere I couldn't follow. My heart pounded as I made the split-second decision to try.

I shot my magic at the vine.

And I missed.

"Lorelei!" I yelled, desperation thick in my voice, but she didn't respond. The vine continued to drag her across the forest floor.

It was clear she was unconscious. A feral need to protect her consumed me, driving me to act. I reached for my power again, focusing everything into the next two bolts. They fired in quick succession, and relief surged through me as one met its mark. The vine snapped.

Lorelei's momentum carried her forward, rolling a few feet before coming to a stop. A hissing noise echoed through the forest, sharp and menacing, as the severed vine writhed on the ground.

With my heart lodged in my throat, I sprinted to her limp form. She was still breathing, but my chest felt like it was being torn open as I took in the small cuts marring her arms, legs, and face. Her bottom lip was split open, crimson blood trailing down her chin.

"Lorelei." My voice was shaky as I crouched down and gently pulled her into my arms. Her body was so still, her face pale beneath the dirt and blood smeared across her skin. The sight of her like this gutted me. I had promised her mother I'd keep her safe, and now she looked like she'd been trampled by a wild horse.

Desperate, I reached down and plucked a handful of vibrant purple and pink flowers from the forest floor. Laying them on her chest, I silently willed her healing magic to awaken. But nothing happened.

No.

My hands trembled as I brushed dirt from her hair and face. She was covered in blood and grime, on her cheeks, her neck, even tangled in her hair. The weight of my failure pressed down on me like a physical force.

Staying alert to our surroundings, I stood with her in my arms and began retracing the path the vine had dragged her through the forest. The trail her body had carved into the ground served as my guide, ensuring we didn't get lost. Thankfully, Lorelei's pack was still strung over her shoulder, not having been lost, and I pulled out the map her mother had sketched for us. After orienting myself, I set off for a small pond marked to the east.

I had underestimated these cursed lands. The warning that the curse would come for us wasn't just a vague threat, it was a brutal reality. Burning rain and killer vines might only be the beginning.

An image of Nellie flashed in my mind. Her freckled face, her wide eyes filled with hope. I had promised her I'd return, that I'd come back to her. But if I wasn't vigilant, if I failed to protect Lorelei again, I might not survive to keep that promise.

I clenched my jaw, the weight of my vow settling like steel in my chest. I wouldn't let my guard down again. I wouldn't let Lorelei out of my sight, or my arms, until this curse was destroyed.

When I reached the pond, I carefully set Lorelei down on the shoreline. Mentally, I thanked the Spring queen for the extra provisions she'd sent with us. Pulling a length of rope from my satchel, I tied one end securely around Lorelei's waist and the other around mine, leaving only about four feet of slack between us.

If something tried to drag her away again, it would have to take me with her.

Using a clean strip of linen I'd gotten from the Spring queen, I dipped it into the pond and began to carefully wash Lorelei's exposed skin. I started with her hands and arms, moving gently to her ankles and shins. Finally, I ended with her perfect face, wiping away the dirt and blood that marred her features.

Seeing her injured like this tore me apart. Small purple bruises were starting to form, and the weight of guilt pressed on my chest so heavily it was hard to breathe.

Lorelei whimpered softly, and my gaze snapped to her face.

"Lorelei?"

Her eyes fluttered open, and she gasped. In the next instant, the grass beneath us began to turn white as if frost had kissed it. Before my eyes, her cuts and bruises vanished, leaving her skin smooth and unblemished.

Thank the fates.

She sat up suddenly, her expression filled with wonder and a touch of fear. When her wide eyes met mine, her voice trembled as she said, "I couldn't control it. The vine that grabbed me had no energy. I couldn't fight it."

The anguish in her voice pierced me, and I wanted nothing more than to pull her into my arms and protect her from whatever came next. But I didn't want to overwhelm her further, so I stayed still, keeping my voice calm and steady. "It's all right. I won't let that happen again," I promised.

Her gaze dropped to the bloody linen strip in my hands, then moved to the rope tied around her waist and looped around mine. Her expression softened, and a small, hesitant smile tugged at her lips. "I'm sorry if I scared you."

I gave a dry chuckle, trying to lighten the mood. "You just healed in seconds after being dragged through half the forest. What's to be scared about?" I teased.

Her smile widened slightly, and she fingered the rope around her waist. "Is this supposed to protect me if the vine comes back?"

I nodded. "Exactly. I'm not letting you out of my sight."

Pink bloomed across her cheeks, and her blush made her even more beautiful. "A handsome lord wants to tie himself to me?" she said with a teasing lilt. "You won't hear me complaining about that."

She thought I was handsome? Her words sent my heart into a chaotic rhythm, thudding wildly in my chest. For a moment, I forgot about the dangers of the Savage Lands, the looming curse, and everything else. All I could focus on was her.

Chapter Twenty-One

DAWN

"It hurtssss," I hissed as Eowyn placed a cool rag against my forehead.

"It's supposed to," she said matter-of-factly. "You're birthing a child."

My entire lower midsection felt like it was being crushed as each contraction rocked my body.

"Can you help with the pain?" Zander asked, his voice tight as he stared at me, looking like he was in as much agony as I was.

"I can," Eowyn replied, "but it won't do her any favors. She won't be able to push properly."

I grunted as another wave of pain tore through me. The contractions were five minutes apart now, and I'd been laboring for over ten hours. Giving birth was taking much longer than I'd anticipated.

A knock at the door interrupted the brief reprieve I felt between contractions. Zander opened the door, and Isolde rushed in, her hair windswept and her traveling cloak still on.

"Dawn!" She ran to my side, her face full of concern. Seeing one of my dearest friends was a relief. Adrien lingered by the door, speaking to Zander in hushed tones.

Isolde kneeled beside me, grabbing my hand and squeezing it tightly. "You're in labor? But it's too soon," she said, her eyes brimming with worry.

I nodded and gestured toward Eowyn with my free hand. "We expected this might happen and have a plan."

"Oh, Dawn. Does it hurt?" she asked softly.

I let out a humorless laugh. "Like a horse sitting on my stomach while someone squeezes my insides like a lemon."

Isolde winced. "Can't they give you a pain tincture?"

"No," Eowyn snapped as she crossed the room to prepare the four little bassinets. "It will cloud her mind and her ability to push."

The bassinets were simple wicker constructions with soft cotton blankets. Eowyn had one of Zander's housemaids attach them to a wheeled table so I could move them with me wherever I went, even to the bathroom. I could take one or two short breaks from the babies each day, but no longer than half an hour. Otherwise, they had to stay within ten feet of me for three months. It was a small price to pay for their survival.

"Why are there four bassinets?" Isolde asked, her tone tinged with horror. She knew I was having multiples but hadn't known how many.

I laughed, a real one this time, but stopped immediately, because it hurt my stomach. I was so sore from pushing for the past several hours.

"Because I'm having four babies," I said, smiling despite myself.

Isolde's breath caught, and she squeezed my hand even tighter. "You poor thing."

Her reaction made me smile wider. Before meeting Zander, the thought of having four children might have horrified me, but now I couldn't wait. Zander was going to be an amazing father, and I was determined to be a warm, nurturing mother—everything mine wasn't. Zander had softened me, and I wanted my children to have a childhood filled with love and affection. Yes, I'd raise them to be warriors, but they'd be warriors who knew they were loved.

"It's going to be fun," I said with a grin.

She shook her head, eyes wide. "Dawn. Four," she whispered, as if saying it louder would make it worse.

"Tell me news of the road. How was the travel?" I asked, trying to distract myself from the pain.

She nodded quickly. "Travel was . . . fine. Seraphina came with us. Thank you for inviting her as well. The trains are full of refugees. The curse has started to grow stronger in the Southern Kingdom. I don't know how much longer we could have lasted there. We're all just hoping that Lorelei and Zane can stop this. And soon."

Her tone betrayed her. She was hiding something. I knew her too well.

"Okay, and what aren't you telling me?" I pressed.

"What? Nothing," she replied far too quickly.

"Isolde, I'm in labor with four children. You don't want to piss me off."

She sighed. "It's nothing, honestly. I've been stressed since I got word about you going into labor early. I haven't slept. The curse has just made my mind jumbled."

My brows furrowed. "Jumbled how? What are you saying?"

She hesitated, glancing toward the door as if hoping someone would come to her rescue.

"Isolde," I scolded, my voice sharp.

Finally, she swallowed hard and said, "I . . . thought I saw your mother when the train was pulling into the station. But when I ran outside to check, she was gone. Now I'm sure it was just a stressed-out delusion."

My mother. Here?

Another contraction tore through me, and a wail escaped my throat as I gripped Isolde's hands. I tried to push the thought of what she'd just said out of my mind, but it had latched on and stuck.

My mother couldn't be here. Right? The mirror portal in the Spring Court wouldn't open for a couple more months. And even then, only Spring royalty could pass through.

No, it couldn't have been my mother. That would be impossible.

But if it was her, she wouldn't be here to meet her grandchildren. My mind whispered the truth I didn't want to hear: she'd be here to kill my husband.

Zander rushed to my side as Isolde pried her hands free, shaking them out as she stepped back.

I stared into Zander's eyes, and I knew Adrien had told him what Isolde thought she'd seen. Fear spiked through me. If anyone could bend the impossible to her will, it was my mother.

"Lock down the castle," I commanded through gritted teeth, my voice strained between contractions. "Only essential staff and family."

"Darling, I'm sure it's fine—"

"Zander, you don't know what my mother is capable of. Lock. It. Down," I roared as another spike of pain ripped through me.

He nodded and left to carry out my orders.

I loved my mother, but if she tried to harm my husband or babies, I wouldn't hesitate. I would remove her head without a second thought.

Chapter Twenty-Two

LORELEI

Zane and I traveled another hour on foot before we made camp under a rock shelf at the base of a mountain. The protruding rock created a natural roof over our heads, which was fortunate because the burning rain was back. The curse was clearly using the land to try to stop us, but although it was slower going without our horses, we were still making good time. If the map my mother had given us was to scale, we'd reach the Tree of Transformation by nightfall tomorrow.

I sat by the fire Zane had built, watching as he pulled out smoked meat and dried fruits to prepare a plate for me. We were still tied together, a precaution Zane insisted on. After the vine dragged me away, I thought I was done for, separated from him forever, hauled across the forest until my skull was smashed against a rock or tree trunk. But Zane had chased after me, his voice panicked as he screamed my name. The way he fought for me revealed his true character, and it made me want to build a life with him. I felt safe with him.

It was a cruel irony to find such a man just days before I was fated to die.

Turning away from Zane, I pulled out the letter again, scanning its contents for what felt like the hundredth time. I prayed I'd misread it or overlooked something, though deep down, I knew there was no hope of that.

When you drink the contents of the vial, your life force will be the price paid to end the curse. This is the ultimate sacrifice.

The words were clear. There was no mistaking them. I would die so that hundreds of thousands could live. This wasn't just about saving the seelie in Faerie anymore. It was about saving all the souls in Ethereum, too.

"Tell me about your realm," I said, rolling up the note and slipping it back into my pack. When I looked up, I found Zane watching me intently.

"Ethereum is actually a lot like Faerie," he said, "in that we have four distinct kingdoms that take on seasonal characteristics, just like your courts here."

I perked up at that. "Oh? And which season would your land most resemble?"

Please say Spring. Or at least not Winter.

"My land would most closely be associated with Fall."

I relaxed slightly. Fall wasn't bad. The Fall Court was stunning with its palette of burnt oranges and vibrant reds. I had particularly loved the cuisine when I visited a few years ago: sweet potato casserole, chicken pot pie, butternut squash soup. And the apples! The juiciest I'd ever eaten. Their cinnamon- and nutmeg-spiced desserts were divine too. My mouth watered just thinking about it.

Yes, Fall was acceptable. Not that it mattered since I was about to die.

"What are the people like?" I asked, trying to push aside my morose thoughts.

Zane smiled then, his expression softening. "Amazing. Diverse. We have unseelie as well as seelie fae, and we all work together for the good of the land. Obviously, we have our challenges. Rebel factions pop up from time to time, but for the most part, we live in peace. I was able to hire workers from all four kingdoms to build a train track that links the whole realm. It's an ongoing project, but it's already been invaluable for moving refugees to safety."

In Faerie, the various courts lived in relative peace with one another, but rarely worked together for the good of the realm as a whole, as Zane described. In fact, I couldn't think of a single time in history when the courts had banded together like they were now to fight against the curse. For the most part, we kept to ourselves. But now, refugees from the other three courts were living in the Spring Court, the only land still untouched by the curse's sinister effects.

When this was all over, I didn't know what our realm would look like anymore. Even if the land was restored to its former glory, I suspected things would be different. Hopefully, for the better.

"Well, I'll take you there when this is all over," Zane promised. "My castle chef makes the best chocolate berry cake in the whole realm."

I gave him a weak smile, but his words only saddened me. I'd never see his realm. I'd never taste that cake.

"I'm tired," I said, feigning a yawn.

He nodded, handing me my plate of food, and we ate quickly.

Zane tried to spark a conversation, but despite my best efforts to remain engaged, my thoughts grew heavier, pulling me into silence. He seemed to sense my mood and stopped trying to talk.

Tomorrow was probably my last day alive. I wasn't ready to let go. I wasn't ready to let him go.

When we finished eating, and fatigue finally tugged at my limbs, I wrapped my cloak around me and nestled close to the fire, trying to find some rest. I glanced up at Zane, who sat next to me, his gaze fixed on the dark forest. He didn't look like he had any intention of sleeping.

"Will you sleep?" I asked softly.

"Yes. When we end the curse and leave these lands," he replied without looking at me.

My mouth dropped open. "That could be days from now."

I was hopeful we'd reach the Tree of Transformation tomorrow, but even then, it would take at least a day or two, if not more, to walk out of this place.

"Then I'll sleep in a few days," he declared with a stubborn set to his jaw.

I thought about arguing but quickly realized it wouldn't do any good. Zane was protective, selfless, the kind of person who put others before himself. He was staying awake to guard me.

And it made me soften to him all the more.

"Wake up, Lorelei." Zane shook my shoulders, pulling me from sleep. I knew he hadn't slept because I looked for his door in my dream void, but it never appeared. I'd just been about to walk through my father's door to say goodbye to him when Zane woke me.

"What is it?" I asked, sitting up, bleary-eyed and disoriented. It was still dark, but the full moon cast its bright light down on us, illuminating his features.

The sound of rushing water reached my ears, jolting me fully awake.

"Black water or some sort of oily liquid," Zane said grimly. "I've dealt with this stuff before. It's nasty. We need to get to higher ground." He grabbed both of our packs, urgency evident in his movements.

As I quickly donned my bag, I peered into the woods. The black liquid was pooling on the ground, and through the trees, a wave of it was coming straight for us, the moonlight reflecting off its surface.

With a yelp, I jumped to my feet, scrambling to get to Zane. He held out his hand, and the moment I grabbed it, he clamped down on mine, pulling me along as we rushed up the side of the rock shelf. But the climb was treacherous. There were no proper handholds or footholds, and every time I found some purchase, my boots slipped. Zane was having the same trouble, climbing three feet only to slide back two.

We weren't climbing fast enough. The black liquid surged toward us, splashing against my ankles. I felt a tug on the rope around my waist and glanced over to see Zane untying the knot that bound us together.

"What are you doing?" I asked, panic rising in my chest.

"Just making sure I don't drag you to your death if this water pulls me away," he said grimly.

"Don't let it pull you away!" I shouted, my voice shaking.

The top of the rock shelf was just above my head but still out of reach. I tried again to climb higher, but the oily substance coating my boots made it impossible.

"Permission to grab your waist?" Zane asked, his tone tense.

"Yes," I cried. This was no time for chivalry.

His firm hands gripped my waist, and he pushed me upward with surprising strength. With a shriek, I scrambled over the top of the ledge I'd been sleeping under only minutes before. Relief, however, was fleeting. Zane was still down below.

"Now you," I yelled, dropping to my belly and reaching down for him.

The black substance had already reached his knees.

He threw the backpacks onto the shelf and leaped, his hands barely gripping the edge of the overhang. I grabbed his forearms, trying to pull him up, but he was far heavier than I could manage.

The rushing noise intensified, and I glanced up to see the oily liquid raging through the forest like a river, gray foamy rapids slamming into trees and bending them in half.

"Don't let go," I shouted over the cacophony.

Zane grunted, kicking his legs in an attempt to push himself up, but one of his hands slipped.

"No!" I screamed, grasping for his missing hand.

My heart pounded as I peered over the edge to see Zane dangling by one hand, the black liquid rising beneath him. If it got much higher, it would sweep him away.

I glanced around desperately, trying to figure out how to help him, when a bolt of lightning wrapped in shadows shot past me, lassoing a tree trunk growing out of the mountainside. I gasped at the sight.

I looked back down at Zane. He still had one hand on the rock shelf, but his other hand held a rope of shadow-encased lightning. His grip seemed strong, but I didn't see how he was going to pull himself up without letting go of the rock. If he did, he'd swing straight into the cliff face.

"There's a tree right behind me, about ten yards. If you lasso it, maybe you can pull yourself up."

He nodded, his face strained, and yelled, "Duck!"

I pressed my cheek to the cool stone, squeezing my eyes shut as he released the rock shelf and shot another bolt of lightning. My heart stopped, fear gripping me. I couldn't look. I didn't want to see if he'd fallen.

Then I heard a grunt and labored breathing.

"Zane?" I opened my eyes to see him using his lightning rope to hoist himself onto the rock shelf.

He collapsed beside me, panting and staring at me with an intensity that made my throat tighten.

"I thought you were going to die," I whispered.

"Not yet," he said, his tone serious, his eyes locked on mine.

"Not ever," I murmured, meaning every word.

He climbed to his feet with effort, his expression shifting. "We need to get to higher ground," he said, his voice flat.

A sinking feeling settled in my stomach. Something had shifted in him, something I didn't understand. And I didn't like it.

Chapter Twenty-Three

DAWN

"I can't," I whimpered to Eowyn, who was tapping my cheek lightly to keep me awake. I'd been in labor for over a day, and I had just pushed the third baby out, a girl to join her two brothers, but I didn't have the strength to birth the fourth.

"I'm exhausted," I told her.

Aribella and Isolde were both in the birthing room along with Zander and Eowyn, assisting however they could. Isolde's sister, Seraphina, had been helping as well, but after she nearly fainted during the first delivery, Eowyn had banished her from the room. Those who remained gave me encouraging words, telling me I could do this, but I wasn't sure I could. I had misjudged how draining it would be when Eowyn tied the babies to me. I was depleted physically, mentally, and magically. I was just a shell of myself, and all I wanted was sleep.

I peered over at the three little bundles, tiny as could be, wrapped in blankets and asleep in their bassinets. Thin protective bubbles surrounded each one, giving the children the nutrients they needed to survive outside my womb, but the cost was great. My energy and magic were being siphoned away. I was tired, hungry, and utterly spent. Yet, I loved them so much.

Two boys and a little girl. Eowyn had been shocked when the girl was born, having assumed I'd give birth only to sons. I'd been ecstatic, but it was the look on Zander's face when he first saw his baby girl that made my heart swell. It was instant love and devotion. I knew I'd carry that moment with me for the rest of my life.

"You're doing great, my love," Zander said, stroking my cheek gently.

Another contraction tightened my belly, but as hard as I tried, I couldn't force myself to push. I had already thrown up four times from exertion. I was done.

"If she doesn't push this baby out, we are going to lose it," Eowyn said grimly.

Panic gripped me, but my body refused to cooperate. My muscles wouldn't respond, and my will was slipping.

My eyes began to close as exhaustion tried to pull me under, but a sharp slap to my cheek snapped them open. I was ready to lash out, but then I saw Isolde kneeling beside me. The fearsome Winter princess had never looked stronger. Married life suited her.

"That hurt," I growled at her.

"I'm sorry, but I'm not going to let you lose this baby," she snapped, her tone firm and unyielding. "You're Dawn Ambrose. Princess of Summer. Lady of the Northern Kingdom. If you can't do this, no one can." A cool breeze filled the warm room, and I felt a flicker of alertness return.

"She's right," Aribella said, nudging Zander aside so she could lean in closer. He moved behind me, stroking my hair soothingly.

"You can do this, Dawn," Aribella said, her voice calm and steady. "Dig deep."

A calming sense of assurance filled me, making me believe I could find the strength to birth this final child. I turned to Aribella skeptically. "Are you using your magic on me?"

She just winked.

The next contraction pressed down hard, and I cried out. Isolde and Aribella were right. I couldn't let anything happen to this child. I was strong enough.

Eowyn positioned herself at the foot of the bed. "I just need one good push. The baby is already halfway there."

With Isolde fanning me with cool air to keep me awake and Aribella bolstering my confidence, I propped myself up on my elbows and bore down. A primal roar tore from my throat as I gave this last push every ounce of strength I had.

Mommy's got you.

There was searing pain, then sweet relief as Eowyn lifted a tiny, screaming baby into the air for me to see before placing her on my chest.

"Another girl," I whispered, a tear slipping down my cheek as my heart expanded even more.

How could I instantly love these babies so much? All I wanted was for them to have the very best in life.

Zander kissed the side of my head. When I looked up at him, he had tears in his eyes. "I'm so proud of you," he said, stepping back as Aribella and Isolde did the same. They knew the drill by now. Eowyn needed space to perform the bonding magic.

Eowyn moved closer, ribbons of silver light swirling around me and the baby as she wove her magic. Slowly, the baby was encased in a thin protective bubble that would keep her safe until she grew stronger.

I smiled faintly as Eowyn worked, even as the bonding magic consumed the last reserves of my energy. I gazed down at my baby girl in awe. She and her siblings were worth every ounce of my magic. They, along with Zander, were my life now. The very beating heart of me. I would do anything for them.

The exhaustion became bone-crushing. Though I wanted to keep my baby close, I could barely hold her. "Take her," I whispered to Zander.

My husband gently lifted his daughter from my arms just as Eowyn finished the protective bubble around her. My head lolled to the side as sleep finally overtook me.

Chapter Twenty-Four

LORELEI

Hiking up a mountain in the dead of night while black floodwaters tried to consume me wasn't exactly what I had planned for this trip. Fatigue pulled at my limbs as we climbed higher and higher.

"The black water will eventually stop rising, right?" I asked Zane.

He'd been quiet, probably tired, but as hard as I tried to put it out of my mind, I couldn't shake the feeling that something was wrong.

"Normally, I would say yes, but I think this place is determined to kill us, so I'm not sure," he answered honestly.

I chewed on my lip. "What if it floods all the way to the Tree of Transformation? What if it washes it away?"

He merely shrugged. It was too dark to see the far-reaching consequences of the flooding, something we'd probably have to wait until morning to figure out.

With a sigh, I trudged on. When we reached a steep incline

just before the top of the mountain, I struggled to scale it. A few steps ahead of me, Zane reached back, offering his hand. I grasped it, and he pulled me up.

Finally, we made it to the summit. I was happy the climbing was over, but I was too exhausted to feel a sense of accomplishment. I collapsed onto my butt, panting, while Zane sat down slowly beside me, so close that our knees were touching.

I peered out at the open expanse. The moonlight cast strange, glowing shadows across the black, oily liquid below, and from what I could see, it covered everything. My view was limited, but it looked endless.

I could feel Zane watching me, so I turned to him. "What are you thinking?"

Rather than answering, he glanced away.

He was silent.

"Hey." I nudged him playfully. "You're too quiet. Tell me what you're thinking."

He sighed, turning back to face me, his gaze dipping to my lips. "I'm thinking that I want nothing more than to spend the rest of my life with you by my side."

I sucked in a breath at the admission.

He turned away again. "Sorry, that was too much."

I shook my head. That wasn't how I felt at all, but he couldn't see my reaction because he was looking away.

I didn't think. I just let my body act.

Reaching out, I grasped his strong jaw and turned his face back toward me. His gaze was questioning, and as I stared into his blue eyes, I searched for the small drop of brown in one of his irises. A tiny reminder of how unique he was.

"It wasn't too much," I said firmly, feeling courage grow in my chest. "Anything with you could never be too much."

Leaning forward, I captured his mouth.

From the moment our lips met, it was as if the world itself shifted, turning from the darkest night to the brightest dawn. A fire ignited deep within me that I never even knew existed.

Zane's lips were warm and soft, and tentative at first, but then he twisted toward me, cupping my face in his hands and taking complete control of the kiss. Deepening it, he stoked my desire, and I gasped lightly, completely overwhelmed by the intensity.

Fireworks exploded inside me. My entire body melted into the kiss, savoring the rightness of it, but then Zane started to pull back, mistaking my gasp for hesitation when it was anything but.

Acting on instinct, my arms looped around his neck, holding him in place, and then I shifted, sliding onto his lap. With my knees bracketing his hips, I leaned into him, parting my lips to let his tongue tease mine.

The world around us seemed to dissolve, leaving only the fire between us. If I could stay in this moment forever, I'd trade every breath I had left for an eternity of this feeling.

As we kissed, tendrils of icy fire unfurled and surged through me, like a second heartbeat coursing through my veins. I didn't even think to stop until something bright flashed behind my closed lids, and I felt Zane grin against my mouth.

My eyes popped open, and I pulled away in shock, finding shimmering black stardust suspended in the air around us. It settled softly on our skin, glowing faintly in the moonlight.

"What is it?" I asked, my voice trembling with a mix of fear and wonder.

Zane, grinning ear to ear, reached up and gently traced my

swollen lips with his fingers. "We call it the soul bond. It happened with my brothers and their wives as well, although the color of the mist is unique to us."

"It's beautiful," I murmured, watching the midnight shimmers slowly fade into the air.

"It's only something the two of us can see when we come together like this," Zane explained, his voice soft and reverent.

My eyes widened. "You mean this will happen every time we kiss?"

He chuckled, a deep, rich sound that vibrated through his chest. "I certainly hope so. It's also confirmation of the mate bond."

My breath hitched.

Mate.

The sparkling particles, shimmering like tiny black diamonds, were undeniable proof that Zane was my mate. And instead of filling me with joy, the realization crushed my heart into a thousand pieces.

Zane's smile faded as he noticed my reaction. I couldn't meet his gaze, unsure of what to say.

Yay, we confirmed we're mates. By the way, I plan to die soon.

A sickening wave of dread settled in my stomach. Nothing about this was okay.

For a fleeting moment, I didn't want to be perfect, self-sacrificing Lorelei. I wanted to be selfish. I wanted to reach into my pack, toss the vial into the black waters below, and live happily ever after with Zane.

"Sorry," I whispered. "It's just . . ."

"I get it. It's a lot to take in. It's all right," he said gently, though I could see the joy slowly seep from his expression.

My chest ached. I did that to him. I caused his pain, and the guilt gutted me.

Still straddling his lap, I suddenly felt awkward and slid off, settling onto the cold, hard stone beside him. But I wasn't ready to break our connection completely, so I leaned my head against his shoulder, trying to offer him what little comfort I could.

He placed a warm hand over my thigh, and we sat there like that for hours until the sun rose. Silent, contemplative, devastated.

Chapter Twenty-Five

ZANE

Lorelei was everything I thought my mate would be and so much more. I could fill pages with what delighted and intrigued me about her, but even so, I hadn't been prepared for the intensity and depth of our kiss.

Having my mouth pressed against the soft pillow of her lips and seeing the midnight sparkles appear afterward, the undeniable evidence of our mate bond, had been nothing short of the most defining moment of my life. I'd never felt anything so strong, pure, and right before. And yet, my heart broke for what I now knew would never be.

Because I had learned the truth she'd been hiding from me.

After she'd been dragged across the forest floor and we sat by the fire together, I'd seen her pull the note from the Wise Ones out of her pack. As her gaze swept over the words, something shifted in her expression, a deep melancholy that hadn't been there a moment before.

I must have caught her rereading that note at least a half-dozen times since we set out for the Tree of Transformation. Each time, that same sadness overtook her. She wouldn't let me see the contents, and I wanted to respect her wishes, but earlier tonight, as she read it by the fire, I knew something wasn't right.

So when she finally fell asleep, I stole the rolled scroll and read it for myself.

Sitting awake by the fire as Lorelei slept beside me, I spent half the night cursing those Wise Ones. I even contemplated throwing the vial into the flames, but if this was the only way to stop the curse, destroying it would doom two worlds and all the souls in them. I couldn't bring myself to do it.

My brothers, their wives, Dawn's unborn babies—they were all counting on us. So I did the only thing I could think of to make this outcome bearable: I stole the vial and resolved to drink it myself.

There was no world in which I could watch Lorelei die. If she died, I would die with her. If not in body, then certainly in spirit.

It was clear now why she'd been so hot and cold, why sadness lingered in her eyes after we shared that incredible kiss.

And why, now, as we walked toward the Tree of Transformation, she was once again quiet and withdrawn.

She was preparing to die.

And I wasn't going to let that happen.

Chapter Twenty-Six

DAWN

I awoke to find it was already midday. I had slept for sixteen hours straight. My body felt weak and exhausted, as though all the life had been drained from me. Rolling over, I spotted Eowyn tending to the little bubbles surrounding the babies. She waved her hands in the air over them, smiling and nodding as if she was pleased with her work.

"Are they okay?" I croaked, my throat dry and desperate for water. A bath would have been heaven.

The healer turned to me and nodded, her eyes misty with emotion. "You are very strong, my lady."

I gave her a sheepish smile. "And we owe you our lives. Thank you." I reached for her hand and she took mine and gave it a light squeeze.

Eowyn helped me sit up and handed me a cup of water. As I sipped, I looked around the room, relieved to see we were alone. I wanted to clean up before seeing Zander again. I felt disgusting.

"Will I always sleep this much? And feel so weak?" I asked.

Her expression softened with understanding and sympathy as she nodded. "You'll feel extra tired and fatigued until the bubbles pop, which will happen naturally when the babies are healthy enough to live outside the womb. You'll regain some strength in a few days, though. You're just extra weary now because you birthed four babies in one day."

"Well, you saved four lives yesterday. You're incredible," I said, meaning every word.

Eowyn ducked her head, clearly embarrassed by the praise, but I caught the pride in her gaze and the small smile on her face. I hoped something inside her had healed. Perhaps, whatever fear she'd carried about delivering babies after the ones she'd lost years ago had been erased by this triumph.

"I'm happy to help, my lady. Would you like me to call your maid so you can have a bath?"

I nodded eagerly. "I would love that. Can they . . ." I gestured toward the babies in their bubbles. "Can they move with me?"

She nodded. "Once your maid arrives, I'll wheel them in after you."

It took some effort to fit myself, the long table with the babies, and my lady's maid, Flora, into the bathroom, but we managed. Flora washed my hair as I soaked in the tub. I was so weak that I couldn't even hold my arms up long enough to do it myself.

"I'm sorry I'm so weak," I murmured, ashamed. Flora wasn't usually required to help me bathe.

"It's perfectly fine, my lady. I'm just glad you and the babies are okay," she replied with a warm smile.

I glanced over my shoulder and found her beaming at the quads, who lay peacefully in their bassinets with their eyes closed, their tiny mouths sucking at the air. Eowyn had told me they didn't need food or water. While in the bubbles, they would take nourishment from me magically, just as they had in my belly.

"The entire realm is making their way to the castle gates, leaving flowers and gifts for the little lords and ladies," Flora said, her voice filled with delight.

Her words made me smile. It felt as though the births were a bright spot in an otherwise dark time.

After helping me from the bath, Flora assisted me in dressing —a task I usually preferred to do on my own. She then braided my hair, adding a few small blue flowers that matched the pale blue dressing gown I wore.

"Where is my husband?" I finally asked.

"He's having lunch with his brothers and their wives. Shall I fetch him?" Flora offered.

"No, thank you. I'd love a walk." I was feeling a bit stronger after the bath.

Using the babies' table for support, I leaned on it slightly, taking my time as I walked down the long corridor to the dining room. My legs wobbled occasionally, but the walk was good for me, so I moved slowly. Flora followed quietly behind me and opened the door when we reached the dining hall.

The moment the babies and I entered the room, Zander's gaze found mine. "Dawn," he exclaimed, leaping up and rushing over to help me. He pressed a soft kiss to my mouth when he reached me, his eyes full of unveiled love and devotion. I'm sure I was giving him the same look.

"Dawn, you should be lying down," Isolde scolded as she came up next to us.

Aribella, Stryker, and Adrien chimed in, telling me I shouldn't be up as well.

I waved them all off as Zander and Isolde led me to a seat at the table. Isolde returned to her spot next to Adrien, and Zander hovered over my shoulders near the babies. I could hear him coo softly at them, and it made my heart melt.

"I needed to stretch my legs," I told them all. "Besides, I just slept sixteen hours. I'm famished."

Without another word, Stryker handed me a huge turkey leg from his plate.

"Honey, she's not going to want your—" Aribella began, but I grabbed it and took a huge bite, moaning in joy as the salty sweetness hit my tongue. It was coated in honey.

"Never mind," Aribella chuckled as I devoured the leg.

"I'll be right back," Zander said, disappearing into the kitchen. He returned shortly with a heaping plate full of all my favorites.

He sat down next to me, and I, abandoning all decorum and princess manners, dug into the food like a starved dog.

"She hasn't eaten in two days," Zander explained, trying to justify my behavior. "They don't let you eat during labor. Did you know that?"

Stryker must have felt bad for me because he slid his plate of chocolate cake onto my side of the table. I accepted it gratefully, taking four big bites.

"Oh, forget that. I'm not having kids if they starve you," Isolde commented.

Adrien laughed. "Are you saying you wouldn't sacrifice a few meals for one of those little bundles of joy?"

"Well, when you put it like that . . ." Isolde trailed off.

Adrien got up and walked over to the babies, making baby noises and scrunching his face to try to get them to laugh. I didn't have the heart to tell him their eyes weren't developed enough yet to make out his features.

I shared a grin with Isolde. "You're next." I winked at her.

She stuck her tongue out at me playfully.

Then I noticed Aribella was unusually quiet. When I looked her way, she quickly pulled her hair forward, trying to hide a purple bruise on her temple I hadn't noticed before.

I froze, pausing mid-bite, and pinned her with a soul-searching gaze.

"Aribella," I said calmly.

She chewed at her lip, casting a nervous glance at Stryker.

Surely he wouldn't hurt her . . . right?

"Yes?" she squeaked.

"What happened to your face?" I pressed.

"Nothing," she said far too quickly.

My gaze flicked to Stryker, whose expression darkened. "I would never," he growled, snatching his half-eaten chocolate cake back as though punishing me for even thinking it.

I turned to my husband, who had "guilty" written all over his face.

"Why in the stars are you treating me like a child?" I snapped. "Who bruised Aribella?"

"I got into a little scuffle in town when I was buying a gift for the babies," Aribella answered, her voice sing-song and far too sweet. "Do you want to see what I got?"

Her deflection only fueled my irritation. Isolde had mentioned seeing my mother on the train, and this was too coincidental.

I leveled Aribella with a serious look. "No. I want to know why you're hiding that bruise from me."

Stryker laid a giant hand over his wife's. "Don't worry. When I find who did it, I will disembowel them," he said, his gaze still dark. "You just focus on healing."

I relaxed a little. "So you don't know who it was? A random angry citizen?"

The brothers exchanged glances, a silent conversation passing between them that told me I wasn't getting the whole story.

I spun toward Zander. "Zander Warrick, don't you lie to me. Who hurt Aribella?"

Zander frowned, a pained expression taking over his face. "Your mother did, my love. I'm sorry, but she's here. Somehow."

No.

Anger rushed through me, and I instinctively reached for my magic. But as I did, a wave of sudden weakness overcame me. One of the babies began to cry, and my head jerked toward them. It was one of the baby girls, the last one to be born.

"Stay calm, Dawn. Just focus on the babies. We'll handle your mother," Isolde said firmly. "If you use any magic, it takes from them."

She was right. I'd reached for my magic without thinking.

Closing my eyes, I took three deep breaths. Slowly, my daughter's cries subsided, and I opened my eyes to find her calm again.

I turned to Zander. "We need to name them. I can't keep calling them girl one and two and boy one and two."

Zander leaped at the distraction, his face softening. "Yes. Do you have any thoughts?"

Standing, I walked over to our first son, the slightly larger of the boys. He was sucking his tiny thumb, his head adorned with a shock of dark brown hair the same shade as Zander's. The baby's light blue-gray eyes reminded me of Stryker's, though, I could see Zane and Adrien in his perfect little face, too. "I think we should call him Callum," I said, wanting to honor the beloved Warrick brother Zander and the others lost before I met them.

"I'd love that," Zander said, his gaze falling on our son with nothing short of complete devotion.

"That's very kind of you," Stryker added, his voice thick with emotion. When I glanced at him, I saw his eyes glistening.

Stryker, the most fearsome and prickly of the brothers, often came across as a hardened warrior. But in moments like this, his softer side shone through. A side that few ever got to see.

"Good choice," Adrien chimed in with a grin.

I moved to the next boy. His hair was lighter, closer to my own color, but he had Zander's striking blue gaze. I loved how I could see a piece of Zander in each of our sons. "Aric," I said softly, "after my father."

Tears misted my eyes as I glanced up at Zander. My father had died when I was just a baby. I'd been told he was a great man and that he and my mother had been deeply in love. Losing him had taken a part of her, and I couldn't help but wonder how different my home might have been if he'd lived.

"Another fine choice," Zander said as he pulled me into his arms, his voice gentle. Leaning down, he whispered in my ear, "Your father would be proud of you."

I nodded, unable to speak past the lump in my throat. Zander and the others gave me a moment to collect myself. When I finally did, I cleared my throat, and Zander's arm dropped from around me to take my hand. He let me stand on my own strength while still letting me know he was there for me. I loved him even more for it.

"And for the girls, I have no idea," I admitted with a laugh. "Any requests?"

"Izzy and Ari?" Isolde suggested, and everyone burst into laughter.

"I have an idea," Aribella said, her tone soft. She gazed at her nieces from across the table, then looked up at me and Zander with a warm smile. "Fay and Ethie," she suggested. "Short for Faerie and Ethereum, which these girls now represent."

My breath caught. It was perfect.

The baby girls were a beautiful blend of Zander and me, just as their names reflected both of our worlds. Fay, with her bright green eyes and corn-silk hair, was the spitting image of me. Ethie, with her dark brown curls and soulful blue gaze, looked so much like Zander.

"I love that," I said, my voice full of emotion. Zander nodded in agreement.

"It's official. Callum, Aric, Fay, and Ethie," I declared.

But even as I spoke, my thoughts turned elsewhere. "Any word on Lorelei and Zane? If my mother's here—"

"She had Lorelei's dagger," Aribella said, cutting in.

My heart stopped. "Her faestone dagger?" I asked, hoping I'd misunderstood her.

Isolde moved to my side, taking one of my hands in hers. "Yes, which is how we think she was able to get here early. We don't know everything about the daggers, but if anyone could find a way to use one of them to get to Ethereum before the Spring equinox, it would be your mother."

"Do you think she harmed Lorelei?" I asked, panic rising. Lorelei was the gentlest of us all. I wanted to believe my mother wouldn't harm someone so innocent, but the truth was, she would go to any lengths to stop the curse.

Zander stood and took my hand, drawing my attention. "No,

we don't believe she did. Zane wouldn't allow that. And we know he's still alive. We'd feel it if he weren't."

I stared at my husband in surprise. It was the first time he'd told me that, though I wasn't shocked. The brothers were connected. I'd seen them use their magic to communicate over long distances. It wasn't a stretch to think their magic linked them in other ways as well.

Glancing down at my babies, I wondered if they would share the same magical connection.

"So what's the plan? If my mother is here, it means she's after one of your hearts," I said, directing my words at the lords in the room.

A horrible thought struck me, chilling my blood. Did my mother hate this world so much that she'd stoop so low as to harm her own grandchildren because they could one day become lords or ladies of Ethereum?

Dizziness washed over me, and my knees buckled. Zander reached out, catching me before I fell, his worried gaze filling my vision.

"Get her to bed, Zander," Isolde said firmly. "We'll take care of everything else."

He nodded, scooping me into his arms. I wanted to protest, but I was too weak to even try. I rested my head against his neck as he carried me, hearing the soft creak of the babies' bassinets being wheeled behind us.

"At least I got food before I fell back asleep," I murmured, the weight of exhaustion pulling at me.

Zander smiled down at me. "Next time you wake, I'll have an entire buffet waiting for you."

I gazed up at him, my heart swelling with love for the man

who held me so tenderly. "Zander, my mom's sick in the head. If you see her, don't make the mistake of thinking you can reason with her."

A flash of fear crossed his face, and I frowned. Zander didn't fear much, and he certainly wouldn't fear my mother.

Then realization hit me. I understood what was troubling him.

"I'll understand if you have to kill her," I said softly. The words hurt to say, but they were true. If my mother had fully lost herself in her mission to save Faerie and was willing to harm Zander, knowing he was my mate . . . She needed to be stopped.

Relief flickered in his eyes. "I'll try not to, my love," he promised.

He kissed my forehead, and as his warmth surrounded me, sleep claimed me once more.

Chapter Twenty-Seven

QUEEN LILIANA

The mirror world was a fascinating place. I might have actually enjoyed exploring it if I weren't so focused on saving my people.

I created a shield around myself as I snuck past the guard at the castle's back gate. Lorelei's powers had turned out to be far greater than I could have ever imagined. When mixed with mine, they created a different kind of magic I was still discovering—this cloaking magic being one of my new abilities.

I moved slowly and purposefully, my gaze fixed on the guard in front of me. While my cloaking magic rendered me invisible to his eyes, he could still hear me if I wasn't careful.

From the locals, I'd learned that all the Ethereum lords were in this city. I had thought it was a stroke of luck to find Aribella in the market earlier, imagining we could team up to save our world. But when I asked for her help in procuring a black heart and showed her Lorelei's dagger, she tried to take it from me.

I escaped before she could use her power on me, but not

before we exchanged blows. The encounter confirmed what I'd already begun to suspect: those delusional, weak princesses I'd sent to this world were incapable of getting the job done. My people were fortunate that I'd come to intervene.

I slipped past the guard and crept around the side of the castle, peeking into windows as I searched for my targets, the Ethereum lords. I didn't know what they looked like, but I assumed they'd be dressed like royalty and possibly accompanied by Aribella. The very thought of her living here with one of them, like a rat scurrying about, disgusted me.

When I glanced into the next window, my breath caught, and the world seemed to tilt.

Dawn.

I'd known there was a chance we might cross paths, so seeing her wasn't entirely unexpected. But what shocked me was her appearance. Her slightly deflated belly, evidence of a recent pregnancy, and the tiny babies in the bassinets in front of her. There were four of them, encased in shimmering bubbles, their small size making it a miracle they were alive at all.

Four.

The room was filled with people, seemingly enjoying lunch in a dining room, but my focus remained on Dawn. My gaze shifted to the dark-haired fae standing next to her, his hand resting possessively on her lower back. He looked at her like she was the most beautiful woman in the world, and my stomach churned with revulsion.

Her mate. An Ethereum lord.

I glanced at the babies again and felt a wave of sickness.

No. How could she?

Looking back at the lord beside my daughter, a deep well of

hatred bubbled up inside me. I wanted to storm into that room and carve his heart from his chest, but there were too many of them. Aribella and Isolde were there, too. I was strong, but I wasn't sure I could take them all on.

Their voices were muffled through the glass, but I saw Dawn's expression change. She looked distressed, then suddenly she stumbled, collapsing into the lord's arms.

I gripped the windowsill, barely restraining myself from smashing through it to rip the villain's hands off my daughter.

I knew what I had to do. Get the heart and bring my daughter back to Faerie. My gaze flicked to the babies in their bassinets. If they weren't tainted by their vile father's evil blood, I'd take them, too. But I'd check first. And if they did have black blood . . . well, then they'd have to be dealt with. Even if Dawn never forgave me, I couldn't allow their evil to spread to our lands.

As the lord carried Dawn out of the room and Isolde wheeled the babies behind them, I followed, peering into windows until I discovered which room belonged to her.

None of them had been strong enough to do what needed to be done, but I was. I didn't relish this task, and I knew Dawn would hate me for it. But I clenched the dagger in my hand, determination solidifying my resolve, and slipped into the castle through an unlocked side door. A guard was distracted, deep in an animated conversation with a pretty nursemaid.

It was time to end this once and for all.

Chapter Twenty-Eight

LORELEI

That kiss with Zane was incredible. My heart ached just thinking about it, remembering the way my soul seemed to sing when his lips moved against mine, the rightness of finally coming together in that way. The magical confirmation of our mate bond should have elated me, but instead, it made me feel sick.

"You're quiet," Zane observed.

I cleared my throat, smoothing my cloak. I didn't want to pretend with him, but I couldn't tell him what I was really thinking. Small talk would have to do. We'd been traveling all day, and night was about to fall. According to the map, we were close to the Tree of Transformation. It should be just over the hill in front of us, but I was extra tense because we hadn't been attacked today. It felt like the curse was just lying in wait, ready to pounce on us the moment we got comfortable.

"Just thinking about what I'll name my new puppy," I lied.

He gave me a winning smile. "And what did you decide?"

I thought about it for a moment. "Peony. After my favorite flower."

Zane glanced at the wildflowers around us: bluebells, chrysanthemums, irises, and jasmine. He leaned in slightly and whispered, as if they could hear him, "Are you even allowed to have a favorite?"

I barked out a laugh. Stars, he was funny, which only made him more attractive. "Yes, I'm allowed to have a favorite. I can assure you, they don't mind. What will you name your puppy?" I asked, curious.

His face fell slightly, though he quickly recovered. Even though I hadn't known him long, the fleeting moment of sadness felt so uncharacteristic that it caught my attention.

"I'll let Nellie name him."

Nellie. Oh, how I would have loved to meet her if Zane and I had been given more time together.

"That's very kind of you. I'm sure she'll be excited to give him a name," I said, though my throat pinched with emotion.

He stopped walking and turned to face me, forcing me to stop as well. He was so tall I had to crane my neck to meet his eyes.

"We have no idea what will happen when the curse is destroyed," he said, his voice low.

I nodded. He wasn't wrong. I knew what would happen to me, but the rest was uncertain.

"Promise me that, should something happen to me, you'll take care of Nellie."

I frowned. "Zane, nothing is going to happen to you."

"You don't know that. This tree could require my heart," he said quietly.

I knew it didn't. It required mine.

"Promise me," he begged when I didn't immediately respond.

Seeing the worry in his gaze, I couldn't bear to deny him. "I promise," I said softly, if only to ease his fears.

His eyes fell to my lips, and a selfish need surged within me. I wanted one more kiss before I met my end, and I wasn't going to deny myself this final wish.

Zane must have been thinking the same thing because we crashed into each other at the exact same moment.

This kiss wasn't like the first. This kiss broke my heart in a million different ways.

I ached for thousands more of them, but I knew this would be the last, so I savored it. I didn't pull away. I panted into his mouth as his hands dropped to my hips and squeezed. Pressing into him, I wrapped my arms around his neck, trying to draw him closer. This was all I would leave Zane in the end, and I wasn't about to squander a second of it.

Then, Zane grabbed my hands, pulling them from his neck and pinning them together in front of me. The gesture was unorthodox, but I was so lost in him that I didn't question it until I felt the bite of restraints around my wrists.

I yanked back, startled, just as another restraint wrapped around my ankles.

My eyes widened as I stared down at the lightning ropes encased in shadows that encircled my wrists. "Zane, what are you doing?"

He took two steps away from me, and I looked up at him, hurt, confused, and in shock.

With a shaking hand, he pulled the vial and the Wise Ones' note from his pocket. Panic shot through me like a lightning strike.

"No. What are you doing?" I yanked against the restraints, but they only burned against my skin when I struggled.

"I'm in love with you," Zane declared, and I froze, my heart thundering in my chest. "And I refuse to watch you die. Please forgive me. Please know I'm doing this so you can live. So you can plant your flowers, enjoy the sunshine, and snuggle your puppy."

He was going to drink the potion. He was going to sacrifice himself.

"Zane, no," I sobbed as the realization hit me, struggling harder against the restraints. I tripped and fell forward, tears blurring my vision.

He caught me, lowering me gently to the ground. "Forgive me," he whispered. "And take care of Nellie. You promised." He kissed my forehead, then turned away.

"Zane, don't do this!" I screamed until my voice went hoarse. "It's me. I'm supposed to do this, not you."

But he began to walk away. As he disappeared over the hill toward the Tree of Transformation, I realized with heartbreaking clarity that I'd fallen in love with him, too. Now, I would have to watch him die. I would have to live on with a hole in my heart that could never be filled.

I could think of no crueler fate.

"Zane, please don't do this to me," I begged, sobbing as uncontrollable grief overwhelmed me. When I read the Wise Ones' letter, I had accepted my own death, but not his.

I couldn't lose him. Not like this. Not now.

The man who had traveled across the realm to rescue me. The man who bought me a puppy because I said I liked them. A man of such noble character, he would take my ill fate and make it his own.

Chapter Twenty-Nine

ZANE

My heart ached as I heard Lorelei's screams. The way she yelled my name, filled with so much anguish, was killing me. But I had to do this. I couldn't let her sacrifice herself. I wasn't capable of sitting back and watching her die.

As I crested the hill leading to the Tree of Transformation, I spotted it, a massive green tree nestled at the bottom of a wide ravine. For a moment, I paused in awe, realizing I was looking at the curse's birthplace.

A bird's piercing screech shattered my thoughts.

I glanced up just in time to see a raven, the size of a large house cat, dive-bombing straight for my face. Throwing up an arm to shield myself, I batted the bird away. But it quickly changed course, circling back to attack me again.

I fought off the creature, but the sound of flapping wings drew my attention over my shoulder. My stomach dropped as I saw over two dozen ravens descending upon me, their caws and croaks creating a deafening roar.

Where in the fates did they come from?

The swarm enveloped me. The birds dove at me in groups of three to five at a time, their sharp talons raking across my skin, their beaks pecking relentlessly. I punched, swung, and blocked, but their sheer numbers overwhelmed me. Pain seared through my arms and face as their attacks landed, scoring my flesh.

This forsaken land was trying to kill me before I reached the cursed tree. But I wasn't about to let that happen.

Summoning my power, I thrust out my hand, releasing a bolt of lightning that struck a raven squarely in the chest. Its body seized mid-air and fell lifelessly to the ground at my feet.

The remaining birds, startled by the sudden storm of magic, scattered, fleeing into the skies.

Panting, I stared at the dead bird, frowning. The Wise Ones' warning replayed in my mind: *Come for the curse and the curse will come for you.*

The attack made no sense, not without the curse's influence. These birds hadn't come out of nowhere. They were sent.

"Sorry, little guy," I murmured, feeling slightly foolish for apologizing to a dead animal. But there was no time to dwell on it.

Hearing Lorelei's grief-stricken screams in the distance and seeing the lifeless bird at my feet only fueled my resolve. I needed to end this curse once and for all. No one, not Lorelei, not anyone, should have to suffer under its malevolent shadow any longer.

Without hesitation, I sprinted down the hill toward the Tree of Transformation. My gaze flicked briefly to the black droplets of blood dotting my arms where the birds had scratched me. Black blood.

In this land, it was seen as a mark of evil, a sign of darkness. But in Ethereum, black blood was the mark of power, of royalty. A birthright that carried both privilege and duty.

As I ran, I couldn't help but wonder if once this curse was destroyed, the seelie here in Faerie could finally shed their centuries of prejudice. Could they end their hatred toward black bleeders? Toward the unseelie?

Would this curse's end be enough to change everything?

If I had a dying wish, it would be that breaking this curse and healing our two worlds might somehow unite everyone as equals. That we could all learn to accept one another despite our differences.

And that Lorelei would be happy.

As I drew closer to the tree in the distance, the unruly, weed-filled ground gave way to a well-manicured field of grass bordered by lavender flowers. The moment my boots touched the grass, an immense wave of power washed over me, crackling through my veins and setting my teeth on edge.

I stared ahead at the towering tree, which had to soar at least a hundred feet into the air, and marveled at its beauty. Its limbs, heavy with bright green leaves and delicate white flowers, twisted and turned as they stretched out toward the heavens. From where I stood, the light brown bark appeared smooth and flawless, radiating a subtle, ethereal glow.

Lorelei's words echoed in my mind: *Over the course of a single day, it cycles through all four seasons.* Judging by the vibrancy of the blooms, it seemed to be in spring at this moment.

The thought made my heart ache all over again. Lorelei should be here to witness this with me. The way the branches fanned out into delicate white buds, each glowing softly as if infused with magic. Sunlight kissed the petals, making them glitter like stardust. The floral scent filled the air, sweet and all-encompassing, leaving me momentarily breathless.

But I couldn't allow myself to linger in awe. That's not what I was here for. I was here to follow the Wise Ones' instructions, to end this curse, and to save both our worlds.

Cautiously, I glanced around, expecting another attack from the cursed land. But nothing came. No ravens, no vines, no burning rain. The silence felt almost sacred as I closed the distance to the tree.

The base of the tree was massive, its trunk wider than I was tall. At its center, right at eye level, was a divot shaped perfectly to fit the Shadow Heart. To think this tree had stood here for thousands of years, waiting for someone to bring the right pieces to end the curse, made my blood boil.

How many of my ancestors had been slaughtered at the hands of a Faerie princess? How many lives were lost when the solution had been sitting here all along? The thought filled me with anger.

But deep down, I knew the truth. It wasn't about just finding the pieces or coming to the tree. It wasn't the right time until now. It took Dawn falling in love with Zander to shift the tides of this centuries-old war. It took Aribella and Stryker retrieving the Shadow Heart and Adrien and Isolde unraveling its secrets.

For reasons beyond my understanding, it had to be us—my brothers and our mates—to finally break this curse that had tormented our worlds for millennia. I should feel honored to be part of this legacy, but instead, all I felt was fury.

Fury that I would never see Nellie again. Fury that I would never kiss Lorelei's sweet lips again. Fury at the cruel fate that had brought us together only to tear us apart.

With a shuddering breath, I pulled the note from my pocket and scanned the instructions once more.

When you arrive, place the pieces of the Shadow Heart within the tree and drink the contents of the vial. Then, place your hand upon the trunk and surrender yourself to the curse. Only through this act can it be healed forever.

I crumpled the note in my fist, letting it fall to the ground.

It was time to end this once and for all.

Digging into my pack, I retrieved the cracked Shadow Heart, carefully holding its pieces together as I pressed them into the indentation on the tree.

The moment the black crystal touched the trunk, the broken pieces fused seamlessly, becoming whole again. A powerful gust of wind swept through the ravine, shaking the massive tree and scattering the flowers from its branches. As the wind howled around me, I watched in awe as the tree absorbed the Shadow Heart, sealing the indentation as though it had never existed.

Then, just as abruptly, the gale ceased, leaving an eerie, expectant silence in its wake.

I froze, watching as white petals floated gently to the ground, resting on my shoulders and in my hair.

Thump-thump. Thump-thump.

The rhythmic thudding of a strong heartbeat reached my ears.

I leaned closer, pressing my ear to the smooth bark. The sound was coming from the tree itself.

Magic was undoubtedly at work, ancient and powerful. I couldn't afford to hesitate, not with the curse already stirring, ready to strike again.

Reaching into my pocket, I retrieved the small vial. Its delicate glass gleamed in the faint light as I held it between my fingers. With a steadying breath, I pulled the cork free.

This was it. The final step. Drink the contents, place my hand on the tree, and it would all be over.

A sudden gust of wind whipped through the ravine, nearly knocking me off balance. I staggered, catching myself just in time.

Was that Lorelei's voice?

Her distant cry carried over the hill, sharp and frantic. Was she okay? Were the bindings hurting her? Would she ever forgive me for what I'd done?

Did forgiveness even matter anymore?

"Fates, protect her all the days of her life," I whispered, my voice trembling.

With shaking hands, I tipped the vial, letting the bitter liquid flow onto my tongue.

The effects were immediate. The fluid seemed to harden in my throat, cutting off my air. I gasped, clutching my chest as my lungs refused to draw breath.

"Zane!" Lorelei's voice rang out again, closer this time, filled with desperation.

She shouldn't have been able to break free from my bindings, but somehow, she had. I didn't dare turn toward her. I couldn't let her see me like this, choking on my final moments.

Stumbling forward, I pressed my hand against the tree.

It reacted instantly, pulling the life from my body. My heart clenched painfully, and I dropped to my knees, slumping forward until my cheek rested against the smooth bark.

The tree's heartbeat filled my ears, louder and stronger with each passing second, drowning out Lorelei's cries. Black dots swarmed at the edges of my vision, narrowing my world.

I couldn't breathe. My chest burned as if a heavy weight were crushing me.

Lorelei's screams grew louder, frantic, and full of anguish, but I couldn't turn to face her.

A low, resonant hum emanated from the tree, vibrating through my bones.

You have your sacrifice. Now end the curse, I demanded silently, forcing the last of my energy into the tree.

A deafening crack split the air.

The world went dark. My soul tore free of my body, and I was no more.

Chapter Thirty

ZANDER

I leaned against the wall in awe, watching my beautiful wife sleep in the soft glow of early evening. My gaze shifted to the four tiny bundles, our children. Dawn had brought them into the world with a strength I hadn't even known she possessed. She wasn't just incredible; she was extraordinary. Two sons and two daughters. Daughters. As an Ethereum lord, I'd never imagined such a thing possible, yet here they were. My heart ached with a love so vast it felt endless.

Dawn had endured so much to bring these babies into the world and was now sacrificing her energy and magic to keep them alive. My role was clear. To protect them at all costs. Yet the talk of her mother's presence in Faerie, combined with the lingering curse, filled me with unease. Sleep would not come easily tonight.

With a sigh, I quietly left the room to let Dawn rest. I padded down the hall to the drink station Zane's maid had thoughtfully set up for the house's guests. Coffee, tea, and drinking chocolate were always available. A small luxury that offered some normalcy amidst the chaos. At the last moment, I chose the drinking chocolate, wanting something comforting right now.

I couldn't shake the disquiet that settled over me. Even with Zane's castle teeming with guards, knowing Queen Liliana was not only in Faerie but here in Westeria made my blood run cold. Stryker had expressed the same unease, especially after Aribella's attack. Adrien, too, was undoubtedly on edge.

I stepped into the library, sipping the warm, rich drink. It wasn't something I often indulged in, but it carried a nostalgic sweetness. It reminded me of simpler times, back when my mother used to stand in the kitchen with the head cook, teaching him her grandmother's recipes.

A smile tugged at my lips as I remembered the time Callum stole the chocolate chunks meant for drinking chocolate and passed them out to the rest of us. We couldn't have been more than six years old, and though Cal, being the oldest, was the obvious culprit, none of us ever gave him up. My mother interrogated us all for hours, but we kept his secret.

The warmth of the memory was shattered in an instant when a dagger came hurtling through the air.

With a gasp, I dropped the mug and barely moved out of its path in time. Reflexes saved me more than anything else. The blade smashed into the stone wall behind me, clattering to the floor.

My breath caught as a strikingly beautiful older woman stepped from the shadows. Her presence radiated power, shimmering with magic that reminded me of the protective bubbles around my children.

Queen Liliana. My mother-in-law.

She had to be. There was no mistaking it. She looked like an older version of Dawn. The same cascade of corn-silk blonde hair, the same piercing green eyes, the same delicate features. But there was one stark difference. The hatred in her gaze burned brighter than anything I'd ever seen. Even when Dawn thought she hated me, she'd never looked at me like this. The chill of it froze me in place.

How in the fates had she gotten here?

I reached down for the fallen dagger, the pink moonstone in the hilt winking up at me, but before I could grab it, a beam of sunlight streaked through the air. It sliced clean through the tip of my left index finger.

Crying out in a mix of pain and fury, I raised my hands and reached inside for my magic. Dawn had given me permission to kill her mother if it came to that, but I feared it would devastate her. The queen thought I was evil. She thought killing me was the only way to delay the curse. But if I could stop her from hurting me and then explain things to her, maybe she would understand, and so as I shot two black shards from my palms, I aimed to pin the Summer queen to the wall by her shoulders, avoiding a fatal blow.

The shards flew through the air, only to strike the shimmering bubble of magic surrounding Liliana. They fell harmlessly to the floor with a metallic clang.

This was bad. Dawn had never mentioned her mother possessing a shield like this.

"Guards!" I shouted, but before the word had fully left my mouth, Liliana charged at me. Her blond hair whipped behind her like a cape as she lunged for the fallen dagger.

I stepped in front of the blade, kicking it aside just as she fired a beam of sunlight at me. I ducked, the heat of her magic brushing past my face.

I'd seen the aftermath of Dawn's power before. It was devastating. If Liliana wanted, she could take my head clean off. But I knew her goal wasn't just to kill me; it was to carve out my black heart. In order for it to stop the curse, she had to do it with the faestone dagger. I needed to incapacitate her before she had a chance to do that.

I scanned the library around me. The quarters were too tight, and I had no backup. Even if guards arrived, they wouldn't stand a chance against a Faerie queen. I was vulnerable, especially with that shield protecting her. I needed space to think, so I did the only thing I could.

I ran to the left and leaped out the window.

The glass shattered as I crashed through, landing on a massive bluebeard bush below. I tucked into a roll, scraping myself on the branches, but I managed to pop up quickly.

Scanning the grounds, I searched for guards, anyone who could help. But instead, I stumbled across two bodies lying motionless on the grass. I couldn't tell if they were unconscious or dead, but I had to assume the Summer queen had taken out a good portion of my guards already. That's what I would have done in her position. To stop a curse. To save a world.

I clenched my fists, suppressing the urge to shout louder for help. If I woke Dawn and the babies, they'd be in danger. The thought of Liliana turning her wrath on them chilled me to my core.

Dropping to my knees, I pressed my fingers into the earth and sent a quick, desperate message through the ground to my brothers inside the castle. It was short, just two words. Anything longer would drain my magic, leaving me even more defenseless.

"Help. Outside."

The faint crunch of footsteps on broken glass made me whirl around. Queen Liliana emerged from the shadows, the faestone dagger now in her hand, her lips curled into a triumphant grin.

"Looking forward to murdering your daughter's husband, are you?" I spat, my voice tight with tension.

Her response was a sharp beam of light aimed directly at me. I twisted to the side, but not fast enough. It tore through the shoulder cap of my right sleeve, leaving the skin underneath stinging from the heat.

I fired two more black shards at her shield, desperate to find a weakness, but they shattered uselessly against the protective barrier. Her grin widened as the fragments fell at her feet.

"Lorelei was seriously under-using her power," she said, her tone almost conversational.

I didn't know what she meant, but if she was talking, I could work with that. Talking meant reasoning, stalling, buying time for my brothers to arrive.

"You have grandchildren," I said, my voice pleading as I grasped at anything that might soften her heart.

Her face twisted into a mask of disgust, and a spear of fear pierced my chest. "I saw. I'll be taking care of them next."

Something inside me snapped. I wouldn't let this woman or anyone else hurt my children. Ever.

Black shards shot from my hands in rapid succession, an unrelenting barrage aimed at her shield. The sheer force made her flinch and cover her face, her magic flickering under the onslaught.

One shard pierced through the weakened barrier and struck her forearm, drawing a hiss of pain from her lips.

Before I could press my advantage, shadows enveloped us, plunging the battlefield into complete darkness.

"Stryker!" I shouted, recognizing my brother's handiwork.

"Does she have a shield?" his voice called from somewhere to my left.

"Yes," I yelled back, my tone tight with urgency. "But if you overwhelm her, it weakens."

A sudden burst of light pierced the shadow fog, Queen Liliana's beam of magic slicing toward Stryker's voice.

"Missed me," Stryker taunted, his voice cool and sharp.

"I've boxed her in. You can drop the shadow fog." Adrien's voice rang out, calm and confident. Relief swept through me, loosening the knot of fear and rage in my gut.

The shadows dissipated, revealing Stryker and Adrien flanking me on either side. In front of us stood a black box of shadows. A prison crafted by Adrien's magic. Queen Liliana was trapped inside, her movements completely obscured.

Adrien's mastery over shadows was formidable. The box would hold her as securely as steel or stone, giving us the time we needed to decide her fate.

"Good work," I told him, my voice edged with cautious optimism. "Now let's—"

A sharp, concentrated beam of light cut through the shadow box like a welder's flame, forcing me to leap out of the way. The edges of the box buckled as Liliana relentlessly slashed at it. Stryker lashed out with a shadow rope to reinforce the structure, but her light beams sliced through it effortlessly, creating a doorway she stepped through with chilling precision.

"Her magic is stronger than ours," Stryker muttered, his tone laced with disbelief.

Queen Liliana stepped forward, her head tilted as she surveyed the three of us. The faestone dagger gleamed in her hand, and her calculating gaze darted between us as if deciding who to carve up first.

The shield. It had to go. Without it, I could kill her.

Summoning another black shard, I prepared to launch it, ready to do whatever was necessary to break her defense. But before I could strike, Liliana froze. Her eyes went wide, her mouth opening in a silent gasp.

Her hand flew to her chest, clutching a locket I hadn't noticed until now. The locket cracked, purple mist escaping in wisps until it revealed a tiny, shriveled black heart no larger than a walnut.

"Is that our ancestor's heart?" Adrien asked, his voice thick with revulsion.

Stryker unsheathed his sword, his movements slow and deliberate. "She dies now."

I was about to agree when a sharp, piercing pain exploded in my chest. It felt as though something vital was being ripped from me.

I staggered, my breath hitching as grief and despair settled like a weight in my chest.

I turned to my brothers and found the same haunted expressions mirrored on their faces.

We all felt it.

Zane.

He was gone. I wanted to deny it to myself, to push the feeling aside, but I couldn't. It was pulsing through me somehow, the loss of my brother.

I'd always shared a connection with my brothers that felt almost physical. Stryker's energy was heavy and unyielding, Adrien's vibrant and resilient, and Zane's—Zane's was pure and brimming with life. That bond had been with me for as long as I could remember, a constant thread tying us together.

When we were twelve, we even tested if we could read each other's minds. We couldn't. But we could always feel each other's presence, until now. Now, there was only a void where Zane's presence had always been.

"He could just be unconscious," Adrien said softly beside me, his voice thick with hope.

"No!" Stryker roared, throwing his head back as anguish tore through his voice, raw and primal.

Zane.

I clenched my fists, my heart heavy with the weight of his absence. Zane was the best of us, full of light and purpose, and he had so much left to live for. How could this have happened? Why did it have to be him?

"They did it," Queen Liliana said, her voice filled with disbelief. "They ended the curse."

"Mother!" someone yelled, and we all glanced up. Dawn was at a window. Looking exhausted and horrified. "If the curse has ended, then it's over. We are all safe. The fae of both lands can live happily side by side in safety. Mother, we are all free."

But Queen Liliana's face twisted with rage as her gaze turned from Dawn and locked on me.

"No," she shouted. "We must rid all lands of the Ethereum lords and their black hearts."

"If you mean that, then you will die," Dawn called down, sadness as well as resignation in her voice.

"They can't be allowed to live," Queen Liliana all but growled. And the look in her eyes made it clear she wouldn't stop until I was dead.

Any lingering guilt I might've had about killing her vanished. She was a monster. A mother that was willing to kill fae who she knew were innocent. And one that her daughter loved and married.

With a flick of Queen Liliana's wrist, three beams of sunlight shot toward me. I dodged, but pain seared across my ear as one of the beams grazed me. Warm blood dripped down my neck as I hit the ground.

Stryker and Adrien roared in unison, their shadow whips and ropes pounding against her shield as her beams of light retaliated with deadly precision.

She was a force of destruction, relentless and merciless.

I pushed to my feet, creating a black shard the length and sharpness of a sword as adrenaline surged through me.

"Stryker, cover me," I shouted.

Adrien continued his relentless attack, hammering at her shield, while Stryker conjured shadow fog to obscure my movements.

And then, just as I was approaching her and she had her eyes on me, Dawn screamed at me. I looked her way, and then she nodded. "It has to be done," she cried, her face the picture of determination even as the tears spilled down her cheeks.

Adrien and Stryker had not let up their attack. Using the distraction Dawn had provided by her scream, I maneuvered behind the queen, my shard gripped tightly in both hands. My heart pounded as I watched the glow of her shield flicker. When it faltered for a split second, I lunged, plunging my blade through her back and straight into her heart.

A guttural scream ripped from her throat as the shield shattered. The faestone dagger clattered to the ground as she collapsed, my shard sword still lodged in her chest.

Her wide, shocked eyes locked on mine as she gasped for breath, her blood pooling around her. She raised a trembling hand.

"Look away, Dawn," Stryker cried.

I turned away, too, unable to watch what came next.

A clean, decisive stroke from Stryker's sword severed her head from her body.

"An enemy is never truly dead until they're headless," Stryker said grimly, his voice like steel.

I nodded, understanding his pragmatism, but her resemblance to Dawn made it impossible for me to strike the final blow myself. At least not head-on, like he'd done.

Adrien approached, his expression somber. "Stryker and I will handle the body. Go to Dawn and the babies."

I glanced back to the window, but Dawn was no longer there.

My hands shook as I nodded. "Do you think Zane could just be injured? I've felt your energy dim before, only to find you gravely hurt."

Stryker and Adrien exchanged a look, their silence heavy with unspoken truth.

"Maybe," Stryker said, though his tone held little conviction. "Once we've stabilized things here, we'll search for him. Maybe there's someone who can help us reach him in Faerie like we did with Isolde. But first, tend to your ear and hand and see your wife."

I glanced down at my blood-soaked shirt and mangled hand, grimacing at the mess.

As I turned to leave, I hesitated. “She said they ended the curse.”

“Don’t trust a word from that witch’s mouth,” Stryker growled.

He was right. I wouldn’t believe it until I saw the proof myself.

I staggered toward the castle, exhaustion and pain threatening to overwhelm me. Inside, I collided with a housemaid who screamed loud enough to wake the entire household. Guards rushed from every direction, their weapons drawn.

Isolde and Aribella appeared at the top of the staircase, their faces pale with alarm. They hurried down, their gazes filled with concern as they took in my battered state.

“Aribella and I were in the library, researching potential ways to locate Queen Liliana. What happened?” Isolde demanded, forming a sharp icicle in one hand. “Did she attack?”

“Oh, Zander, are you okay?” Aribella asked, pressing a cotton apron to the side of my head as blood trickled down.

I apologized to the maid for scaring her, and she hurried off to fetch the healer. Turning to the guards, I ordered them to assist my brothers outside. Then I met the gazes of both Isolde and Aribella.

“Queen Liliana is dead,” I said, my voice steady despite the turmoil inside me. “And she claimed the curse has been destroyed.”

I wanted to add that Zane might be dead, too, but the words refused to form. Saying it aloud felt like accepting it, and I wasn’t ready for that.

Behind me, a sharp intake of breath sent a chill down my spine. Even without turning, I knew it was Dawn.

Spinning around, I found her gripping the babies' table for support, using it like a walker as she rolled closer to me.

Her eyes roamed over me, taking in the blood dripping from my finger and the cloth pressed to my head by Aribella.

"Are you okay?" she asked, her voice weak, her expression a mix of worry and heartbreak. Her eyes were red from the tears she'd already shed. I could see the pain of overhearing what had happened to her mother reflected in her gaze.

"Yes," I assured her quickly. "Dawn, I'm sorry. I tried not to kill her, but she—"

She nodded before I could finish, relief washing over her features. Her eyes fell to the bassinets where our children slept peacefully. "They're safe now. You did good," she said. There was an unmistakable sadness in her tone, and it sent a crack through my own heart. She had just lost her mother, and she was affirming my decision. How was I worthy of such an amazing princess?

I hesitated, then asked, "Dawn, she said they ended the curse. You know your mother better than anyone. Do you think she was telling the truth?"

She frowned, uncertainty clouding her expression. "I wish I could tell you she was, but I'm not sure. I'm not sure of anything about my mother anymore."

I nodded, though the lack of clarity did little to ease my mind. "She was wearing the necklace you told me about, but it cracked, and purple mist came out of it."

All three women gasped in unison: Dawn, Isolde, and Aribella.

"What?" I asked, glancing between them.

Dawn stepped out from behind the table, her green eyes shimmering with unshed tears. But this time, they were tears of joy. "That's never happened before. What else could it mean but that the curse was destroyed? Can you help me get to the city hospital? I want to check on Nysa. If the curse is gone, maybe she'll finally be healed."

I frowned, my gaze darting to the babies. Dawn was far too weak to walk that distance, and there was no way I could allow her to roll our newborns through town. It wasn't safe.

"How about I check on Nysa and the others?" I offered. "If she's awake, I'll bring her here."

Dawn's lips pressed into a thin line, her stubbornness flaring briefly before she glanced down at the babies and sighed. "Only if you promise to get those injuries looked at while you're there."

I'd nearly forgotten the state I was in. Bloodied and bruised.

Leaning down, I kissed her forehead, careful not to get any blood on her. "I promise."

Her lips curved into a small smile. Although her eyes still glistened with tears, there was a flicker of hope in her expression that made my chest tighten.

I turned to leave, but Isolde's voice stopped me. "Aribella, will you stay with Dawn and help her back to her room? I'll go with Zander."

"Of course," Aribella replied, stepping to Dawn's side and slipping her arm around her shoulders for support.

Isolde and I stepped outside, and the moment we did, she grabbed my arm, forcing me to face her. Her blue eyes glistened with unshed tears, and her grip on my arm was firm but trembling.

"What's wrong?" I asked, my voice barely above a whisper.

She bit her lip, hesitating before speaking. "I just wonder . . . if Lorelei and Zane really did break the curse . . . at what cost?"

Her words struck like a blade, slicing through the fragile wall I'd built to contain my grief. A wave of anguish crashed over me, and Isolde gasped, her sharp eyes catching the truth, or at least some of it, in my expression.

"I don't know," I said, my voice tight with emotion. "But I fear to find out."

Chapter Thirty-One

LORELEI

The scream that tore from my throat was barely recognizable. Zane stood with his back to me, facing what I could only assume was the Tree of Transformation at the bottom of the hill.

I yelled his name, but he didn't turn.

Sprinting as fast as I could without tripping down the steep incline, I ran to him, my wrists and ankles bleeding from the strength it took to rip free of his bindings. My heart beat a furious cadence in my chest, ramming itself against my ribs. Terror gripped me. I was too late. He'd already drunk the potion.

As I neared, I saw Zane place his hand on the tree. A moment later, he sank to his knees.

"No!" I screamed, a sob forming in my throat.

This wasn't happening. It was supposed to be me, not him. *Me.*

A cracking noise rent the air, and a powerful shockwave

knocked me off my feet. I was thrown backward, landing hard on my back, my teeth snapping together painfully.

I groaned, my body battered and sore.

Zane.

Scrambling to my feet, I gasped when I looked at the tree. It had split in two, revealing . . . a mountainous landscape with a gaping cave.

A portal. The tree had cracked in half, creating a portal to some unknown place.

But then my eyes fell on Zane's limp body crumpled at the base of the tree, and my world crashed down around me.

Desperation clawed at me as I gathered as much power as I could muster, sending my magic along the lines of the earth. I searched for every sign of life. I sensed every tree, every flower, every weed within a ten-mile radius. Not only that, I felt the presence of animals, insects, every living thing.

But not Zane.

"No. No. No," I whimpered, the word becoming a mantra of despair.

I ran to him, hope battling against the crushing weight of reality. My tears blurred my vision, but I pushed forward, stumbling toward him.

Zane couldn't be gone. Fate couldn't be that cruel.

When I reached the tree, my heart shattered. Zane lay on his back, his chest unmoving, his lips a sickly purple, his unseeing eyes fixed on the sky.

A guttural scream of despair tore from my chest and burst from my lips. I collapsed onto him, throwing my body over his lifeless form. Sobs racked my frame, my tears wetting his face, chest, and hair.

"Why?" I cried, my voice cracking. "Why did you do this?"

It felt like someone had carved my heart from my chest, leaving only a raw, empty, bleeding void in its place.

"It was supposed to be me," I sobbed. "Not you."

He had taken a fate that was meant for me, and that wasn't right. I couldn't accept this. I wouldn't. I had to do everything in my power to reverse it. I'd healed the dying many times, but I'd never brought someone back from the dead. It was something I had never dared to try before, but for Zane, I would do anything, give anything.

Taking a shaky breath, I lifted myself off Zane's chest. Pressing a hand to his cheek, I found it still warm to the touch. Gently, I closed his lids, and as I gazed down at him, I could almost convince myself he was only asleep, not truly gone.

Leaning forward, I whispered in his ear, "I love you too, and I'm not going to let you go."

Closing my eyes, I began to pull the life from every bush, tree, flower, and blade of grass around me, filling my wellspring of power. What I was about to attempt would require a tremendous amount of magic, more than I'd ever channeled before.

I continued pulling power, filling myself with more magic than I'd ever held before. I went far past my limits, until it felt like I might combust.

When I could take no more, I opened my eyes. The world around me was drained of life, washed in gray. The plants and vegetation were shriveled and dead as far as the eye could see. I knew it extended beyond the ravine. I'd likely drained the life from everything within a two-or three-mile radius.

Sadness pierced my heart for what I'd done to the land, but I vowed to restore it if I survived this.

Peering down at Zane, I was struck again by how peaceful he looked, as if he were only resting. I pressed a kiss to his stubbled cheek, then laid both hands on his chest and began to push my magic into him.

As I funneled my magic into Zane, I searched for a spark within him to ignite his healing. But it wasn't working. Just my magic wasn't enough.

Usually, when I healed someone, I poured my magic into their life force, their very essence, helping their body heal itself. But Zane didn't have a life force anymore. For all intents and purposes, he was an empty shell, so as I poured my magic into him, there was no anchor, so it wouldn't stay inside of him. The only thing I could think to do was to push some of my life force into him as well to act as a tether.

It was an idea I wouldn't have considered if Queen Liliana hadn't done something similar to me using the faestone dagger. She hadn't been just pulling my magic from me, but my very life force as well. But unlike her, I would be willingly giving my magic to Zane rather than taking something from him. I wasn't sure if it would work, but it was the only option I could think of.

Without hesitation, I dug deep into myself. If I died saving Zane, it would be a worthy sacrifice.

Reaching into the depths of my being, I visualized my center of power as a glowing orb in my chest. With a mental blade, I sliced it in two. Agony ripped through me, worse than anything I'd ever experienced. I didn't know how I remained upright, but I did.

With a roar, I shoved the glowing essence into Zane. Even though I was giving my life force willingly, the process was excruciating. Pain shot through me as if I were being torn apart.

I bit my lip to keep from crying out and tasted the coppery

tang of blood, but as soon as I transferred some of my life force into him, his body jolted as if struck by lightning. Relief flooded me when my magic circled the essence, anchoring it inside him as I'd hoped.

I wasted no time funneling healing magic into Zane, feeding the spark until it grew into a roaring fire. The pain only intensified, but I refused to stop.

Minutes ticked by. Or perhaps even hours. Time was whittled down to just two things now: the agony that ripped through me and the healing fire burning inside of Zane.

Then, suddenly, I felt him. Zane's presence brushed against me like a soothing balm, lessening the pain. For a moment, I couldn't tell where I ended and he began.

But his heart still wasn't beating, and his chest wasn't rising. It wasn't enough.

I pushed harder, emptying myself completely. I gave him all my magic, then took his fledgling energy into myself to fuel my efforts, filtering it and sending it back into him.

Finally, I felt it. A faint, weak thump beneath my palm.

My heart leaped as the beats grew stronger and faster. With a gasp, Zane's eyes snapped open.

Completely spent, I collapsed forward onto his chest, my muscles like jelly, and my mind clouded with exhaustion. But I was alive.

And so was he.

Zane wrapped his arms around me, sitting up and cradling me in his embrace. He looked down at me, his blue eyes wide with wonder as they searched my face.

My gaze fell on the dead grass, shriveled flowers, and dry

bushes behind Zane. I had drained the entire area of its life to heal him, and I'd do it again without hesitation.

"Thank you," I whispered to the earth, acknowledging the tremendous sacrifice it had made.

"What happened?" Zane asked, his voice filled with confusion. "The last thing I remember—" He broke off, his eyes catching on the gaping portal beside us. His expression darkened with realization. "But . . . the sacrifice. I died."

He turned to me, questions written all over his face. I nodded. "You did. But I saved you," I said simply. The details could wait. All that mattered now was that he was here with me. I had brought him back, and I was determined never to lose him again.

Concern flashed across his features. "Are you okay?" he asked softly.

A laugh bubbled up inside me, a mix of joy and relief. He had just returned from the brink of death, and yet he was worried about me.

Grinning, I nodded. "I'm perfect. Now."

Reaching up, I brushed a lock of hair away from his face. My hand trembled, but it wasn't from weakness. It was the sheer gravity of the moment. As my fingers lingered near his cheek, both of us stilled, our eyes falling to my wrists.

The wounds from when Zane had bound me were still there, minor but unmistakable. What shocked us both was the blood seeping from the small cuts. It wasn't red as it should have been. It was black.

Black, like the blood of an Ethereum lord. Like Zane's.

He gently grasped my wrist, holding it as if it might shatter. "Why are you bleeding black? How?"

"I . . . don't know," I admitted, my voice barely a whisper.

It had to have something to do with the way I'd healed him. When I gave him my life force and essence, when our energies intertwined and flowed into each other, something must have shifted, fundamentally altering me.

If I were being honest, I felt different. Not in who I was because, at my core, I was still me, but my magic had changed. It was sharper, deeper, more complex, though I couldn't yet articulate the exact nature of the transformation. If this was the price I had to pay to bring him back, it was worth it. Still, I was alive, and I could already feel my strength returning.

Movement caught my attention, and a shadow flickered at the edge of my vision. I turned toward the portal and gasped. Four cloaked figures stepped through the swirling gateway, crossing from their world into ours.

Zane scrambled to his feet and reached for me, helping me up. His movements were swift, his instincts protective as he immediately tucked me behind him.

"*We will not hurt either of you, Zane, Lord of the Western Kingdom, and Lorelei, Princess of the Spring Court.*"

The words echoed directly into my mind, sharp and sudden, making me flinch.

Zane's voice was low, filled with awe and disbelief. "The Wise Ones?"

The Wise Ones? The beings who had left me that fateful note?

Cautiously, I peeked out from behind Zane and got my first glimpse of the figures before us. They were slightly shorter than average, their forms glowing softly with an otherworldly light. Their radiant, white-tinged skin seemed to shimmer, casting a faint aura around them. Small, curved horns peeked out from their wild, unkempt hair, and their eyes—entirely white—held a piercing, ethereal quality as they regarded us.

Unseelie. The first unseelie I had ever seen.

"*We are pleased you have ended the curse,*" one of them said, his voice resonating in my mind rather than my ears. "*It will bless your lands and people for generations to come.*"

Another spoke, his tone equally reverent yet firm. "*And now, we can come home.*"

Even though none of their mouths moved, I instinctively knew which one was speaking and turned my attention to him.

"Is this your home?" I asked, stepping out from behind Zane. He immediately wrapped an arm around my waist, pulling me close. I didn't mind at all.

"*It is,*" the Wise One replied. "*We were banished along with the other unseelie when the curse was created. Locked in a cave until the time at which the curse would be destroyed and we would be set free. We waited millennia for the right Faerie princesses and Ethereum lords to be born, those who would be capable of seeing past the prejudices they were taught, embracing love and sacrifice instead. Those strong enough to bear the weight of all fae, seelie and unseelie alike, and one day unite the two worlds.*"

I stared at the Wise Ones in awe. They were talking about me and Zane, and the others. We were the ones they had waited for. A swell of pride filled my chest. I was grateful to have the opportunity to unite the worlds, but something still didn't make sense.

"If you were locked in a cave all this time, how did you get the note and the poison into the Shadow Heart?" I asked.

The Wise One to my left gave what I thought was meant to be

a smile, though it looked awkward, like someone attempting it for the first time. Lifting a hand, he tapped a finger against his temple. "*We see many years into the future. The note and vial were planted in the Shadow Heart before we were banished to Ethereum.*"

I gasped. They'd known they would be trapped in that cave for thousands of years before it even happened? And then, they had to wait centuries for me, Dawn, and the others to be born. How terrible.

Suddenly, all four Wise Ones bowed low, their forms dipping with solemnity before Zane and me. "*We thank you for your sacrifice and for finally freeing us. Because of what you have done today, both Faerie and Ethereum will see many years of peace.*"

Tears pricked my eyes, blurring my vision. The weight of their words hit me hard. Not only did I have the chance to live a life with Zane, but both our worlds would prosper because of what we'd done. My heart felt like it might burst with emotion.

Straightening, the Wise Ones turned toward the portal. Through the shimmering opening, I could see the dim interior of the cave they'd been imprisoned in for so long. For a moment, I thought they intended to return to Ethereum, but as one, they raised their arms.

I gasped as golden ribbons of magic flowed from their hands. The magic swirled in the air, twisting and weaving before cascading toward the split in the tree, blanketing the portal in a radiant, golden glow.

"What are they doing?" I asked Zane.

He glanced down at me, his brow furrowed. "I don't know."

The golden magic accumulated along the edges of the portal, and before our eyes, an intricate arch began to take shape. The shimmering gold vines intertwined, forming a delicate yet imposing frame. The base of the portal flattened and straightened, creating a smooth threshold. The split tree now resembled a massive arched doorway, at least thirty feet wide and twice as high.

A blinding flash of golden light burst outward. I shielded my eyes, wincing at the intensity. Moments later, the brightness faded, and I blinked rapidly to clear my vision. When I looked again, the cave was gone.

In its place, I saw a platform with tracks stretching into the distance. It reminded me of the train station Zane had described to me.

We had small trains in Faerie, mainly for transporting goods and materials down mining mountains, but nothing like the railcars Zane had explained. He had spoken of massive carriages ferrying fae across Ethereum's kingdoms far more advanced than anything I'd seen here.

It was nighttime on the other side of the portal, just as it was here, and the platform appeared empty. That was probably for the best. If anyone had been there when the portal appeared, they would've been scared out of their wits.

"Is that one of your train stations?" I asked, my voice tinged with awe.

Zane nodded, his eyes fixed on the scene. "The one in the village of Weldstone, I believe. It's not far from my castle in Windreum."

I glanced at the Wise Ones, who had turned to face us again. One of the figures in the middle gestured toward the newly formed portal. "*And now there is a way for fae to travel safely back and forth between the realms.*"

I was awestruck. The Wise Ones were unimaginably powerful. They had remade the portal, shifting its location from their cave to a village in Zane's kingdom. It was clear to me what this was. A gift. A more accessible connection between the two worlds was created for the benefit of both realms' citizens.

As the Wise Ones began to walk away, Zane tightened his grip on my hand and then lifted my wrist to show them. "Do you know why she bleeds black now?" he asked, his voice steady but full of urgency.

They paused and then spoke as one, their voices merging in an eerie yet harmonious symphony that sent shivers down my spine. "*Lord Zane, we always knew you would drink the vial. We also knew that Princess Lorelei's power could bring you back. We had to present the task in a way that would ensure the Tree of Transformation received the willing sacrifice it needed to end the curse. A descendant of Balazar Warrick. Someone of black blood. When Lorelei shared her essence with you to bring you back, you, in turn, shared a part of yourself with her. Your bond is now even deeper than before. Her heart is now black because of it, and yours is red.*"

I heard Zane release a soft sigh of relief. "So she'll be all right?" he pressed.

The Wise One furthest to the left nodded and added, "*She is fine. However, you will both find that your magic has been altered in some ways.*"

Altered? What did that mean? I frowned, but before I could ask, Zane seemed unbothered by the revelation and continued.

"You know," he said, "I would have gladly drunk the vial if you'd simply asked."

The Wise Ones glanced at one another, their expressions unreadable but tinged with what might have been amusement. "*Had we done that,*" the central Wise One replied, "*Lorelei would have drunk the vial to save you, and she would have died. You would not have been able to bring her back.*"

Zane turned to me then, gently cupping my face in his hands. "Is that true?" he asked, his voice low and searching. "Would you have sacrificed yourself to save my life?"

"A thousand times over," I said without hesitation. "If I had known you would go behind my back and read the note, I would have hidden it from you in the first place."

His gaze softened as he searched my eyes. "When it comes to you," he said, his voice thick with emotion, "there are no lengths I won't go to in order to make sure you are happy, safe, protected, and loved."

And then his lips were on mine. The kiss was full of tenderness, and my heart melted at his touch. It was done. The curse was broken, Zane was alive, and we were together. We did it.

When we finally parted, I noticed the Wise Ones had left, their shadowy forms now distant silhouettes at the top of the hill.

"*One more thing,*" their combined voice echoed in my mind. "*The faestones from each of the princesses' daggers have the power to restore what the curse destroyed. Plant them in the earth and combine your powers to heal the lands. What is healed in Faerie will also heal in Ethereum.*"

With that, they crested the ridge and disappeared from view.

"They're kind of freaky," I said, breaking the silence. Zane's laugh was rich and warm, filling the space around us.

He glanced back at the portal nestled between the halves of the split tree. A whistle echoed through the air, and further down the tracks, I saw a light moving steadily toward us. The train was arriving.

"Did you say this village was on the outskirts of Windreum?" I asked.

He nodded, a curious look in his eyes.

With a grin, I tightened my grip on his hand and took off running toward the portal, dragging him behind me.

"Wait, Lorelei, what are you doing?" he called after me, his tone filled with equal parts amusement and confusion.

"The curse is destroyed. I want to see the other princesses, and I'm sure you want to see your brothers. I want to see where you live and ride on your train," I said, excitement bubbling over.

Zane yanked me to a stop just before I could step through the portal. "I would love that, but I have Nellie waiting for me back home and the puppies we bought," he said, his tone gentle but cautious. "And the Wise Ones just told us we need to heal the land with the daggers." He patted the pouch at his side. "What if we go through and can't come back?"

I stopped pulling on him, his words giving me pause. He was right. I hadn't thought about that possibility. "I don't think it's a one-way portal," I said with hope. "The Wise Ones said we could travel safely back and forth between the worlds. Can't we just go for one day? We can return tomorrow to head back to the Spring Court and plan our journey to the other Courts to heal the land. I used up so much magic bringing you back, that I need to replenish anyway."

Zane rubbed his bottom lip contemplatively, his gaze fixed on the shimmering portal behind me. I turned to follow his line of sight just as a train pulled into the station on the other side. Its loud whistle pierced the air, startling me.

Before I could say anything, Zane let go of my hand and suddenly leaped through the portal. My heart stopped for a moment, but he quickly reappeared, stepping back through with an exhilarated grin on his face.

"It's open," he exclaimed, his eyes shining with delight.

We laughed, holding hands as we ran together through the portal and boarded the train.

I wasn't going to wait one more second to start living my happily ever after.

Chapter Thirty-Two

DAWN

I slept for another few hours. I could feel more of my strength returning each time I rested, so I allowed myself to continue to do so. After I woke, Aribella helped me roll the babies into the sitting room to wait for Zander and Isolde to return from the hospital. Aribella tried to convince me to sit while we waited, but there was a restless energy inside of me that wouldn't let me just relax, so I paced back and forth.

It couldn't have been more than a half hour before my husband and best friend returned. When he first walked into the room, I noted that he didn't look great, but he looked infinitely better than the last time I saw him. He was still in his dirty and bloodied clothes, but his face and hands had been scrubbed clean, his finger was wrapped, and a small bandage covered his ear.

"Is it true? Is the curse—?"

Nysa walked in behind him, and I swallowed a sob. Her light green skin was healthy and fresh. The black streaks that had marred her complexion were gone, and her eyes were bright and clear.

She looked from me to my still, slightly swollen belly and then to the babies with wide eyes.

"Dawn, the last I saw you was at your wedding. How?"

I rushed forward and pulled her into my arms. She was frail, skinnier than before from having spent so many months bedridden, but she was alive. Healthy.

And most importantly, free of the curse.

I pulled back, my grin wide. "There's so much to tell you. I'm not even sure where to start."

I turned to Zander, excitement bubbling over inside me, only to see that my husband looked despondent. Something was wrong.

The grin dropped off my face. "Zander?"

He and Isolde shared a look, and then Zander smiled at me, but it didn't reach his eyes.

"Zander, what's wrong?" I asked, releasing Nysa and stepping toward him.

Aribella and Isolde both walked over to Nysa and started explaining what she'd missed in low, hushed tones as I went to meet Zander in the doorway of the small sitting room.

"The curse is broken, but . . ." A shadow passed across his face, and my stomach sank.

"But what?"

"Zane's gone."

No. I shook my head. It couldn't be true. I didn't want it to be true. Not sweet Zane.

"Are you sure?"

Zander swallowed hard. "I'm sure. We all felt it."

When he said, *we all*, Stryker and Adrien came up behind him, looking freshly washed and dressed, as opposed to my husband. They nodded to both of us as they entered the room, their gazes going toward their wives, who were still speaking with Nysa across the room before turning back to us.

The atmosphere turned somber.

The curse had ended, which was miraculous, but if Zane had sacrificed his life to end it . . .

I thought of Lorelei then, sweet Lorelei. She and Zane were perfect for each other. Had she succumbed, too? We Faerie princesses didn't have a connection with each other like the Ethereum lord brothers did, so if Lorelei had perished as well, we wouldn't have felt it.

"I . . . I don't know what to say," I told them. There had been so much joy recently with our babies being born healthy and with the curse ending. But it was mixed with sorrow.

Zane and my mother were gone.

Although my mother had allowed her bloodthirsty quest to stop the curse to supersede any morals she once had, going so far as to try to kill my husband, I'd still loved her. I hated what she became, but I loved the mother she had been before all of this.

At the same time, I was relieved she was gone, knowing my babies and my love were safe. Yet, I missed her. I felt . . . discombobulated.

We rejoined Aribella, Isolde, and Nysa, and then all just stood there in a strange, melancholy haze, watching the babies doing cute things like hiccupping or blowing bubbles on their lips while talking about the latest news as messengers arrived.

It was late, past nine in the evening, but word was spreading fast.

The unseelie who had been cursed with disease, were now healed. We assumed the lands were still damaged, but in time, we hoped they could heal as well.

In the last hour, ravens had started to arrive from the nearest parts of the other kingdoms, letting us know the black waters had disappeared.

The curse was well and truly destroyed. Zane and Lorelei had done it.

But we didn't celebrate.

"I'm not sure who wants this or what good it will do now," Stryker said as he pulled Lorelei's faestone dagger from a sheath at his hip and handed it to Aribella, who stood closest to him.

She took it gingerly and pressed it to her chest in reverence.

"They did it," she whispered. "They sacrificed so that we could live on for generations."

I guessed she was assuming Lorelei was dead, too, but I was still holding onto hope. I wasn't ready to let go. I wasn't ready to give up.

Zander nodded. "To Zane and Lorelei." He placed a fist over his chest, and one by one, everyone did the same, even Nysa, who didn't know who Lorelei was and had only met Zane for all of three seconds at our wedding.

My eyes filled with tears as I met Zander's gaze.

He needed this. He needed a moment to bury his brother in his heart, because we would never get a body.

We were cut off from Faerie, probably forever.

As we were all lowering our hands, Zander, Stryker, and Adrien all simultaneously gasped, their faces reflecting shock.

"What's wrong?" I asked.

It was Zander who answered, wearing a huge grin.

"Zane lives. I feel him."

"I feel him too," Stryker said, and then a crease formed on his brow. "But something feels different."

Adrien nodded. "I agree, but I still know it's him. He's alive!"

Isolde let out a whoop. Stryker picked up Aribella, swirling her in midair, and we all burst into laughter and joy, so much so that one of the babies woke and started fussing.

Everyone quieted, but we still smiled and hugged. Until we heard the scream coming from down the hall in the direction of the throne room.

Stryker, who was nearest the door, had his sword drawn and ready before anyone could even react.

The men told us to stay back as they ran to investigate, but we, of course, ignored them. Nysa stayed behind to guard the babies as Aribella, Isolde, and I followed in our husband's wake.

The boys burst into the throne room up ahead, swords drawn and shadows poised, ready to cut down any enemy. Adrien, realizing we'd followed them, threw up a shadow wall in front of us, preventing us from coming into the room behind them.

Isolde bared her teeth in frustration at her husband and then lifted her hands, preparing to use her magic to get through the wall, when it suddenly dissolved in front of us, just in time to see one of Zander's shards drop to the ground harmlessly at his feet, shattering like glass before dissolving.

We burst into the room behind them and took in the scene.

One of Zane's household staff appeared to have been dusting his throne and had dropped the duster to the ground. She now stood in front of a mirror portal, her hands covering her mouth in shock and awe.

Aribella, Isolde, and I moved closer. The mirror was identical to the ones we all had back in our palaces, but instead of reflecting an image, it was fused open, revealing a woman on the other side standing in a throne room. And not just any woman.

"The Spring queen, Lorelei's mom," I gasped.

As Queen Gloriana stared open-mouthed through the portal at us, she shook her head as if to clear her thoughts.

"Girls?" She leaned closer, reaching out to try to touch the mirror's surface, but her hand passed through to our side.

With a gasp of shock, she recoiled. Isolde walked right up to the mirror, getting as close as she could without passing through.

"Is Lorelei with you? The curse no longer holds this land," Isolde told Queen Gloriana.

Queen Gloriana slowly shook her head, looking downtrodden. "She hasn't returned yet. But we've received word that the curse has lifted here, too." She leaned forward, peering at Isolde with a look of wonder on her face. "Isolde, is it really you?"

"It is," Isolde said. "Is my family all right? Did they make it to the Spring Court like I told them to?"

Queen Gloriana nodded. "Yes, they're safe. They're all staying here with us at the Spring Palace. So are the Fall queen and king," she added, and Aribella made a noise next to me.

I glanced over to see tears in her eyes as Stryker pulled her into his arms, cooing softly in her ear that her parents were okay.

Aribella hadn't spoken much about her parents back in Faerie. I got the impression it was too painful for her, but it was clear now, from the look of relief on her face, how much that news meant to her.

When I turned my focus back to the mirror, Queen Gloriana reached forward again. This time, Isolde gently grasped her hand when it appeared in our world, and the queen yelped. Yanking her hand back, the Spring queen took a shaky step away from the mirror.

"Go get Sera," Isolde told the housemaid who had discovered the mirror portal. Then she glanced over at Adrien. "I'll be right back, my love." Without waiting for him to respond, she stepped through the mirror and into the throne room on the other side.

"Isolde," Adrien scolded, moving to follow her, but Zander stopped him.

"We don't know if they will accept us, brother. Let her handle this."

Adrien ran a nervous hand through his hair, staring at the mirror portal with apprehension. I could understand his hesitancy. What if Isolde got stuck in Faerie?

Aribella turned to me, her eyes bright with excitement. "Do you think that it will stay open? That we can visit our families?"

Families?

I no longer had family in Faerie. It had always just been my mother and me. No siblings, no father.

Someone took my hand, and I looked over to find Zander at my side, smiling down at me. My heart filled. My family was here now, in Ethereum. But I knew what she meant, and who was to say if the portals would remain open? I hoped they would.

I started to tell her I wasn't sure when a familiar voice called out from the other side of the mirror.

"Dawn!"

I snapped my head up to see Master Duncan standing in the Spring Palace's throne room. A small crowd was lining up behind him. I recognized Aribella's mother, Queen Beatrice, among them.

"Where's my daughter?" Queen Beatrice shouted as she pushed her way forward.

"Can we come over?" Master Duncan asked, inspecting the mirror. He peered at the edging, seemingly deeming it safe.

I glanced at Zander to confirm it was okay, and he nodded before I told Master Duncan it was safe to cross.

This was a historic moment. The leaders of Faerie entering the mirror world.

Master Duncan and Queen Beatrice came through first. As I went to greet Master Duncan, Aribella ran into her mother's arms, the pair sobbing as they embraced.

Then Adrien passed through the mirror to Faerie to check on Isolde.

Just as Serafina, Isolde's sister, arrived, looking flushed as though she had run the length of Zane's castle to get here, her sisters—all five of them, minus Isolde—came through the mirror portal. Before we knew it, we were all moving back and forth at will without issue.

From what we could gather, Queen Gloriana had just returned the mirror to the Spring Palace's throne room. She explained that my mother had stolen it, but she'd sent her soldiers to retrieve it. It turned out that the portal opened the moment the mirror was returned to its place in the throne room, connecting it directly to Zane's throne room here in the Western Kingdom.

I had to wonder if the same was happening with the other mirror portals, connecting the different Faerie courts with the Ethereum kingdoms. But since we'd all been forced to abandon the other palaces and castles because of the curse, we wouldn't yet know until we returned.

We told Master Duncan and the others that my mother had been killed. We didn't share the details of how, and they didn't ask.

Master Duncan mentioned that I would need to be sworn in

as queen and sent a messenger to the Summer Court to check on its status. Since we didn't have train stations or any fast mode of travel, it would take days, even with a raven delivering the reply.

I was overwhelmed yet filled with joy. Isolde and Seraphina had been reunited with their entire family, as well as Aribella with her parents.

The only fae missing were Zane and Lorelei. If Zane was truly alive, where were they? Stryker's comment about something feeling different about Zane ran through my mind, but I had to hope that wherever the Western lord and Spring princess were, they were safe with each other.

Though it was late, Zander had the kitchen prepare a full five-course meal and had tables brought into the throne room. We were having a celebration.

One of Lorelei's younger sisters, her name escaped me, approached with a young red-haired girl. Judging by her clothes, she wasn't royalty.

"Is this Zane's house?" the girl asked, seeming unsure.

I nodded. "Yes, it is. Who are you?"

"I'm Nellie. Have you seen Zane?" she asked, hope shining in her eyes. I'd overheard her asking Isolde the same thing a few minutes ago.

I shook my head gently. "I'm sorry, I haven't. How do you know him?"

She chewed on her lip, looking like she was about to cry. My heart ached for her.

"He's my friend, and he said he was coming back," she whispered.

As she turned to leave, I caught her arm gently. She turned

back to me, her eyes brimming with tears so full I was sure she could barely see.

"If Zane said he was coming back for you, then he's coming back for you," I promised her.

If any of my husband's brothers were a man of his word, it was Zane. I didn't know how they were connected, but it was clear Zane had touched this young girl's heart, and I wanted her to know he wouldn't abandon her.

"Would you like to stay and have a meal with us while we wait for him?" I offered.

Lifting her chin, she nodded, doing her best to put on a brave face. My heart ached for her.

I called for Nysa to bring the babies since it wasn't good for me to be away from them for long. When they arrived, fae from both worlds stopped to offer Zander and me their congratulations.

As I glanced around the room, with Zander at my side and our children close, seelie and unseelie alike mingled, gazing around in wonder and passing in and out of the portal with ease.

It was the best feeling in the world. There was a rightness to this. To have the two worlds open, to being one people.

I watched as Stryker extended his hand to Aribella's father, King Leonard, and created a small horse out of shadows. When it dissolved, they shook hands, smiling.

Zander slipped his hand into mine and glanced at me. "Queen, huh?" he teased.

I gave a nervous laugh. "Yeah, we might need to figure that out."

He nodded. "I've always wanted to live in a place that's hot and sunny."

I laughed. "You liar. You love the snow."

Grinning, he pulled me into his arms. "I do. But I'll go wherever you go. We can spend equal time in both places if your people need you. We'll figure it out."

Stars, I married the most understanding man in the realm.

"I love you."

"I love you too, little bird."

He leaned in to kiss me, but Nellie's squeal ripped through the air.

"Zane!" she screamed.

I pulled myself from Zander's arms and looked toward the open doorway to the throne room.

Zane stood there with Lorelei, holding hands, both wearing smiles.

And I knew just from looking at them that the Spring princess had found her mate.

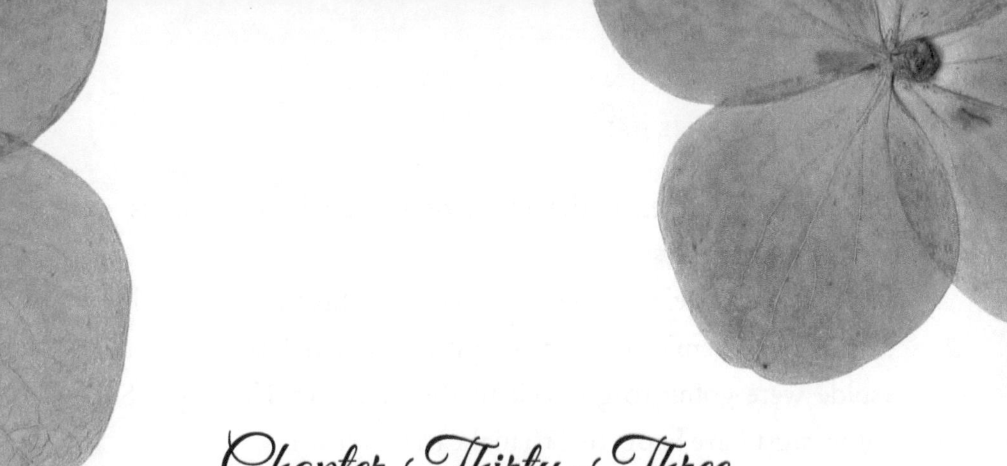

Chapter Thirty-Three

ZANE

Lorelei was amazed by the train system I'd built, and I couldn't help but feel a burst of pride at that. Her gaze flitted here and there, her eyes wide as saucers as she took everything in: the wood-lacquered benches, the paneled walls, the electric lights, and the Western Kingdom landscape flying by the windows.

The staff onboard were overjoyed to see me, and I was thrilled that we were only a short stop away from Windreum. It was well into the night when we arrived at the main train station, but even with the lateness of the hour, fae danced in the streets. They cheered and threw flower petals as we passed.

"The curse is destroyed! The plague is gone!" they shouted.

Lorelei just smiled, peering at me as she took it all in. "Oh, Zane, these shops are so quaint," she said as we passed the boutiques.

"I'll take you tomorrow when they open. Whatever you want is yours," I told her, and she blushed.

When we reached the front of my castle, my guards were visibly shocked to see me.

"My lord. We've been so worried. Your brothers are inside."

"All of them?" I asked, surprised. When I left, Adrien and Isolde were going to go back to the Southern Kingdom. Something must have happened to make them return.

He nodded. "Lady Dawn had her babies early. Everyone is healthy," he added quickly, when he saw my brows knit together in concern.

Lorelei squeezed my hand beside me, and my guards opened the front gates to let us in.

"My lord!" Jessie, my favorite housemaid, an elderly unseelie with pointed teeth and gray skin, greeted me with a deep bow as we entered. "Oh, you must come and see what's happened."

"I heard. Dawn had her babies," I told her as we followed her.

"No, my lord. I mean, *yes*, but it's not that." She scurried along the hallway, leading us to my throne room.

I kept a tight grip on Lorelei's hand as she looked around my castle in wonder. I hoped she liked it, but if she didn't, that was fine too. I'd let her redecorate the entire thing if she wanted.

When we reached the double doors leading to my throne room, a large crowd of voices could be heard from behind them.

My maid cracked the door open and then bowed before disappearing behind me.

"Are they having a party for Dawn?" Lorelei wondered aloud, echoing what I was thinking.

When I stepped inside and scanned the space, shock rippled through me.

These were not all my people. I recognized Lorelei's mother, Glori, right away. Seelie from Faerie were in my house.

How?

Then I spotted the mirror on the far wall. It looked identical to the one I'd seen when I rescued Lorelei from Queen Liliana's Summer Court manor house. And through it, rather than reflecting the scene in front of us, I could see into what I recognized as the Spring Palace's throne room.

"Zane!" Nellie's voice pulled my head to the right, where she was sitting at a table with Lorelei's sisters, eating what looked like chocolate cake.

I grinned, releasing Lorelei's hand and opening my arms as Nellie ran into them.

"You came back for me," she whimpered into my ear and sniffled.

"I told you I would. Were you a good girl for Queen Glori?" I asked.

She nodded, pulling back and wiping at her eyes. "But she said I need to learn better table manners."

We both laughed at that.

Lorelei squatted down beside us. "Hey, Nellie."

"Hey." Nellie hugged Lorelei like she already knew her, which surprised me.

When they separated, Lorelei glanced over at me and laughed. "I might have been visiting her in her dreams to make sure she knew you were okay. And to get to know her."

I smiled. Now it made sense. "Did you tell her about the puppy?" I asked.

"What puppy?" Nellie said excitedly as Lorelei smacked my arm.

"No. That was supposed to be a surprise."

"What puppy?" Stryker's voice came from behind me, and

standing, I spun around to find my eldest and most stoic brother staring back at me with something that looked almost close to a smile.

It was good to see him. It was good to see everyone, considering I thought I never would again.

"Still too grumpy for a hug?" I asked.

He grinned, the expression still looking a little foreign on his face as the jagged scar on his cheek puckered. "That depends. Did you get me a puppy?"

I laughed, pulling him in for a hug anyway, which he returned.

"Well done, brother," he said, patting my back. When he pulled back, there was a suspicious shine in his eyes that I would swear were tears if it was anyone but him. "We thought we'd lost you for a second there," he said, his voice gruff.

Looking into his gaze, I sobered a little, realizing they'd felt me die. "For a second there, you did," I said, but then glanced over at Lorelei. "But someone was too stubborn to let me go."

Lorelei ducked her head, her cheeks turning a pretty shade of pink.

It seemed like Stryker was going to ask something when Zander and Adrien appeared and swallowed me in a hug.

"We're so glad you're all right," Zander said right before he released me. Adrien, looking overcome with emotion, just nodded his agreement.

"Excuse me." I felt a tug on my jacket and looked down to see Nellie. "What puppy?"

I noticed that Lorelei had left my side to join her mother and sisters.

"Your puppy. And one for Lorelei," I told her.

Nellie whooped, fist-pumping in the air, while my brothers looked at me with raised eyebrows.

"Who is she?" Zander asked.

"My . . ." I hesitated. *Daughter* felt weird. I'd had to have been ten years old to have her. "Sister," I said, watching her for a reaction.

She grinned at me, nodding with tears in her eyes.

"Sister?" Zander repeated. I hoped he wasn't going to make a big deal of it and risk offending Nellie. I hadn't had any time to explain how I found her and that she had no one to go home to.

"Well, does she know she has three other brothers now, too?" Zander asked.

"Thank you," I mouthed to him as he took Nellie's hand and began introducing her to everyone in the room, including her two new "brothers," Stryker and Adrien.

Seeing my throne room filled to the brim with fae from Faerie and Ethereum alike brought tears to my eyes. An unseelie housemaid handed Aribella's mother a napkin, and she flinched for only a second before taking it with a smile. It would take time to break down the walls of lies that the previous generations had built, but I knew that together we could do it, making way for a new generation to come.

"Zane," Lorelei called to me, waving me over to where she stood with her family.

I cleared my throat and walked over to her. We still had work to do, but as long as she was by my side, we could get through anything. Together.

Chapter Thirty-Four

LORELEI

I had the best time last night after destroying the curse. I met Zane's brothers and his staff, mingled with my parents and the other princesses, ate good food, had good conversations, and snuck glances at Zane whenever I wanted. It was wonderful, and for the first time in months, everyone seemed excited and optimistic about the future.

Zane had offered to have a room made up for me in his castle when the festivities started to wrap up, but my mother reminded us sharply that we were not yet married and that I was a princess. So I stayed the night at the Spring Palace while Zane slept at his castle. He'd given me the sweetest kiss just before I went through the mirror portal back to Faerie that had put a silly smile on my face that lasted until I'd finally fallen asleep in my own bed.

Although the atmosphere was infinitely lighter with the curse destroyed and Queen Liliana gone, Zane and I still had work to do. We needed to restore the lands using the daggers and our combined power, just as the Wise Ones had instructed.

This morning, I woke up early, changed into a pretty dress, put on some light makeup, and snuck over to Zane's castle through the open mirror portal. I found him alone in a small study, the same one from the first dream I'd visited him in. He was seated at a round table, holding a steaming cup of coffee when I approached. The way he grinned at me made my insides flip.

I was glad to see him alone. There had been so much excitement the night before that we'd celebrated until a late hour, never finding a moment to ourselves.

When Zane had wished me goodnight last night, in front of my mother who had been waiting to make sure I got safely to my bed, alone, he'd whispered in my ear to meet him for breakfast.

As he stood and pulled out a chair for me, I bypassed it and boldly stepped up to him, pressing against him and peering into his eyes. They flared to life with desire.

I'd been thinking about something all night, and I had to ask him about it before I burst.

"What does *mates* mean?" I asked. "I know it means a couple or that we're supposed to be together, but in your world, what does it mean?"

Zane gave me a sweet smile, reaching up to trace a patch of freckles at my collarbone. The simple touch sent tendrils of heat down my spine.

"Mates means that when the fates made you, they made me, too," he whispered. "It means I'll never have another, even if you were to perish tomorrow. You are the only one for me, Lorelei. Mates means 'the one whom my soul has chosen.'"

My heart melted. That was way more romantic than I'd expected.

Leaning down, his lips brushed mine softly, causing a heady longing to spark inside of me right before he pulled back.

"But I know that mates are not a part of your culture," he said gently. "So I'm willing to take this as fast or as slow as you want."

I relaxed a little, pleased to hear him address the one thing that had been heavy on my mind.

"I want you. I love you. I just . . . it's a lot," I told him.

He froze, his gaze widening.

"What?" I asked.

"You . . . love me?"

Oh, right. I'd told him when he was dead. He wouldn't remember.

"Yes, I love you." I grinned. "I just don't know what I'm ready for yet."

He nodded, giving me an understanding look. "We can slow down."

He took a step back from me, but I stepped forward, closing the distance. "I don't want to slow down. I just want to date for a little before we get engaged, then be engaged for a little before we get married. And then be married for a bit before we have babies."

Zane smirked. "Dawn and her fast marriage with four babies put a little fear in you, didn't it?"

It wasn't just Dawn. All the girls seemed to have married within weeks of meeting their husbands. I mean, I got it. We were mates, and everything was electric and wonderful, but I wanted to slow down and enjoy each season with Zane. I thought I'd only have days with him, but now that I knew we'd have a lifetime together, I wanted to savor every stage, every experience, every moment with him. I didn't want to skip anything.

I nodded playfully, and he laughed. "Date for a bit, then engaged, then married, then babies," he said almost to himself.

I smiled. "But don't take *too* long."

He chuckled again, pulling me into his arms. "You just tell me when you're ready for each phase of life, and I'll happily walk through it with you."

"Okay," I said.

"Okay," he agreed, gesturing for me to sit, and when I did, he pulled the silver dome off a plate to reveal poached eggs, hashed potatoes, and strips of bacon.

We tucked into our breakfast, my heart full and hopeful about the future.

"I got my dagger back last night, so we have all four faestones now," I told him. Although my court and Zane's kingdom hadn't experienced the effects of the curse and so I didn't think we would need my faestone to heal our lands, I wanted it with us just in case.

He nodded. "We'll travel to each court in Faerie, healing it, and move on to the next. If the Wise Ones were right, the kingdoms here in Ethereum should start healing as well."

"I hope that's true."

"We'll see," he said.

After breakfast, I had a quick visit with Aribella and Isolde again, along with their husbands, who I had to admit were amazing. Then I went to check on Dawn. I'd learned last night how she was keeping the babies alive outside the womb at such a young age, and it was clearly taking a toll on her. She looked exhausted and so I kept my visit with her brief.

Finally, Zane and I grabbed our packed bags and went to the throne room, easily slipping through the portal and into the Spring Court. Nellie, who'd stayed with my sisters last night, was waiting for us, her backpack slung over her shoulders and a traveling cloak wrapped around her.

Zane cast me a questioning look, as if asking whether I'd told her she could come. I shook my head lightly.

"Nellie, we're only going to be gone a short time. A couple weeks at most," Zane told her.

She pointed a finger at him. "You promised we'd be together now, and I can help you if anyone gets hurt."

Zane looked at me. "Lorelei can heal me if I get hurt."

Zane had told me about her magic and how, in order to heal someone, she took on their injury. I hoped to work with her on being able to heal without that awful side effect, but I felt we needed to build a better rapport first. In order to truly help her, she needed to trust me first.

"I think I will need an assistant," I said.

Zane raised an eyebrow at me. "Are you two ganging up on me?"

Nellie ran to my side, folding her arms over her chest, and nodded. "I'm going. I'm Lorelei's assistant."

Zane broke into a grin. It was clear he had such a soft spot for her. She was already family to him, and I loved that about him.

"Fine," he relented.

With that and my mother's blessing, we grabbed mounted horses and headed for the Summer Court.

We reached the border between the Spring and Summer Courts sooner than I had expected. From there, we could see the dry and cracked soil where the curse had tried, and failed, to bleed into the

Spring Court. A shiver ran down my spine when I remembered trying to escape Queen Liliana. How the air had been filled with ash and the ground leeched completely of life.

We rode for another hour into the desolate lands before stopping. We wanted to make sure we were well enough into the Summer Court for the faestone to heal the land, but we were hesitant to travel any further considering the condition the curse had left it in. It didn't feel safe.

Nellie scanned the surroundings with a frown and a touch of fear in her eyes.

"Nellie," I called, drawing her attention. "I know Zane has offered you a room in his castle, but I would like to offer you a place to stay in the Spring Palace as well. My sisters and parents have already grown so fond of you. They wanted you to know you'll always have a place there."

She and my sister Octavia had become quite close, as my mother had told me. Nellie's eyes grew misty. "I'd like that sometimes. Like having a sleepover?"

I nodded. "Yes, like that. Anytime you want."

She swallowed hard and then rushed into my arms, hugging me. I met Zane's gaze over her head to find him giving me an adoring look.

When she pulled away, Zane brought out the faestones from the daggers that had been melted down, along with the daggers that were still whole. He held them in front of us.

"All right," he said, "the Wise Ones mentioned the dagger and our combined power. I'm guessing Dawn's faestone would heal this land?"

"I think so, yes," I agreed.

Zane handed me Dawn's orange faestone before putting away the others.

"If anyone gets hurt, I'll be right here, ready to help," Nellie announced.

"No, you won't," Zane told her sternly. "You will never heal again because, in order to do that, you have to hurt yourself."

His words were out of love, but I saw Nellie shrink into herself.

"Actually, Zane," I interjected, "I think Nellie has a milder, untrained form of my power. With practice, I could teach her to transfer the illness to the plants and flowers instead."

Nellie's eyes grew wide. "Really? Cool!"

I winked at her. "But until then, I think you need to sit out any healings and let me handle them."

She frowned but nodded. "Fine."

"Here, hold this." Zane handed her his bag, probably just to make her feel useful, and then got on his knees on a patch of blackened earth.

I did the same, letting my power fan out around me. It felt different.

"My magic feels different," Zane said. "My brothers even said that I feel differently to them now."

"My magic feels different as well," I commented. "I think because when I saved you, it . . . meshed us."

He reached out and grasped my hands. "That's why we do this together."

Nellie snickered beside us, and I grinned.

Placing our interlocked fingers over the faestone resting on the ground in front of us, I reached for my power and then used it to scan the plants and trees around us. At least what was left of them. They were low on energy, hurting but not dead.

I sucked in a breath, also feeling an energy in the sky, something I'd never felt before, and wondered if it was Zane's power. It was electric.

Snapping my gaze over to Zane, I could tell from the look on his face that he was feeling energy unfamiliar to him as well.

"I have no idea what to do," Zane said.

"Me neither. But you feel the plants as well?"

He nodded, a look of awe on his face. I'm sure I was wearing a similar expression.

"Maybe we just start flooding the faestone with power?" I offered.

"It's worth a try."

"And I'm here to assist if needed," Nellie added, causing both Zane and me to smile.

"Ready?" Zane asked, and when I nodded, we both pushed our magic into the faestone. I gasped when it began to sink into the ground.

"Keep going," he said with a grunt.

I did, pushing everything I had into the earth. Thunder rolled overhead as lightning crackled in the sky.

"Is that you?" I asked.

"I think it's you," Zane responded.

Weird. I did feel a connection to the sky's energy, but I couldn't tease it apart from the earth. This was all so new.

A vine grew up from the ground and sprouted a white flower right beside us.

"Good job, Lorelei," Zane encouraged me.

I smiled. "That's not me." I was familiar enough with my nature magic to know I wasn't making that flower grow.

Zane stared at me in shock.

"Keep going," I encouraged, just like he had.

It seemed that when I saved him, and my heart turned black, we'd fused ourselves together in such a way that we now shared powers. I could call lightning from the sky, and he could make flowers bloom. In that way, it was actually beautiful that we could share such a thing.

"Whoa," Nellie exclaimed when a shockwave of energy exploded out from us, instantly turning every blade of grass green and restoring the flowers and trees.

Then, just as suddenly as it happened, our magic cut off.

We stood, looking around in wonder at the beauty we had just created. The trees were now heavy with green leaves and dotted with flowers. A carpet of thick green grass blanketed everything, and the flowers—oh, the flowers—were gorgeous. Pinks, purples, yellows . . . the colors were vibrant and alive.

I peered down at the earth, which seemed to have taken the crystal as a sacrifice and amplified our powers to create this.

"Thank you," I whispered to it.

"Can I try at the next court?" Nellie asked, holding up Isolde's dagger.

"No," Zane and I said simultaneously, and then we laughed.

We spent the next several days traveling to the edges of the Fall Court and then the Winter Court, my least favorite because it was so cold, to heal the lands. Each time, our combined power caused the crystal to sink into the earth and spread its magic throughout the land, restoring it.

But there was still one place I wanted to fix.

"You guys mind if we take a little detour?" I asked. "Well, actually, it would be quite a big detour."

Zane gave me a questioning look.

"Where? Somewhere fun? Will there be sweets?" Nellie peppered me with questions as she leaned her head on my shoulder inside the carriage.

Over the past few days, we'd really bonded, and she'd cemented a place inside my heart. Every morning, I did her hair, and she kept asking for more elaborate styles with braids. She told me she had always wanted braided hair, but her nana's fingers couldn't manage it in her old age. I felt for the girl and was so glad that Zane had brought her into our lives.

I laughed, looking down at her. "Not only will there be sweets, but there will also be puppies," I told her.

Zane jerked his head in my direction, realization dawning. "You want to go to the Savage Lands?"

I nodded. "What if we made them . . . less savage? This is the portal the citizens of Faerie will be able to use to visit Ethereum. What if we cleaned them up and made it a travel hub of sorts?"

Zane's eyes grew wide. "I love that idea. My men could put in a road. Or maybe I could help the courts build a train system here like the one we have in Ethereum?"

I nodded, feeling my excitement build. "We would need approval from the other courts, but I don't see why not. Oh, it would make travel so much easier."

It was settled. We traveled to the town where Zane had bought our puppies first and played with them, promising to return once they were weaned. After taking a night's rest in an inn, we set off for the heart of the Savage Lands to show Nellie the tree where Zane had lost his life and saved our worlds.

Since the curse wasn't trying to stop us, we moved quickly and with far more ease than before, but as we'd traveled, we'd taken in the devastation from the flood of black liquid that had tried to kill us. Half of the trees and foliage had been washed away. The areas that weren't affected by the black flood were wild and unruly, with darkened trees and thick overgrowth. An ominous-looking place that was difficult to travel through.

When we finally reached the Tree of Transformation, the golden vine arch the Wise Ones had created with their magic was just as beautiful and awe-inspiring as I remembered.

"Whoa, this portal is pretty," Nellie said as she slid off the back of her horse and took a few tentative steps forward.

"What are you thinking?" Zane asked me, looking around at the dead landscape around us.

I pulled out my dagger, the last one, and palmed it.

"I don't want this to be used as a weapon ever again," I told him, kneeling as I set it on the ground. "I wonder if the earth will take it and allow me to . . . redecorate." I winked.

Technically, the Savage Lands, located at the very center of our converged courts, weren't part of any one court but were still part of Faerie. The faestones seemed to carry magic we had never fully understood, so I was hoping that the pink moonstone would still work here.

Zane kneeled beside me. "Worth a try."

"Okay, this time, when we feed it with magic, I'm going to try to guide it to do what I want," I told him, and he nodded.

I had a vision for this place. I wanted fae to feel welcome here, for it to be a place where all of Faerie could come to embark on a tour of Ethereum, and in return, a beautiful first introduction to our world for the citizens of Ethereum as well.

Nellie was sulking off to the side because in every court, she'd asked if we needed help, and every time, I'd told her no. This time was different. This was the faestone from my court, and I believed that meant I was going to have more control over it than I'd had with the others.

"Nellie, come assist me," I called out.

"Me?" she said, shocked, her tongue red from gummy candies we'd picked up for her at the last village.

"Yes. Come help me."

She bolted over, eagerly looking down at me.

"Place your hands on my back, and when I say to, I want you to push some of your magic into me," I told her.

She frowned. "I don't usually push. I pull."

I nodded. "That's the problem. You take sickness into yourself, but I'm going to teach you another way."

She pressed her mouth into a firm line, concentrating. "Let's do this." She rolled out her neck, and Zane and I smiled at each other.

Zane and I pressed our interlocked fingers over the faestone like we had in other courts, and then, with Nellie's help, all three of us poured our magic into the stone. It took Nellie a few minutes to get the hang of pushing her magic rather than pulling, but eventually, I felt a burst of fresh magic feeding Zane's and mine, and I knew it was time.

Taking a deep breath, I closed my eyes and began to imagine the layout of the land Zane and I had crossed over in the past two days, as well as what I knew about it from the maps I'd seen.

I started with the trees, creating a wide path, large enough for two carriages to pass side by side, that wove its way through the Savage Lands to create roads to all four Faerie courts. I then made the trees shift into a variety of species: oaks, maples, weeping willows, and cherry blossoms.

At one point, Nellie gasped, but I kept going.

Next, I worked on the ground cover. Instead of dead brush and gnarled ferns, I arranged things in a more orderly fashion, transforming large sections of the landscape into a well-thought-out garden while still keeping some patches throughout the territory the same. It was important to me not to completely change the Savage Lands. There was a wild beauty to this place that I still wanted to preserve.

Next, I made moss flourish along the tree trunks and then covered the exposed ground in a thick blanket of grass or fields of wildflowers. With the help of Zane and Nellie's magic adding to mine, I made flowers from all four kingdoms spout up along pathways and in open fields. I coaxed trees to bloom and some to grow to almost impossible heights.

By the time I was done, I was utterly exhausted.

"I'm finished," I said, opening my eyes and pulling my hands away from Zane's.

When I looked at the result of our combined magic, I gasped. It was even more beautiful than I had imagined.

A wide dirt path lined with stones now flowed through the ravine, straight to the golden portal. Along its edges were rows of purple and pink flowers, with a second row of blue and yellow blooms behind them. The mixture of trees in the surrounding area was breathtaking, especially with the vibrant green moss growing along their trunks.

"It's so pretty," Nellie said behind me, and I glanced over my shoulder at her.

"And you helped make it that way," I told her. "I couldn't have done it without your magic. You're very powerful."

She smiled shyly and ducked her head, her cheeks turning as red as her hair.

Still smiling, I glanced over at Zane to see him peering through the portal at the small village thoughtfully.

"You know," he said. "I'd always intended for one of these outer villages to be a hub of sorts for trading and additional train connections. What if Weldstone Village became the first train station to connect to Faerie?"

I blinked at him. "Connect to Faerie. Are you talking about running a train through the portal?" I never would have thought of that idea on my own, but the portal was huge, so there'd be enough room to lay track and run a train through it.

Zane nodded. "We are one people now. What better way to show that?"

Excitement coursed through me at the thought. I could already imagine where the train platform would go. Just off to our right, near the giant willow tree.

"It's a perfect idea," I said, taking his hands in mine.

"You're perfect," he muttered, looking into my eyes as he pulled me closer.

"Eww, are you going to kiss?" Nellie said, and I grinned.

Zane shot Nellie a look. "All right, time to head back to the Spring Court," he said before turning to me. "Then I'm taking you out. Alone."

Nellie stuck her tongue out at him, but her gaze reflected happiness.

I laid a hand on Zane's stubbly cheek, looking into his gorgeous blue-and-brown specked eyes, and my heart swelled. He was so handsome. So kind. So much more than I even knew to hope for. I couldn't imagine my future without him, and I was just so glad that now I didn't have to. There was nothing I was looking forward to more than spending time with him and getting to know him better.

"I can't think of anything I'd rather do more," I said honestly, and he smiled, and then a wicked gleam entered his gaze.

"I can think of one thing," he said, and then, much to Nellie's distress, he leaned forward and captured my mouth. And just like every other time we'd kissed, the world fell away until it was just the two of us, lost in the warmth and certainty that we were exactly where we were meant to be.

Three months later...

LORELEI

When we used the faestones to heal each of the Faerie courts, the lands in Ethereum were restored as well as we'd hoped. Refugees from the courts in Faerie and the kingdoms in Ethereum started to return to their homes and work to rebuild what they'd lost. It was going to be a long road to recovery for everyone, but we were hopeful the worlds we were now building would be even stronger than before.

Less than a week after we returned from the Savage Lands, Dawn, Isolde, and Aribella returned with their husbands to the lords' kingdoms. It was sad to see them go, but each lord had his own kingdom to rule.

As the monarchs from each of the courts and kingdoms returned to their lands and homes, it was discovered that there was a mirror portal connecting the two realms in each of the throne rooms, just like the connection between the Spring Court and the Western Kingdom. That meant that the princesses could live with their husbands, but still help their courts as well.

With his brothers now returned to their respective kingdoms, it was just Zane in his castle in Ethereum now. I visited daily. Sometimes, immediately after waking up, I'd rush over to have breakfast with him.

Nellie had taken up my offer to stay in the Spring Palace with my family and me. It started by having sleepovers in our palace, and eventually, she just never left. Both of our dogs slept beside her every night. She had the room next to Octavia's, and the two of them had become inseparable. She also visited Zane daily and had even started asking when we were all going to share a home like a "normal family."

Zane and I had been having such an amazing time together, taking turns showing each other our favorite places in both Faerie and Ethereum. Every day we spent together, I fell a little more in love with him, and every night when we said goodbye, it was a little harder to leave him.

For the last month, I'd been dreaming of becoming Zane's wife. I was ready for the next step, and I'd even dropped hints about what type of ring I wanted. Just last week, I'd pointed out a pink sapphire in the shop window of one of the boutiques in Windreum, going on and on about how beautiful it was, but rather than picking up on the hint, he'd gotten distracted by a street vendor selling candied almonds and rushed off to buy us some.

I'd told him I wanted to take things slow, but now I feared he was going to take years to propose. I was done waiting for him to catch my hints. It was time to ask for what I wanted and hope his heart hadn't changed.

"What do you have planned for today?" I asked Zane as we ate a late breakfast in his study. The cozy little room in the corner of his castle was fast becoming a favorite spot of ours.

"Today's a big day," he said as he picked up his coffee cup. "I have to oversee the train extension in Weldstone. We're connecting the tracks between Faerie and Ethereum this week."

He sounded excited, and it *was* exciting. The people of Faerie had taken very well to the idea of a train running from the mirror world into Faerie and then extending throughout our realm. The queens from all four courts had signed off on the project, and now it was just a matter of time.

"Oh, that's too bad. I thought maybe we could get engaged today," I said casually, just as he took a sip of his coffee.

He started choking immediately, his eyes going wide as he cleared his throat.

"I'm sorry, what?" he said when he finally cleared his windpipe.

I pretended to itch my nose to cover a smile. The look on his face, half-shock, half-hopeful, was priceless.

"I know I said I wanted to wait and take things slow, but it's *too* slow, Zane."

"Is that so?" Zane said, and as his shock faded, a smirk started to lift the corners of his mouth.

I nodded. "It is. Spending time with you these past months has been amazing. But now I want more. Don't you?" I asked, feeling a little unsure as nerves crept up on me.

What if he needed time now, and I was pushing him? I didn't want that. Zane had been so understanding and patient with me. Shouldn't I be offering him the same? If Zane needed time now, then that's what I would—

He stood and pulled something from his pocket and then

placed it on the table in front of me, cutting off my runaway thoughts immediately.

It was the pink sapphire ring I'd seen in the shop.

My mouth dropped open, and I looked up at him. He had been paying attention.

"I've been driving myself mad, wondering if this was a hint or not. I didn't want to push you away by giving it to you too soon," he said.

The vulnerability that I felt a moment before fell completely away as joy started to fill me.

"It *was* a hint. One I dropped over a month ago," I laughed.

He smiled, looking relieved. "Well then, forgive me for not doing this a month ago."

He dropped to one knee, and my heart thumped with giddy anticipation.

"Lorelei Maebry, I have grown to love you more in the past three months of courtship than I ever thought possible. Your kind heart and sweet spirit are unmatched. Would you do me the honor of—"

"Yes," I blurted, shoving my ring finger in his face.

He was shocked for a moment but then bellowed with laughter. Slipping the ring onto my finger, he stood and pulled me into his arms.

"Now," he said. "You just tell me exactly how long you want to be engaged."

Three more months later...

LORELEI

"Will you braid my hair in a crown like you did last time for Octavia's party?" Nellie asked as she sat in the chair before me.

"Of course," I told her, running the brush through her thick red strands and smoothing it out. Peony and Potato sat at our feet, asleep, and I smiled at the name Nellie had given the boy dog. So much had happened in the last three months . . . I couldn't believe I was going to be Zane's wife today.

We'd decided to have the nuptials here in Spring Court. Fae had been traveling in from both realms all week. Dawn and Zander brought the babies, who were now healthy and out of their bubbles. Dawn was back to her strong and energetic self despite the late-night feedings. She told me that lack of sleep was nothing compared to the amount of energy that had been drained from her while the babies were still in their healing bubbles.

It was reassuring to hear because, after her mother's death, Dawn had taken on the role of Summer queen. Balancing her responsibilities as a new monarch, caring for her newborns, and being married to Zander, a lord of Ethereum with his own kingdom to manage, seemed almost impossible.

I believe the only way she managed it all was by having Zander steadfastly by her side. It was clear to anyone who came across the pair how supportive they were of each other. Zane had confessed to me that he thought Zander might eventually step down as an Ethereum lord to help Dawn rule the Summer Court. The lords had nephews who could step up to rule one of the Ethereum kingdoms, whereas Dawn was the last in her royal line.

Aribella and Stryker, and Isolde and Adrien had all come in for the wedding as well and were staying at Zane's castle. When Aribella and Stryker arrived, they'd had some exciting news to share with us. Aribella was pregnant. Stryker had seemed both overjoyed and terrified at the prospect of being a father, but I knew in my soul that he was going to be the best daddy.

After hearing the news about Aribella, Isolde was very proud to announce that she was *not*, in fact, pregnant. But she was excited to tell us that after our wedding, she and Adrien were planning on taking an extended trip. They planned to sail around Ethereum to visit all the different seas. Besides being able to make up for the honeymoon they couldn't take while the curse ravaged their lands, they wanted to check on the water unseelie around the realm to see how they were fairing.

"You shouldn't have to do her hair on your wedding day, my lady. Allow me?" my lady's maid said, but I shooed her off.

"No, thank you, Esmelie. I like doing her hair," I told her while I smiled at Nellie in the mirror as she beamed up at me.

It was our thing now. Almost every day, we sat down, and she requested some elaborate braid. It usually took me almost an hour, and during that time, we talked, laughed, and bonded. It was a precious time that I wouldn't have traded for the world, not even on my wedding day.

After I finished Nellie's hair, I let Esmelie do my hair and makeup and I got into my pink gown made of tulle and satin. I was finally ready.

My sisters and Nellie walked down the aisle ahead of me, scattering pink and white flower petals as they went before standing off to the side. I caught the smile on my mother's face and the tears in her eyes as I took my father's arm and began my walk. But the moment I saw Zane, my gaze locked on him, and I couldn't look away for the rest of the ceremony. His eyes never left mine either, until the moment when he wrapped me in his arms, sealing our bond with a kiss.

The Spring Palace ballroom wasn't large enough to accommodate all the fae we wanted to invite to our wedding. So, after the ceremony, we took a carriage ride through the fields of grass and flowers surrounding the palace. Our subjects, both seelie and unseelie, gathered on the fields to wish us well.

The reception was a whirlwind. We barely had a chance to eat as we danced and mingled with our guests. Before I knew it, the hour had grown late. Zane caught my eye and tipped his head toward the exit, a playful gesture that made me grin.

I peered at Dawn, who was dancing with Zander and smiling as she gazed adoringly into his eyes. Then I sought out Aribella and found her sitting on Stryker's lap as he rubbed circles on her back. Next, I spotted Isolde making out with Adrien in a dark corner, and I giggled.

I was overjoyed to see that what had started as a curse to divide and punish our people had ended up uniting us stronger than ever before.

Leaning into Zane's ear, I whispered, "Take me to bed, husband."

He swallowed hard. Grabbing my hand, he guided me off the dance floor.

I caught Dawn's gaze as we were leaving, and she gave me a grin and a nod. Laughing, we ran through the palace and into my mother's throne room toward the mirror portal, not even hesitating before stepping through to Zane's castle.

Picking me up, Zane ran through the corridors toward his bedroom. Well, our bedroom, now. We'd decided we would live together in Ethereum until my mother passed the queenly duties on to me, and then we could decide where to go next.

When we reached his bedroom door, Zane paused and then slowly lowered me to the ground, letting his eyes roam up and down my body. "I know you've wanted to take things slower, so if you're not ready to share a room, that's okay."

I gave him a devilish grin, leaning forward so that my lips brushed his. "I've been dreaming of this day for months," I panted, and then we crashed into each other.

He opened the door and pulled me inside, slamming it shut behind us. A fever of passion washed over me as I tore his shirt open, reaching for his bare skin and raking my fingers over the muscles there.

He pulled back from me, his wide eyes full of surprise.

I grinned, and then he yanked the strings on my dress, causing the whole thing to fall to the floor so that I stood before him in nothing but my underclothes. But rather than feeling shy like I thought I might when his gaze raked over me hungrily, I felt strong and beautiful.

With an encouraging nod from me, Zane scooped me into his arms and took me to bed. As we came together as one, I couldn't help but feel the truth of what Zane had said so many months ago about mates. He truly was the one whom my soul had chosen, and I'd choose him over and over again if given the choice.

The End.

Please Write a Review

Reviews are the lifeblood of authors and your opinion will help others decide to read our books.

If you want to see more co-written books from Leia and Julie, please leave a review on Amazon.

About Leia Stone

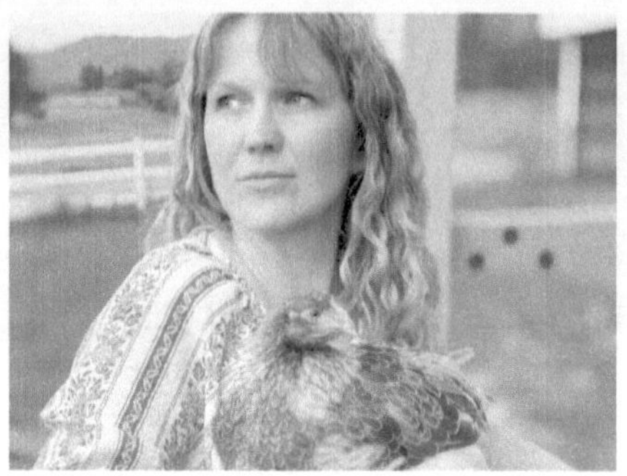

Leia Stone is the USA Today bestselling author of multiple bestselling series including Matefinder and Wolf Girl. She's sold over three million books and her Fallen Academy series has been optioned for film. Her novels have been translated into five languages and she even dabbles in script writing.

Leia writes urban fantasy and paranormal romance with sassy kick-butt heroines and irresistible love interests. She lives in Spokane, WA with her husband and two children.

www.LeiaStone.com

About Julie Hall

Julie Hall is a *USA Today* bestselling, multiple award-winning author. Before diving into the world of publishing, she was publicist and marketer for Sony, Summit Entertainment, Paramount, The Weinstein Company, and the National Geographic Channel.

Now, she crafts addictive action-packed fantasy stories that leave readers with epic book hangovers. Julie's books have been translated to four languages and won or were finalists in over 20 national and international awards.

Julie currently lives in Colorado with her four favorite people–her husband, daughter, and two fur babies.

www.JulieHallAuthor.com

Join the Fan Clubs

Get involved, make some friends, and get exclusive sneak peeks before anyone else.

 *Leia & Julie*

Acknowledgments

A big thank you to my amazing co-author and best friend Julie for being my ride or die and sending me gluten free cookies. You deserve a pet otter. A huge thank you to my agents Flavia and Meire at Bookcase Literary for all they do and a special thanks to our readers for supporting us all these years.

~ Leia

My first thanks goes to Leia for putting up with all my quirks and keeping our co-writing ship moving forward. It's such a pleasure to get to work with such a talented co-author and amazing friend. I couldn't be more excited to be writing this series with you! Thank you to my husband, Lucas, for being both the shoulder I cry on and my biggest cheerleader. You're my fun buddy for life and I adore you. And finally, thanks to all our amazing readers. You're the reason we get to do what we love!

~ Julie

Books by Leia Stone

LEIASTONE.COM/BOOKS

FANTASY

Vampire Hunter Society

Shifter Island Series

Wolf Girl Series

Daughter of Light Series

The Titan's Saga

Supernatural Bounty Hunter Series

Dream Wars Series

Fallen Academy Series

Dragons & Druids Series

Matefinder Series

Matefinder: Next Generation

Hive Trilogy

NYC Mecca Series

Night War Saga

Water Realm Series

The Kings of Avalier Series

Gilded City Series

ALL TITLES

LeiaStone.com/books

Books by Julie Hall

JULIEHALLAUTHOR.COM/BOOKS

CREATURES OF CHAOS SERIES

Creatures of Chaos

Kingdom of Chaos

FALLEN LEGACIES SERIES

Stealing Embers

Forging Darkness

Unleashing Fire

Supernova

LIFE AFTER SERIES

Huntress

Warfare

Dominion

Logan

SHADOW ANGEL SERIES

Shadow Angel Book One

Shadow Angel Book Two

Shadow Angel Book Three

Julie's books have won or were finalists in over 20 awards.

www.ingramcontent.com/pod-product-compliance
Lightning Source LLC
Chambersburg PA
CBHW020247030826
48979CB00030B/2650/J

* 9 7 8 1 9 5 1 5 7 8 5 3 4 *